Wong Chung-shun, 1896

PROLOGUE

It is a lonely place where the Jesus-ghosts preach. They preach about love, about a god who died of love, yet in the street the people sneer and call out and spit, then on Sundays sing in the Jesus-house.

Their god is a white ghost. You see the pictures. He has pale skin and a big nose and a glow of moonlight round his long brown hair. He has many names, just as we *Tongyan* have many names. We have a milk name, an adult name, perhaps a scholar or chosen name. The Jesus-ghosts call their god Holy Ghost. Even they know he is a ghost. People are like their gods, just as they are like their animals. They even call him Father. We do not need to name them, these *gweilo*. Even they know they are ghosts.

Yung says, We do not need to recognise their words; we do not need to interpret the raised syllable. It is there in a flicker of the eyes, the slight curl of a lip, in the muscles of the face, the way they set against us. He says, The body has its own language, as fluid as poetry, as coarse as polemic.

Yung has a way with words. He says the language of the body can be used as a weapon.

Now that Yung is here, I do not have to pay a clansman. One of us can go to the market while the other keeps shop; one can sort bananas while the other trims vegetables. Now that he is here, I can save to

1

bring out a wife. I can save the fare and the poll tax. It will take a good many years.

When Yung first arrived we did not recognise each other. We had not seen each other for over ten years. He is eighteen now, and books have affected his brain. He dreams big, impossible dreams. He does not understand life, and he does not understand this land. He is full of too many feelings like wild animals caught and caged in a zoo. He likes to talk, and his words are quick, quicker than his understanding. He is very young – fifteen years younger. My brother is like a son, an only, foolish son.

AS THE EARTH TURNS SILVER

AS THE EARTH TURNS SILVER

novel

ALISON WONG

PICADOR

First published by the Penguin Group (NZ) 2009

First published in Great Britain 2010 by Picador
an imprint of Pan Macmillan, a division of Macmillan Publishers Limited
Pan Macmillan, 20 New Wharf Road, London N1 9RR
Basingstoke and Oxford
Associated companies throughout the world
www.panmacmillan.com

ISBN 978-0-330-51898-7

1 3 5 7 9 8 6 4 2

A CIP catalogue record for this book is available
from the British Library.

Printed by CPI Mackays, Chatham ME5 8TD

Visit **www.picador.com** to read more about all our books
and to buy them. You will also find features, author interviews and
news of any author events, and you can sign up for e-newsletters
so that you're always first to hear about our new releases.

For my father Henry Wong, who did not live to see this come to fruition, for my mother Doris Wong and the generations that came before, and for my son Jackson Forbes and the generations that come after.

PART 1
WELLINGTON
1905–1909

A SHILLING

They had just turned into Tory Street, past Mount Cook Police Station, Chung-shun and his younger brother Chung-yung, on their way to Haining Street for soupy wontons and noodles. A late Sunday morning, the sun shining with the heat of ripening fruit, the wind for once not too vigorous. Yung whistled some folk ditty, oblivious to *gweilo* rules that made whistling, singing anything but hymns, and playing the piano on Sundays frowned upon. Shun merely frowned. His leg ached and made him lose all appreciation of the one day of the week when the shop was closed. He did not notice the calmness of the day, the lack of dust and grit swirling from the road to assail their eyes and coat their skin and clothes and hair. He did not notice the man approach them.

Yung saw the man coming. Even from a distance there was something strange about the way he walked, an ambling stiffness. As they got closer, Yung saw the man's eyes focus upon him, saw his face spread into a toothless grin. He watched as the man walked up to them, stood too close (the stink of stale piss and unwashed clothes) and said through sunken cheeks, 'Gif me a shilling.'

Yung held his breath and stepped back, looked the man over. He was a good four inches shorter and very thin, and there was something wrong with his eyes. His hands were hidden in the pockets of his dirty, oversized coat, and for a moment Yung considered whether he might be concealing a weapon.

'What for?' he asked.

Yung could see him thinking. 'Haaaf yoou aaany muun-neee?' the man said slowly, his face loose, his lips hollowing into his gums. 'Muun-neeee.'

Yung smiled. 'I haaf muuneee,' he said. He slapped his pocket, rattling the coins.

The man pulled his hands out of his pockets, held up his fists. 'Gif it to me or I'll . . .'

Yung laughed. *Muuneee.*

He turned and walked back towards the police station. He hummed. He liked the solid red brick building, the black and white brickwork forming arches above the windows and doors, the imprints of arrows stamped into the bricks. If he didn't think about the prisoners who'd made them, then he found it amusing, the way the bricks were placed so randomly, sometimes with the arrow facing inwards and hidden from sight, sometimes out, sometimes pointing to the left, sometimes to the right. They were like clues left behind at the scene of a crime, a scene that had been contaminated by reporters, curious onlookers, bumbling policemen.

He walked into the coolness of the building, across the geometric tiled floor, past the staircase, to the room where Constable Walters sat in the depths of the building. They knew each other well. The constable often passed by the shop on his nightly patrol and Yung would offer him a banana or a ripe pear, taking comfort from knowing the police were around.

Constable Walters rose from his desk, and as they came back out onto the street they saw the man hurry in the opposite direction and disappear down Frederick Street. The constable followed but soon lost him.

When he returned, red faced and breathing heavily, he asked what the man had looked like. Yung described a man in his forties, no, thirties (*gweilo* always look older than *Tongyan*), about this high – he motioned with his hand – light hair, no teeth . . . Shun described the man's big red nose.

'Shun Goh,' Yung said, addressing him politely as elder brother, 'all *gweilo* have big red noses.' He turned back to the constable. 'Nose just like you,' he said, 'and here . . .' He touched the right side of his jaw, trying to describe a scar but not knowing the words. 'He velly stupid,' he added.

After the constable had gone, Shun berated his brother, throwing his hands in the air. Why tell the *gweilo* he had money *la*? Why shake his pockets? Was he mad? After he walked off the *gweilo* harassed him for money too!

Yung wanted to laugh but he had to show respect. He tried to explain – after all the man was harmless, a simpleton, no more – but Shun wasn't listening. How come Yung was so stupid? Just two months ago Ah Chan was beaten up in the street. Didn't he know how dangerous it was?

Yung closed his ears. Already he was dreaming up a couplet. About a man with no teeth and half a mind, about a confusion of arrows and no idea which way to go.

NAORILAND

Sometimes under the weight, the shape, of his brother's expectation, Yung felt death-weary.

He stood before the washtubs out the back of the shop and gazed at his red-stained hands. He pulled the last beetroot from the water, brought down the blade quickly, once, twice, watched the leaves with their fine red stalks, the long end of the root, thin as a wet rat's tail, fall into the wooden box. Then he tossed the trimmed beetroot onto the others, carried the enamel basin to the wash-house and tipped them onto the purple-red mass in the copper. It would take half an hour for the water to come to the boil and then another hour, bleached worms, beetles, spiders slowly boiling on the surface of the red dirt water.

He went back and cleaned the tubs, tipped in half a sack of carrots, covered them with water, then took the broom and pushed it under then up through the vegetables, sweeping, tumbling them clean in the ever murkier liquid. He could feel a layer of sweat forming on his brow, the dampness of his white singlet, his shirt, under his arms. He loosened his grip, relaxed his arms for a moment, then pushed down again. Once he'd had tender hands, hands that knew only the calligrapher's brush, the grinding of ink stick with water. They were still soft, pale, not cracked and brown like his elder brother's, but now calluses had formed on his palms, on the fleshy pads below his fingers.

He remembered the first time he'd done this, the rhythmic push and pull of wood and bristle, the sting of his skin rubbing, folding in on itself.

He pulled the plugs, watched the rushing, sucking waters, stepped back as the pipes drained onto the concrete pad. He picked out the cleaned carrots, dropped them into a bamboo basket, tipped the rest of the sack into the tubs and filled them again with water. How many years had he been here boiling beetroot, washing carrots, and trimming cabbages and cauliflowers? Eight? Nine? Almost ten years.

Standing on the deck of the *Wakatipu* as it heaved into port, he had been astonished by the landscape. Dusty clay and rock where men had hacked a footing. Where they had tried to anchor themselves, their wooden shacks and macadam roads from Antarctic southerlies. Hills thick with bush and curling foliage falling to the bays. Ships loaded with coal or logs from the West Coast or human cargo from Sydney. Wellington: a town built of wood and dust and wind.

Shun Goh told him *gweilo* gave this land a strange, mystical name. The name of the dark-skinned people, the people of the land. He said Maoris were dying. In fifty years they would be wiped out, the way a white handkerchief wipes sweat from the face. They would become a story passed from mother to son, like the giant birds they'd heard of. Fierce birds that could not fly. *Moa*, the people said, like a lament . . . *Maori* . . . their absence a desolation.

In those early days Yung thought he saw a Maori, but the man selling rabbits door to door turned out to be Assyrian. And the man selling vegetables was Hindoo. This is what all the dark-skinned people were – Assyrian or Hindoo – the ones who lived in Haining Street.

Over months, years, he did see Maoris, their status and appearance as varied as *gweilo*. When the *gweilo* Duke and Duchess visited, *Tongyan* adorned a huge arch with flags outside Chow Fong's shop in Manners Street. *Chinese Citizens Welcome*, it said. Everyone lined up along the route: *gweilo, Tongyan,* Maoris.

'Who these Maolis?' Yung asked Mrs Paterson from the bakery next door, referring to the proud people in their finest *gweilo* top hats, pressed black suits and gold watch chains he saw welcome *gweilo* royalty, the groups of them he sometimes saw near Parliament.

'They're from up north,' Mrs Paterson said. 'They come to petition the government.'

'What is *petition*?' Yung asked.

'They want their land back,' she said, and then asked about the price of potatoes.

Sometimes Yung saw Maori fishermen or hawkers of sweet potato and watercress. They dressed in old ghost clothes and heavy boots, or wrapped an army blanket fastened with rope or a belt around the waist, sometimes even a blanket around their shoulders. But whatever their standing they never called out names or pulled his braid. They smiled, cigarette in hand, as if to a brother.

The first time Yung saw them he turned to Shun, looking for a sign. But his brother did not smile back. 'Be careful,' he said. *Have a small heart.* Yung looked at the tobacco-stained teeth, the blue-green markings etched all over the dark faces. One of the men was young, perhaps his own age, and he had a straggly beard that partially obscured his tattoos. Yung looked him in the eye and smiled, just the corners of his mouth, then followed his brother, unsure of what he should do.

Yung pushed the broom down into brown water. Almost a decade, and he'd barely spoken to a Maori. Proudly tipped his hat to an old woman perhaps – the way he'd seen ghost-men meet, greet and pass their women – or to Maori men he'd smiled a hello. Only once one had come into the shop.

The man's face was fully tattooed and he'd held himself so very erect and with such dignity in his top hat and pressed black suit, a white handkerchief neatly folded in his jacket pocket, that Yung had been at a loss for words. Yung could imagine him waving from a shiny black motorcar as crowds lined the parade.

The man had nodded his head slightly. 'Good afternoon,' he said.

'Good afternoon, sir.'

The man smiled, flashing a gold tooth. He looked at the strawberries and grapes.

He only wants the best fruit, Yung thought. The most expensive. 'Stlawbelly go lotten. No good,' he said. 'Glape best quality. Velly sweet.' He walked over, selected the best cluster – each grape plump, juicy, purple-black. 'Please tly,' he said, offering it up.

The man took a grape and placed it delicately in his mouth. He smiled again. 'Very good,' he said. 'I'll take two bunches.' Then he looked around again. 'How is the pineapple?'

Yung lifted a pineapple to his nose and sniffed. He tugged gently at one of the inner leaves, then put the pineapple back on the stack. He picked up another, smelled it and tugged at a leaf, which came away. 'Good pineapple,' he said. 'Lipe and sweet.'

As he handed over the packaged fruit, the man thanked him.

'Good luck,' Yung said.

The man looked at him quizzically.

'Your land,' Yung said.

'Yes,' the man said.

They almost bowed to each other before the man walked out into the southerly.

What *gweilo* had ever treated him as respectfully? How many had even looked in his eyes?

Each day he worked in the shop. Each day but Sunday white ghosts came in and out. He handed them vegetables wrapped in newspaper or paper bags filled with fruit. They put money on the wooden counter and he counted out their change. Good day. Good day.

He wanted to talk. He wanted to understand. But how to say? His English was improving. But how many customers truly invited his stumbling conversation?

On Sundays and other afternoons or nights when his brother gave him time off, he would go to a clansman's – to another fruit and vegetable shop or laundry – or go down Haining Street, Taranaki, Frederick or Tory. They called the area *Tongyangai* – Chinese people's street, where people of the *Tong* dynasty lived. In shop or cook-house or gambling joint, or even outside on a warm summer evening, they'd gather together to gossip and drink tea. His best friend Ng Fong-man, Cousin Gok-nam, everyone would be there. Everyone but women. Chinese women, wives. Even as he visited greengrocery, laundry, market garden, as he drummed up support and donations for the Revolution, how many women did he see? Who could afford the poll tax or even the fare?

Yung shut his eyes. He tried to remember his wife's face, the way her brow furrowed in concentration when he wrote the first line of a couplet, when he challenged her to complete it. He tried to remember her voice, the sound of her laughter ...

No, *everyone* would be there in Haining Street, and *gweilo* also, placing bets, or after work, crowded in with *Tongyan*, checking their *pakapoo* tickets. *Aaaaiyaa. Aaaaiyaa.* The thumping of tables. The smell of pork soup. The sizzle of garlic and ginger. White ghosts shoulder to shoulder, familiar faces without names. Their only intercourse green-inked characters marked on white tickets.

'Beetroot cooked *la*! What are you doing? Why aren't the carrots out in the shop?'

Yung started. 'All right *la*!' He dropped the last of the carrots into the basket. Watched the back of his brother's head as it disappeared inside again, his shiny shaven skin, the long oiled braid running down.

DREAMS OF SUN YAT-SEN

Shun Goh had given him the rest of the afternoon off – enough time to walk to Fong-man's, have a cup of tea, play a game of cards and maybe argue about politics. Yung was relieved to get away from his brother, and out of doors. Usually spring was windy, unpredictably wet, yet today he didn't have to hold his hat to stop it from flying away. He almost had to squint for the blue glare of sky.

He walked around the Basin Reserve where he'd seen men in funereal white play a strange game with a piece of wood and a ball. Once he'd seen the ball hit three sticks in the ground and all the men cry out and throw their hands in the air – everyone except the man holding the flat piece of wood. Today there were only children rolling down the grassy banks and a group of boys on the common with a stick. He continued up Webb Street, then turned right into Cuba, delighting in the warmth of the day, in the jostle of horse and cart and tram, in the noisy ducking and weaving of humanity.

He paused outside the fishmonger's with its window piled high with rabbits, the little curtain of them that hung across the top of the entrance. Rabbit tails would brush his face when he entered, the soft fur smelling of grass and gaminess against his skin. Rabbit stewed in an earthenware pot. One shilling each, or maybe only tenpence. He licked his lips and walked on, humming a song he couldn't quite remember the name of, a song that had lost its words but not its tune. He hummed as if he had all the time in the world – waving to Mr Paterson, breathing in the yeasty smell of hot bread as he drove past in his cart, only just becoming aware of children behind him.

He turned, saw the boys – half a dozen of them, maybe more, seven- to ten-year-olds, one fat, the rest skinny, each with a little tweed cap and dirty knees. The tallest was carrying a stick.

'Ching Chong Chinaman,' they sang. 'Born in a jar, christened in a teapot, ha, ha, ha.'

Yung kept walking. He felt his hat being knocked to the ground, his braid uncoiling, falling down his back, hands grabbing and yanking. Bursts of laughter and another yank.

He turned around and charged at them. 'Pigs! Dog-shit!' he shouted in Chinese. 'Drop dead in the street!'

The kids laughed and ran off. He wanted to chase them, grab hold of them, push their faces in the dirt. The tall one, the one who'd pushed his hat off with the stick. The redhead or, even better, the fat one – he would have been easy to catch.

'Ignore the barbarians,' his brother always said. 'Never give them an excuse to retaliate.'

But he was sick of it. He was educated. He was respected. Back home he could have been an official. Even now people came to him to read and write their letters, their New Year couplets. He went to meet the newcomers off the ships, to help them with customs and immigration.

One night when his brother was down Haining Street a couple of young hooligans had come to the shop and started throwing cabbages around. Yung had been so incensed he'd tossed them out, both of them, into the street. He could still see the dust settle round them. They never came back.

Yung smiled. His brother never knew. He picked up his hat, recoiled his braid and covered it again, carried on.

He had walked this way so many times before – past the drapery,

13

the pharmacy, over the tram tracks – yet only now did the saloon catch his attention. It was the veranda posts at first, the bright red, white and blue spiralling paint, and a similarly painted pole sticking out from above the doorway with the sign *S. Gibson* hanging from it. In the window there was a poster of a man in a suit and bun hat, pipe hanging from his mouth: *pipe tobacco in its most enjoyable form.*

Yung appreciated a well-laid out display, the aesthetics of colour and shape and categorisation. Arranged on shelves were blue tins of Capstan, Marcovitch Black and White, pale lemon State Express 555. There were matches in cardboard containers shaped like miniature hatboxes, as well as copper and tin versions, cylindrical and rectangular, wooden pipes and a brown ceramic tobacco jar inscribed with writing. Yung couldn't see all the words, and he didn't recognise them all either – *When all Things were made . . . better than Tobacco . . . a Bachelor's Friend* (what did Bachelor mean?) – but he did recognise the different tins and packets they sold in the greengrocery. He admired the china shaving mugs, each displayed with its own brush, the chrome hand clippers, Rolls Razors, cigar cutters, long leather razor strops, bottles of Scurf and Dandruff Lotion, and a Black Beauty Razor Hone with a long blue fish decorating the box.

A wooden partition separated the display from the interior. Even from the door onto the street he could only see another lead-light door with the words *Gents' Saloon* in the stained glass. He stepped back as the inner door opened, as a man emerged from the yellow-tinged, smoky light. As he walked past, Yung saw how neatly cut he was, how smoothly shaved. Yung smelled the tobacco and cinnamon. Another man entered the shop, and the smell of tobacco puffed out again before the door closed.

Yung could see his reflection in the window, his forehead shaved smooth, nothing of his tonsure or of the hair coiled under his hat. He'd had the braid for as long as he could remember. Some men cut theirs off. Some to stop the hair pulling, some for the Revolution. Even back home there were those who cut off their braids and then had to wear

14

hats or wigs when they went out or chance execution.

Yung dreamed of the end of the dynasty. He dreamed of a new and powerful China, free of corruption, free from Manchu and foreign domination. He dreamed of Sun Yat-sen heading the new Republic, a man from Heung Shan who spoke English and not only the Peking dialect of the northerners, but also Yung's language, their language, Cantonese. Now he dreamed of a haircut like Sun Yat-sen's, like that of the man he'd seen walking out of the shop.

But *gweilo* saloons didn't cut Chinamen's hair, everyone knew that; and if, even if he had the courage, the foolhardiness, what would happen then? He would sit back in a chair, waiting for a barbarian to run a blade across his cheek, over his jaw, across his throat. The room would be wreathed with smoke. He would be surrounded by ocean ghosts, looking, watching, in an afternoon of no natural light, just the yellow glow of gas mantles. He thought of Fong-man, beaten in his shop in this very same street. He would sit back in the chair and feel the blade as it cut across his throat, and no one would notice if he didn't come out.

That night, Yung took the scissors from the drawer in the kitchen and cut off his braid. He heard the swish of the blades and the crunch as he cut through, his head strangely light, hair falling loosely at the back of his neck. He held the braid heavy in his hand, feeling terrifyingly liberated, and yet as if he had amputated a limb, as if already the sword had come down on his neck. He didn't know what to do. He looked in the mirror, the one he used every few days for plucking facial hair. He did not recognise himself. He felt as if he were growing paler or maybe pinker – because that was the true colour of barbarians, not white but pink, something like the colour of domesticated pigs. He looked at his face, at his hair. He felt as if even his name was translating. He put the braid at the bottom of a drawer and covered it with his most intimate apparel.

Why had he looked in the window of that saloon? Why had he not simply gone to Ah Fung's, the Haining Street barber, like everyone else? Why did he always want whatever he could not have?

He swallowed his shame. It would take time for the shaven parts of his head to grow, but tomorrow he would go. He would get Ah Fung to style his hair. He would buy bay rum. He would go out into the street, slick and sweet, smelling of bay oil and cinnamon.

Onions

Edie McKechnie was digging in the woodpile searching for slaters, spiders, beetles, anything wriggly with lots of legs, when her brother, Robbie, came racing home with his friends: the show-off big kid, Billy, who always bossed the others around; Wally, who looked like he'd eaten a chelsea bun too many; some other silly, dirty boys.

'Want to see a trick, Edie?' Billy asked.

Edie glanced up, then ignored him. She lifted a piece of wood. Underneath, in the dirt and damp wood dust, she found four slaters. She flipped one onto its back with her nail, watched the pale eyelash legs wave, the soft grey armour curl.

'Look!' yelled Billy.

Edie noticed the stick for the first time when Billy reached out and flicked off Wally's cap.

'Hey,' said Wally as he scrambled to catch it, then picked it up from the ground.

'Let me, let me try,' said Robbie.

As he grabbed the stick and aimed at Wally's head, Edie noticed dirt all over her brother's clothes, grass and who-knows-what in the mess of his thick red hair.

'Ow! Ya bounder!' yelled Wally. 'I'll knock yer blimmin' head off!'

'No blimmin' way!' Robbie laughed and ran off, with Wally and the other boys chasing.

'Was that Robbie?' Their mother stood in the doorway, her face flushed from thumping irons onto sheets, shirts, petticoats, skirts, swapping them as they cooled with a hot iron from the range.

'He's taken off with Wally and Billy again.'

'Bother. I need him to chop wood. You'd better come in and help me cook dinner.'

Edie looked down. Her slaters had disappeared, even the one she'd flipped onto its back. She'd have to come out later with a jar. She wiped her hands on her skirt, stood up and went into the house, trying to remember what slaters ate for dinner.

Katherine McKechnie's neck and shoulders ached. She still felt the effects of hauling yesterday's wet washing and today the effort of lifting heavy irons. In winter, the range and the irons and the work kept her warm, but now sweat plastered her bodice, her petticoats, to her skin.

She stood at the bench and lopped the top and bottom off an onion, peeled away the skin. She should have started earlier, not finished ironing shirts that Donald wouldn't need till Thursday or Friday . . . Ow! She examined her nail. Thank goodness, no blood. She blinked. What was God thinking when he created onions? She wiped her eyes, hurriedly chopped, shoved the pieces into the hot fat, tossed a second onion into the bottom of the pantry. Glanced at Edie.

'Careful . . . If you cut off a finger it won't grow back, you know . . . Here . . .' She took the knife from her daughter and showed her again. 'Keep your fingers out of the way. As you cut, you have to keep moving your hand down the carrot away from the knife . . . That's more like it . . . When it gets too little, just leave it and start another. I'll finish off.'

'Mum?'

18

'Yes?'

'What do slaters eat?'

Katherine looked up from the kidney she was slicing. 'Well, I don't know. What do other insects eat?'

Edie stopped chopping. 'They're not insects, Mum.'

'What?'

'Insects have six legs.'

Katherine stared at her daughter. She wasn't even seven. 'Where did you get that from?' she asked.

'You know – that book we got from the library.'

Katherine laughed. Of course. Both the children could read beyond their years. How could they not with their father a newspaperman, *a purveyor of words*, as he liked to say. But it was Edie, the youngest, who seemed the most eager, dragging Katherine to the Newtown library each week, bringing her novels by Jane Austen or George Eliot – surely she couldn't really understand them – and non-fiction books with beautiful colour illustrations on any subject – ornithology, Egyptian history, Etruscan architecture. Robbie, on the other hand, seemed to thrive on the exploits of Revolver Dick or Jim, the Slayer of the Prairies. If he'd been old enough, one of his favourite pastimes would have been the games evenings at the library. But they were shut down for 'destructiveness and rowdiness'. Katherine smiled grimly. Give him a few years and he'd likely be one of the chief culprits.

She scraped chunks of beef and kidney into the pot, looked across at Edie. 'So how many legs do slaters have?'

'Fourteen.' Edie grinned. 'I counted.'

'So what do you call slaters if they're not insects? Did it tell you that in—?'

The front door slammed and Robbie came running down the hall to the kitchen. Peered into the smoking pot. 'Steak and kidney . . . Can I have something to eat?' He reached for the biscuit tin.

Katherine smacked away his hand. 'Go and chop some wood and bring it in, and then you can help yourself to a slice of bread and dripping.' She looked at his filthy face, the grass stains and dirt on his clothes, his black-edged nails. 'But wash your hands first. I don't want dirty marks on the loaf.'

After he'd gone out, Edie asked, 'Do you think slaters might like bread?'

'I don't know, dear. Ants do. And birds.' She noticed a chunk pulled out of the loaf. 'And naughty boys.'

An hour later, Robbie put down his fork after just one mouthful. 'I'm not hungry,' he said.

Katherine sighed. 'Well, you shouldn't have eaten so much bread then, should you? I did say *one* slice.'

Donald McKechnie spat into his plate. 'No wonder the boy can't eat! How long did you cook this for? Five minutes? How many times do I have to tell you?'

'Then perhaps you shouldn't insist on steak and kidney on Tuesdays. It takes all day to do the ironing and that doesn't leave much time for cooking.'

'Then put the dinner on in the morning, woman! Haven't you got anything in that skull of yours?'

Katherine examined Donald's red face, his twitching moustache. She had more teeth in that skull of hers than he did, that's for sure. What did he say? Fed up to the back teeth? It was his back teeth, or lack thereof, that was the problem. She imagined his mouth stuffed full of tough, sinewy stew, his jaw working and working, gravy leaking from the corner of his mouth, from his ears. She looked down and tried not to smile.

'Eat it tomorrow,' she muttered without meeting his eyes.

She took his plate into the kitchen and scraped the stew back into the pot, sliced the last piece of Sunday's roast, cooked till it fell from the bone (thank goodness on wash days they ate leftover roast), and laid it on the remains of Donald's gravy. She could have told him that

Mac had run out of kidneys, that he'd told her to come back in the afternoon. She could have told him to wait another hour for dinner instead of always insisting it be on the table at six. She spooned more gravy over the top and took the plate back out.

Donald was telling Robbie about some incident at work: '. . . and then the peabrain . . .'

Katherine could hear them laughing but she didn't know, didn't care why. She felt tired. Very tired.

She'd met him at her sister's wedding. She noticed the way people listened to his stories, laughed at his jokes. The way women could not help but flirt with him. Even her mother and sister. She watched, fascinated, almost horrified at how he moved through the room, a steamer moving through water, leaving a wake behind him.

Did he feel her watching? He looked up, directly at her, made some excuse and made his way across the dance floor.

He told her the radiance of her dress brought out the light in her eyes like the wings of a *Doxocopa cherubina*. A butterfly, he said. From Venezuela. Peru. Had she heard of those places? Its uniqueness, he said, lay in its iridescence. You might look once and see only a plain but lovely green, but look again, down its wings, and it was like gazing into a prism – shimmering strips of blue and green.

'What about the whites of my eyes?' she'd said recklessly. 'Do they remind you of cabbage butterflies?'

He'd stared at her, surprised, and she blushed. She turned to leave, but he caught her by the arm – she could feel the tingle of his hand on her skin. He looked deeply into her eyes and said, 'You should come and see my collection. It is but a small affair, but the *Doxocopa cherubina* is well worth perusing.'

Within the week he was walking her around his parlour, stopping at each framed, winged body. 'Katherine,' he said. 'Kate . . .' He placed the palm of his hand upon her back as he guided her from one specimen

21

to another, told her butterflies and moths belonged to the same order – only butterflies were the more beautiful. Later she discovered he'd bought them from a lepidopterist he'd interviewed for the *Post*. He'd memorised the Latin names, country of origin, distinguishing features of male and female.

The *Doxocopa cherubina* was still pinned and framed on the wall of their parlour. Breathtaking if, as he said, you looked down, not up, its wings. It was very still. It had lost the capacity to breathe.

As Katherine watched her husband eat soft meat and gravy and cauliflower boiled till its grey lumpiness mashed in the mouth like small brains, she saw very clearly – had she not always known, if not for a temporary madness? – all of Donald's women were *Lepidoptera*: either a moth to the flame or merely part of his silent collection.

'. . . the gravy's not bad, I suppose, considering . . .'

Katherine felt Donald's gaze.

'. . . but put in some more onion, for godsake. Didn't you learn anything when Mother came to stay? God bless her soul, may she rest in peace.'

Katherine gathered up the plates and took them into the kitchen – Donald's and Edie's eaten clean, hers and Robbie's barely touched. She could hear Donald getting down the dictionary that had passed from McKechnie father to McKechnie son. '*Procrustean*,' Donald was saying. 'Robbie, what does *procrustean* mean?'

Katherine's finger stung where a line of blood pooled beneath her nail. She scraped the uneaten food back into the pot. Left the onions to rot in the pantry.

A FINE EXAMPLE OF A BRITISH GENTLEMAN

When Donald came home in the wee hours reeking of whisky and tobacco, Katherine pulled the eiderdown over her face and feigned sleep.

'Met a fascinating gentleman tonight,' he said, his words slurred and slow. Katherine pictured a giant snail, with Donald's waxed moustache, sliming across the room. *But snails do not lurch drunkenly into bed,* she thought. *I'm being unkind to snails.*

'. . . Terry's a splendid specimen of a man,' he said. 'And don't you get any funny ideas about it . . . We had a few drinks with . . .'

A few?

Donald rattled off names of *prominent* Members of Parliament, as he called them.

Katherine waited, but before he could say more he had slumped over the bed, letting out loud, *immelodious* snores.

Katherine smiled. Did Donald know that word? Had he found it in his dictionary? Now, such words came to her only in his absence. *Immelodious.* The sound of birdsong, even more beautiful than *melodious.* The sound of contradiction. Like waking in the night and seeing for the first time. Like falling out of love.

For days Donald couldn't speak of anything but Lionel Terry. *Terry, graduate of Eton and Oxford. Terry, descendant of Napoleon Bonaparte. Terry in the Transvaal fighting the savage Matabeles. Terry, friend of Cecil Rhodes and Paul Kruger. Terry the poet and painter.* How could Donald remember? Hadn't he been drunk? Was he having lunch with the *splendid specimen* every other day? (And wasn't that the word you used to describe dead things? Things you collected and pinned under glass?) Katherine swept around Donald's feet with the hearth brush, making him move one foot, then the other. She swept in front of the fireplace and then came back again – and again – imitating the perversions of a small, obstinate fly, but nothing could dampen Donald's enthusiasm.

'He walked all the way from Mangonui to Wellington carrying just a walking stick and a knapsack. Bet you a shilling you have no idea where Mangonui is, eh. Kate, he pretty much walked the entire length of the North Island!'

Katherine swallowed. He hadn't called her Kate for years.

'Damned fine poet, too,' Donald continued. 'Gave me one of his tracts.' He waved it at her, but she excused herself to empty the dustpan.

'Yes indeed, a fine example of a British gentleman,' he was saying as she left the room.

Katherine had a suspicion of British gentlemen. They had the right accent and excellent manners, which concealed any number of vices. Good riddance to bad rubbish, she thought as she watched coal dust and ash fall into the bin in a small cloud.

'I've invited him for dinner Sunday,' Donald called from the parlour.

Katherine examined Mr Terry upon his arrival. He was at least six foot five. Athletic. Handsome. He stood very erect – obviously a man with military experience. She had to admit, reluctantly, that he did *appear* a splendid specimen of a man, though his abundant hair had turned prematurely grey.

'Mrs McKechnie,' he said, 'a pleasure.' He smiled. 'Is that roast mutton I smell cooking? I'm sure you are an excellent cook, Mrs McKechnie, but regretfully I do not eat meat. Our carnivorous tendencies are an unhealthy obsession and play havoc with our constitutions.'

Katherine was at a loss for words. She had never heard of anyone who did not eat meat. All she could do was summon the children to set the table.

Terry ruffled Robbie's hair. 'Let the boy join us in the parlour,' he said.

From the kitchen, Katherine could hear their outbursts of laughter. Edie sniffed.

'Blow your nose, Edie. It does a young lady no favours to sniff like a dog.' Katherine bit her lip. She could hear her own mother's voice – the same words, the exact same tone. My sakes, she didn't want to be like her mother!

She watched Edie wipe her eyes and blow into an embroidered handkerchief. She put her hand lightly on her daughter's shoulder.

'If you hurry and set the table, then you can call them straight in for dinner.'

'Mrs McKechnie,' Terry said as he entered the dining room, 'where may I ask do you buy your vegetables? From an honest Briton or do you buy them from the heathen?'

Katherine stepped back, for Terry towered above her. 'The Chinaman's fruit and vegetables are cheaper,' she said, 'and fresher.'

Terry smiled. His upper lip twitched. He looked her in the eye and then, as if the leading man in some theatrical production, he began to recite, his voice resonant, deliberate, his bearing, his hands somehow embellishing each word:

See, advancing, grim, relentless, as a scourge sent forth from hell,
Comes the blighting curse of Mammon, in the white man's land to
   dwell;
Mongol, Ethiop, nameless horror, human brute from many a clime,
Vomited from earth's dark pest holes; bred of plague, diseases, and
   crime.
Swathed in rags and noisome odours, gaunt and fleshless, dwarfed of
   limb,
Visages like the grisly jackal seeking dead midst shadows dim;
See the horde of drug besotten, sin begotten, fiends of filth,
Swarming o'er thy nation's bulwarks; pillaging thy nation's wealth.

He pulled tracts from his suit pocket and handed them to the children. Katherine saw the brightness, the flush of excitement on Robbie's face, the fascination and uncertainty of Edie.

Suddenly, inexplicably, she wished the bowl of carrots in her hands were not chopped and boiled, but still whole and raw, sharpened, hardened like arrows. For one long moment she imagined tipping a water-filled pot of them; imagined Terry's astonished expression as he lay soaked and pinned to the floor, half a dozen carrots passing through his chest and into the floorboards. She could hear the tinny, frenzied piano accompaniment, the quick, jerky black and white motion of his neck, his arms, his legs, as he tried to pick himself up. She almost laughed, nervously, astonished at her ludicrous imagination. Instead she placed the bowl on the table and showed Terry to his seat while Donald carved the mutton.

Terry asked Robbie to pass a tract to his mother. Katherine pressed her lips into a thin smile. No one noticed. Terry had the poetic gift. He and Donald had enough conversation in them for the whole family.

'We cannot eradicate the natural hatred between races with civilisation,' Terry was saying as Katherine passed vegetables around the table. 'We have to end this insane practice of importing alien races . . . No, thank you. I'm sure you are a fine cook, Mrs McKechnie, but I do not eat food contaminated by Chinamen . . . This employment of alien labour is a criminal injustice to the British workman. It's the chief cause of poverty, crime, degeneracy and disease throughout the Empire . . .'

Donald raised his glass. 'Hear, hear!'

'Robbie,' Terry continued, 'where do leprosy and bubonic plague come from?'

When Robbie could not answer, Terry said, 'Why, from the filthy heathen, son. The Mongols and black savages . . .'

Katherine gritted her teeth. Robbie was *not* Terry's son. But Donald smiled, nodded, patted Robbie on the back.

Terry spread butter on a slice of Katherine's home-baked bread. He turned to Donald. 'The presence of Asiatics in this country jeopardises the rights of our fellow Britons. We have to take drastic measures before it's too late . . .'

Terry chewed on his bread. 'A wholesome loaf, Mrs McKechnie.'

To Donald he said, 'As for the Maoris, there has never in the history of the world been a case of two races living together in the same country without the deterioration and decay of one or the other. The weakest race is always doomed . . .'

Katherine tried to consider at least some of Terry's words. After all, didn't the politicians say precisely this – that the Maoris required protection, that they were in danger of extinction?

Terry reached for another slice of bread. 'The Maoris are now in such a state of moral, mental and physical degeneration that without complete and utter separation, their race will be beyond salvation. I see no practical solution but to exchange all lands in Maori possession for islands such as Stewart and the Chathams . . .'

Katherine wondered how much land was still in Maori possession. And how many Maoris were there left to be crammed onto the islands?

'An interesting proposition,' Donald said. 'But how to achieve the desired result – now that's the challenge.'

Terry swallowed. 'McKechnie, my man, nothing worth its salt comes without hard work and sacrifice . . . As for race-adulterers, they should be transferred to outlying islands also. Mark my words . . .'

Race-adulterers? Katherine had never even considered the mixing of races, but to use the term adultery seemed absurd. She accepted Terry's exhortation and drew a thick black line through every one of his words.

'My petitions to members of Parliament, the Commissioner of Customs, the Minister of Native Affairs, etcetera, etcetera, have been to no avail,' Terry was saying.

He declined the roast mutton, the vegetables, even Katherine's bread and butter pudding. He did not eat foreign foods. Sugar, he said. He did not even drink tea. Katherine went to the meat safe to fetch him milk. She didn't know whether to be alarmed or to be sorry for the man.

Early the next morning before anyone else rose, Katherine searched for the tracts. She knew Donald had his, but hadn't Terry left another three? Where were they all? She found two and fed them, deliciously, to the coal range, filled the kettle and set it on top. How she would savour her porridge this morning, her sweet, milky tea.

A BAG OF PEANUTS

The news spread from one shop to another, from laundry to greengrocery to market garden. There had been the shooting in Naseby the previous year, and then the murder of Ham Sing-tong in Tapanui only a few weeks before, but this was Haining Street. This was where Cousin Gok-nam lived, where Shun and his brother Yung went on Sundays for wontons and roast pig, for tea and gossip.

Joe Kum-yung was not a clansman, but with maybe three hundred in all of Wellington, every Chinese was a brother, especially one shot at point-blank range. Yung heard from Fong-man, who heard from Joe Toy, that Kum-yung had been walking home when a man came up behind him and shot him twice in the head. No one got a good look at the murderer. It was a Sunday evening. It was dark. Haining Street was almost deserted. The man with the revolver wore a long grey coat. He was tall. He was *gweilo*. When Joe Toy got there, his cousin was lying outside Number 13 in a dark pool of blood, a paper bag of peanuts scattered about him.

Shun wondered whether the locks on the doors were adequate. Kum-yung had been in New Zealand thirty years – a cripple from his gold-mining days on the West Coast. His clansmen had raised the money to return him to China, to return him to his wife, but instead the fool had gone up the coast to try his hand at market gardening.

And lost everything! He'd only been back in Wellington a few weeks. Why hadn't he gone home? When he'd had the chance . . .

Shun rubbed his gammy leg. He told his brother not to go out after dusk. Not to go out at all, not unless absolutely necessary.

But the murder had barely passed three hundred pairs of lips when stranger, even more compelling news broke. A man had turned himself in. The murderer was in custody.

THE TRIAL

A crowd began to gather early on the morning of the trial, eager to see Lionel Terry brought down from the Terrace Gaol. Donald half-ran down Lambton Quay, and by the time he arrived at the Supreme Court his armpits felt uncomfortably wet and his shirt stuck to his back in a film of sweat.

'Damned hot for November,' he said as he joined a group of reporters.

'We get this in Auckland all the time,' one of them laughed. 'But not the blinking wind!'

Thompson, whom Donald used to work with at the *Evening Post,* offered a cigarette. 'I hear you've met Terry.'

'Yeah. Good bloke, Terry.'

Thompson struck a match and held it up, sheltering it from the breeze. 'Did you have any inkling he was going to do this?'

Donald drew on his cigarette, blew out. 'Hell no,' he said. 'Didn't like Chinks, that's for sure. A scourge, he called them. Wanted them sent back. Who doesn't? But . . .' Donald shook his head sadly, drew on his cigarette and blew a long plume of smoke. 'Sure knows how to make a point . . .'

They stood on the steps of the courthouse, shifting their weight from foot to foot, discussing the case as the crowd grew and became more boisterous and spilled across the road, threatening to close Stout Street.

When the doors finally opened and Terry still hadn't appeared, Donald and the press and a mass of spectators charged for the main courtroom doors; yet more snaked up to the public gallery by the steep staircases on either side. Donald found a place in the press area. There was not enough room and some reporters ended up sitting with Chinamen and other spectators. The doors closed with hundreds still amassed outside.

Perhaps it was the sheer number of chattering, excitable people, the sour taste of stale sweat, everywhere the darkness of stained wood. Donald gazed upwards where the walls were paler, off-white, where faint light filtered through second-floor windows. This was not some inexplicable error, some minor indiscretion. His friend was on trial. For murder.

The crier called out and the crowd fell silent and rose. The Chief Justice, Sir Robert Stout, entered and sat at the bench.

Donald took a pencil and pad from his pocket.

Even as Terry came up from the cells, as he stood tall between his guards, a white handkerchief neatly folded in his suit pocket, Donald noted that he had a dignity uncommon in those who frequented the dock. He caught his eye and Terry smiled, nodded slightly.

He had declined counsel. If anyone could defend himself with honour, then surely that was Terry, yet a vague uneasiness stirred in Donald's stomach. He watched as the registrar read the charge and asked how Terry pleaded.

Terry lifted his chin and peered down at the man. He objected to the word guilty. He had nothing to say except that his action was right and justifiable.

'That means not guilty,' said His Honour.

Not guilty. The words reverberated in Donald's mind. As the jury was empanelled, he listened to the names, good British names, examined each face, speculating on each man's views. How could they

32

not agree on the Asiatic problem?

He listened as the Crown opened with Charles William Harris, who was in Taranaki Street on 24 September at 7.35 p.m. Harris had heard a report from the direction of Haining Street and seen a man standing on the footpath. He saw a flash and heard a second report, then saw the man come towards him. The man was tall and wore a long, light overcoat. Only then did he notice a Chinaman lying on the footpath twenty to twenty-five feet from where the man had been standing.

Terry looked on implacably. He had no questions for Mr Harris or for the next witness, Constable Fitzgerald.

Now Joe Duck, a resident of Haining Street, was sworn in. *Joe Duck. What kind of name is that?* Donald watched the scorn on Terry's face as the interpreter lit a match, handed it to Duck, mumbled something unintelligible and waited for him to blow it out.

Duck had lengthy discussions with the interpreter.

'We need an interpreter for the interpreter,' the Prosecutor said.

Donald, Terry and half the court snickered.

If the interpreter was to be believed, the Chinaman saw a man in a light overcoat fire a gun in Haining Street. The man who fired walked off. The man who fell was Joe Kum-yung.

For the first time Terry asked questions. Was Joe Kum-yung taller than Duck? How tall was Duck, how many English feet were there in five Chinese feet . . .

Donald smiled. *Confound the bugger with irrelevant questions.*

Dr Ewart gave evidence that death was caused by injury to the brain from the bullet wound.

Then Ngan Ping of Molesworth Street swore on the Bible and spoke without an interpreter. One Friday night Terry had come into Number 5 Haining Street where Ping and others were playing cards.

'You were gambling,' Terry said.

Yes. Undermine his credibility – that of every Chinaman – by revealing his criminal nature.

'No gambling,' the Chink said. 'Only Chinese cash. Cannot spend it here,'

'Are you a Christian?' Terry asked.

'Yes.'

'You believe the Bible is better than your own religion?'

Ha! As Terry continued to interrogate, he reminded Donald of a boy pulling off the wings, then the legs of a fly.

Now Constable Young and Inspector Ellison stated that Terry had come into the station and given up his revolver. He'd shot a Chinaman to call attention to the evil of alien immigration. He'd signed a written statement.

Damn.

Horace Clare Waterfield, Private Secretary to His Excellency the Governor, produced the letter which His Excellency had received through the post the morning after Joe Kum-yung was shot. The letter, signed 'Lionel Terry, British subject', stated that to protect the rights of Britons against alien immigration he had 'deemed it necessary to put a Chinaman to death' that evening in the Chinese quarter known as Haining Street.

Oh damn.

Terry cross-examined Dr Martin as to the nature of the wound, and the Crown closed its case.

Terry declined to call evidence. He had nothing to give except a short statement.

Donald leaned forward in his seat.

Terry pulled out a thick pile of papers and addressed the jury. He objected to His Majesty being placed in the position of protector of unnaturalised race aliens, he said. He was surprised at the number of Asiatic witnesses and officials. Evidently the vast difference between European and Asiatic veracity had yet to be realised. The evidence given by the Chinese witnesses, especially that of Ngan Ping, the Christian, was distinctly Asiatic in quality, and he suspected the Chinese interpreter of being more shrewd than honest. Although in any other case he would decline to reply to a charge in which so many aliens were concerned – he glanced at Donald – he had brought this charge against himself for the purpose of protesting against this very evil.

Not entirely unreasonable.

Terry denied emphatically that he was the victim of an insane delusion or that his intellect had been impaired by sunstroke or any other ailment.

No.

Donald stared at Terry. Of course he agreed with Terry about the Chinese, but this was a capital charge. Surely it would be easier to excuse his action if there were some underlying condition. Something as innocent as sunstroke.

Terry continued with a long explanation of his position. The New Zealand Government needed to ship its aliens to other shores, so that it would be a country fit for white settlement . . . Upwards of 100,000 people were dependent upon the Asiatic alien for staple food products . . . The enemy was tampering with the food supplies, polluting the source from which the country derived its strength . . .

Donald tried to concentrate. He'd always enjoyed Terry's speeches, but this time his mind started to drift. Terry's *short* statement was full of polysyllabic words and contorted legal statements. It was too long.

'I did murder one Chinaman, presumably Joe Kum-yung,' Terry was saying, 'but the murder was committed to test the law relating to the protection of aliens . . .'

Donald examined the Chief Justice's face. How would he interpret this? At least, as a fellow member of the Anti-Chinese League, His Honour hated the Chinese too.

'As it is naturally impossible for people of two distinct races to possess the same characteristics, therefore it is equally impossible for the laws of the people of one race to govern those of another.'

Well, well, well . . . Donald stabbed his pad with his pencil.

'As the laws representing one race cannot be applied to people of another race, therefore it is unlawful for people of two or more distinct races to dwell together in the same country.'

Mmmmm . . .

'Therefore, there cannot be a law according protection to or in any way recognising the presence of unnaturalised race aliens in British possessions.

'In reply to the charge that I killed *this* alien,' Terry paused, looked at Donald, the jury, 'the Chinaman, being a race alien, is not a man within the meaning of the statute.'

Donald closed his eyes. Opened them again. There were few men he'd met who could match Terry's charisma or indeed his powers of rhetoric. Of course he agreed that decisive action was required. But the audacity of the man!

As the Chief Justice summed up, Donald gripped his pencil. The law applied to every human being in New Zealand, His Honour said. There was no answer to the charge.

God! Here was the Chief Justice, fellow hater of the Asiatic element, having to protect Chinamen!

The only possible question, His Honour said, was whether the prisoner knew the nature of his act and was responsible for his actions. Donald's knuckles, his fingers, turned white. There was no evidence of mental aberration, the Chief Justice continued, and the prisoner himself plainly contradicted it. He paused, surveyed the courtroom. Therefore, it was the duty of the jury to find the prisoner guilty.

Donald wanted to jump up and shout, 'This is an honourable man. You know that, Your Honour. You agree with his position. I've seen you at the meetings . . . He's a Briton. A gentleman . . . Perhaps a little misguided . . .' Why the devil had Terry denied any mental incapacity? Surely it could have been sunstroke? Why did he refuse counsel?

Terry caught Donald's eye as he was led away, head held high, emotionless.

The jury retired. Donald sighed and took out his pocket-watch. Seven minutes to one. He stood up and glanced at the gallery, at the crowd of spectators. There, behind that woman with the outrageous hat, the grapes and the pineapples and the fiddly blue ribbons – damn it, if he'd had to sit behind her, he would have given her an earful – as she moved, behind her, suddenly he saw Robbie. The boy was wagging again, but for once Donald didn't mind. He would have done the same himself, had he been in his shoes.

He went out into the breezy blue-eyed day, lit a cigarette and walked from Stout Street into Whitmore, from Ballance into Lambton Quay and back to the main entrance on Stout. He took a piss, then hurried back towards the courtroom.

The jury returned at 1.25 p.m. with its verdict:

'GUILTY, with a strong recommendation to mercy . . .'

Donald did not hear all the words.

'. . . not responsible for his actions . . . suffering . . . from a craze . . . his intense hatred . . . mixing of British and alien races.'

The registrar asked Terry if he had anything to say. Was there any reason why he should not receive the death sentence?

Terry stood very tall and straight, his voice strong and clear. 'Nothing except to repeat what I said formerly, that my action was a right and justifiable action.'

'Prisoner Lionel Terry,' the Chief Justice said, 'the recommendation of the jury will be duly forwarded to his Excellency, the Governor . . . The sentence of the Court is that you be taken . . . to His Majesty's prison at Wellington, and thence to the place of execution,' Donald broke the lead of his pencil on his pad, 'and there be hanged by the neck till you be dead . . . may the Lord have mercy upon your soul.'

A hush fell on the court. All eyes were directed at Terry, who stood very still, his blue eyes calm.

Donald watched as Terry was led out. He sat in his seat as others leapt up and chatted excitedly. He would write about his friend – how he'd held the court spellbound by his oratory, how he'd risked all for the honour of his race, how he'd stood clear-eyed and erect, a knight errant lifted from the pages of chivalry.

NO CONTINENTS OR SEAS

Katherine watched helplessly as Robbie lived and breathed Lionel Terry. His father talked through his reports even before he published. 'What do you think, Robbie? Enough drama for you?'

Robbie wanted to sign the petition that ran throughout the country, but his father said, 'When you're older, son, you'll have your turn.'

Donald tried to get Katherine to sign. It was the only time she remembered him swearing at her. She could feel every movement of her body, the heaviness of her arms, her legs, as she turned her back and walked out of the room. She could feel herself quivering, could feel his eyes burning at the back of her neck. The blackness of his rage, his stunned disbelief.

The petition collected thousands of names, but in the end it wasn't needed. The Government had already decided: Terry's sentence was commuted to life imprisonment.

Father and son tracked Terry's progress from Wellington Gaol to Lyttelton, from Lyttelton Gaol to Sunnyside (mental hospital, indeed! – the papers didn't say lunatic asylum any more), from the madhouse to his escapes into the countryside. Donald and Robbie told each other stories, embellishing them more and more with each telling – why, you'd think he was some modern-day Robin Hood, the way people talked, the way they helped him.

'Terry's adventures certainly add spice to the paper,' Donald said as he poured more whisky. 'We could run a series of cartoons, Robbie. Terry swimming the Waimakariri. Terry in the abandoned hut at Burnt Hill eating raw vegetables and grasses . . .'

So they weren't Chinamen's vegetables, Katherine thought.

They were all sitting in the parlour, Edie reading a book, Katherine mending yet another hole in Robbie's sock. This one didn't deserve the name 'sock'. More a mass of darning held together by wool scrap. Why couldn't Donald give her more money?

'How about a cartoon of the man in Oxford giving him his handkerchief and check cap with the caption – *Good on you, Terry. Keep up the good work . . .*'

Damn. Katherine sucked her finger where she'd pricked it with the needle.

'We could have Terry lecturing about the alien problem before the crowd at Sheffield . . . Sure they caught him in the end, carted him back to Sunnyside, but you can't keep a good man down. I hear with his latest escape the Chinks throughout Canterbury locked up their shops and didn't even work their gardens. Now there's a good cartoon.'

Katherine sighed. Now she listened as Donald read aloud yet another letter:

My friend,

During my recent excursion I enjoyed a right royal time amongst the mountains and rivers, though the water was a little too cold and I had to indulge in a good run up hill to get what the silly little medicos call the 'red blood corpuscles' smiling again. I cannot understand why people choose to live on the stagnant flat when they might as easily live at altitude where the air is pure and life is infinitely more wholesome . . .

The madhouse is thoroughly tiresome. I miss the conversation of intelligent companions, this being the primary motivation for my numerous excursions. Your continued encouragement and strong support are a great comfort to me. Please give my kind wishes to all our mutual friends.

I remain,
Yours as ever,
Lionel Terry.

'We need to start a petition for Terry's release, Robbie,' Donald said. 'The madhouse is no place for a man of his intellect. It would be enough to send a sane man mad.' He sat, hands steepled in concentration, Robbie beside him, a mirror image of his father.

As Katherine put away her sewing basket and went to cook dinner she noticed Edie, head raised from *The Story of the Earth*, quietly observing. Katherine did not need to tell her that women (and girls) of good breeding did not read Donald's newspaper. Katherine always banished any unattended copy to a pile near the fireplace. Stories of avaricious doctors, filthy foods in restaurants, fallen women all went up in flames.

Nevertheless, Katherine worried. Not only about Donald's influence but also about Edie's own eccentricities. Once, in the library, Katherine caught her up on the shelves, fingers wrapped around *Gray's Anatomy: Descriptive and Surgical*. She was seven, for heaven's sake. All right, almost eight. Did she understand anything of what she read or did she just enjoy the illustrations, the challenge of impossible words? Thank goodness she hadn't dropped it. Katherine was in no mood for an argument with the librarian. Nor did she fancy having to explain to Donald why they were paying for an expensive damaged book. He'd put on his shirt that morning complaining that even a Chinaman could do a better job of the ironing. As she'd pulled Edie down from the shelf, as she scolded her and slapped her hand, Katherine could hear Donald's mother calling from the grave, her voice like a noose round her throat. *Such stubbornness in a girl*, she was saying, *such peculiarity! Beat it out of her now, Donald, before it's too late. What man will have her if you don't nip it in the bud? How can this not lead to unhappiness?*

Alone in the kitchen, Katherine sliced the top from an onion, stared at its translucent creamy-green rings. She could see a tree stump

– the end of life, all the rings of its history. She was throwing a stone, watching the ripples of water.

It was easier not to think. Or feel. Perhaps intelligence was not a blessing. More a test of character.

She saw her daughter's face, the long curls of red hair, a scattering of freckles over her upturned nose, her big hazel eyes. She sliced the bottom from the onion and her eyes watered. Once she'd looked like that too. Like her daughter.

She peeled the skin, held the naked onion in her hand. For a moment she saw a lopped-off globe with no continents or seas, a world that had lost its shape. And all its boundaries.

RISING TO THE SURFACE

In the early hours of Monday morning – that time of the day and week when sleep is deepest and life is at its most vulnerable – Katherine woke, then, stretching across the cold white sheets, fell immediately back into sleep. Later that morning, as she heated the copper, a constable came to see her, told her Donald had been drunk when he fell into the water.

Katherine did not stop to cry. She thanked the constable and waved him away, sent the children to school with apples, a bagful of biscuits. She added two tablespoons of kerosene to the copper, let the bedclothes boil in yellow-soaped water.

All day she scrubbed the skin from her knuckles, pulling linen, frocks, seven white shirts through the mangle and into blued water. The rain came down as Katherine pegged the last of the wash on the line. Inside she watched the slanting cuts of water, five pairs of trousers – brown, blue, black – blown full of cold air.

Every evening he came home with the *Post*, devouring it with whisky and half a pack of cigarettes before dinner. A pack of wowsers, he'd say, as he mocked the Women's Christian Temperance Union or the three women who'd just crossed the Southern Alps by the Copland

Pass. 'If Misses Perkins and Barnicoat spent more time developing their womanly arts, then perhaps they'd find husbands. As for Mr Thomson—' Donald roared with laughter. 'How the devil did he snare a wife like that?'

Katherine watched a column of ash fall from his shaking hand. *Let the house burn,* she thought, but she walked into curling white smoke and stubbed it out with her shoe.

Afterwards as he sat at the table, hands and the cuffs of his sleeves still smudged with ink from the paper, Donald expounded the victories of his day. The latest in a war of words. As Katherine served sago and stewed apple or banana, he smiled, gave Robbie a wink. Pulled a word he'd rehearsed out of the print of his mind. 'Robbie, spell me: *enatant.*'

Robbie gazed up out of the corner of his eye, as if to catch the black letters as they swept by. 'E,' he said, 'E-N-A—'

Donald filled in the blanks, overwriting the incorrect letters. 'So what does it mean, son?'

Robbie thought for a while, a flurry of questions creasing his brow. 'Something that's very hard, Father.'

Donald laughed, praising his son for an excellent answer. Then looked at Edie.

Edie wrapped the white tablecloth round her fingers. Her lower lip quivered, her lips parted slightly, as if a word, or perhaps just an expectation of a word, might slip from her tongue and tumble into the unsuspecting hands of her father. And yet she said nothing, only looked into the face of her mother.

Katherine could not bear to see herself in her daughter. She gazed out the window at a small piece of sky – a piece of blue-grey fabric sewn over and over as if to cover a hole. She hesitated. Turned to see Donald laughing furiously. What had she said? What do you say over and over when no one hears you?

Now Katherine watched his empty clothes on the line. He was not coming home. She did not have to conjure up the meaning of words – *his* words; watch as he listened and laughed at her. Or tell anyone who asked that he was a newspaperman, neglecting to mention *Truth*. She did not have to find Robbie, on Saturday afternoons, reading the sex scandals passed down from the hands of his father. She gazed at Donald's chair, closed her eyes. What would she tell the children?

That night Katherine lay on the left side of the bed, feeling the space beside her. Robbie had stopped sobbing. Only the rattle of a tram as it slid down the tracks of Riddiford Street, the thud and wheel of a horse-cart, a drunk's thick call as he passed on his way from the Caledonian, the Tramways, some godforsaken hotel.

She woke sprawled across the double bed, filling Donald's absence with her own body. Breathing in the freshly starched sheets, two fat pillows squashed beneath her. *Nothing left of him, nothing conjugal.* She turned, her face brushing his pillow. Even now with its new white slip, a faintly familiar smell. *His* smell.

He would come with the closing of her eyes – a rough groping and thrusting of body parts. Rolling off into sleep, leaving her wet, suddenly cold with his sweat. The first night she'd lain in the dark, her face startled like a silent *oh*. Later she learned to press her mind into a thin black line. She'd tell him her period had come – two and a half weeks out of four. Or perhaps she was pregnant – surely he didn't want her to miscarry.

After two years of marriage her mother had said, 'Katie, it's time you were getting on with the business of life. Doesn't Donald deserve a son?' She spoke quietly, as one who had borne nine children, five of whom had survived.

And so it was that Robbie was born. And within the year, Edie. Another pregnancy followed. Morning sickness. Excruciating pain. The rush to hospital in the back of a cart. The sweet, lingering dizziness of chloroform.

When she woke, the doctor said he had removed the embryo. Katherine blinked and looked away.

The doctor cleared his throat; told her there would be no more children.

Katherine bit her lip. Wasn't this what she wanted?

She vomited.

The doctor waited until she was finished, then said her tubes were blocked with scar tissue – not only the left side where the embryo had implanted. She'd had pelvic inflammation some time in the past. He paused; told her she should be careful. Gave her a look that made her blush.

'I expect, Mrs McKechnie,' he said, 'you do not want to be the subject of your husband's newspaper.'

Katherine opened her eyes. The relief of waking in half-light, the slow roll towards summer. She almost pulled herself out from under the bedclothes. And then she remembered. She lay back again, watching night fade, sunlight slip through the blinds, leaving, unexpectedly, a window of brightness over the bed. This, she decided, was pleasure. A luxury to be grasped. To be hoarded greedily.

Every morning she had risen at 5.30, leaving Donald to sleep another hour. She would empty cold ashes onto a copy of *Truth*. Blacklead the grate and polish the hearth. Strike a Vesta – burn its red head into a new day's fire.

Today she would burn the Bible. Not the Lord's Authorised Version but *Mrs Beeton's Everyday Cookery and Housekeeping Book*. The one Donald's mother had sent upon news of their betrothal.

Before work each day, as if he'd learned Mrs Beeton's precepts by heart, Donald would inspect his collar and the cuffs of his sleeves and God forbid if he found even the merest hint of uncleanness; he only

45

gave out five shillings at a time, expecting her to account for every penny, and when he came home he ran his hand over the furniture and if he found dust, admonished her.

As sunlight crept slowly up the bed, up to her face, into her mind, Katherine remembered the dictionary – the one with gilt-edged pages, the one that had passed from McKechnie father to son, the instrument he had fashioned against her. She wanted to burn it in the brown-edged lap of Mrs Beeton – and yet she was afraid.

BROKEN BISCUITS

Katherine sat in the front row of the church wondering which of the women Donald had slept with. Plump Mrs Paterson, the baker's wife, who had fussed so effusively? 'Poor, poor thing,' she kept saying. 'Such a loss, such a terrible, terrible loss.' Geraldine McCorkindale, the eighteen-year-old with pouty lips from the office? Or perhaps the pretty brunette sitting at the back, slender hands clutching a wet kerchief over her growing belly?

Katherine closed her eyes. The fragrance of lily of the valley bloomed in her mind. She listened to Donald's friends pay homage – to a dedicated family man; passionate wordsmith and newspaperman; avid cricketer (who hadn't seen him down at the Basin on a Saturday afternoon with his son?); good ole mate, always in for a drink and many a fine tale.

She needed to hear people speak of his life, his tragic, untimely death. To give his absence form. Solidity. She gazed at his casket, its profusion of flowers. Which has more colour, she wondered. A man's life? Or his death? Draped in black, she sat quite upright, willing herself, unwilling herself, silently to believe.

Afterwards – after the endless cups of tea and polite farewells – Katherine returned home with her children, Edie dry eyed and utterly silent, Robbie tearful and clutching his father's pocket-watch, stopped at 3.05, the exact time he had hit the water.

Since his death, every window had remained covered, like Donald's dead eyes; each day darkened like water closing over. Yet even as Katherine raised each blind, her spirit did not lighten. After her initial delight, lying in bed luxuriating in a tumult of wicked thoughts, she had been suitably morose, relief giving way to a rising fear.

She took in laundry and sewing and a succession of distasteful boarders. Edie learned even better how to cook and sew and wash and iron. Robbie got a job selling newspapers, which Katherine disliked intensely, but how else could they get by? When the boarders didn't work out, Katherine had to find somewhere smaller, shabbier: a rundown two-bedroom villa on Adelaide Road with no bathroom or hot water. Edie shared a room with her mother.

They'd received a little money from Donald's colleagues at the paper and from Mr *Truth* himself, John Norton, but this did not last long, not after funeral expenses. They received a couple of shillings each week from the charitable aid board, but Katherine hated the way the inspector wiped his fingers on the door frame and across the grate, the way he checked that she bought nothing extravagant like butter or oranges, the way he inquired with the neighbours about any unsuitable men who might come calling.

Sometimes Katherine had hated Donald for living; now when the bills arrived she could hate him for dying. *I'm so, so sorry,* she would write after she'd deliberately sent an empty envelope and then received a polite but firm reply. *It is the shock of it all. I do not know how I shall recover from my poor husband's sudden passing. Please find the cheque enclosed.*

The first time she visited the neighbourhood fruit and vegetable shop, the Chinaman added free unblemished fruit to her bag of cheap, speckled ones. She felt the heat rise in her face and left quickly. Afterwards she didn't even know if she'd given the courtesy of a thank you.

Sometimes they went to the soup kitchen, and again Katherine felt ashamed. What would the neighbours think? What would her mother? Yet the children needed to be fed, and Mother Mary Aubert and the sisters were kind – there was never a hint of condescension.

Robbie got a job as a butcher's boy after school, something he was far too young for, but as a favour from Mac Mackenzie, who'd enjoyed a beer with Donald in his time. Mac taught Robbie how to sling the basket of meat over one arm and urge on his mount with the other. It was a job Robbie loved, especially racing the boys from Kuch's and Preston's; and they got the odd free mutton bone, knuckle or kidney, and some money to help pay the rent.

They ate bread and dripping or bread and jam, broken biscuits, turnips and carrots and cabbage, marked-down apples or the occasional overripe banana, the good fruit the Chinaman gave them, and meat once or sometimes twice a week. Katherine quietly despaired, searching the newspaper's *Wanted* columns, inquiring at offices, factories, shop counters, even knocking door to door, seeking work.

APPLES

The first time she came into the shop, Yung was polishing apples, rubbing them with a soft grey cloth till the skin gleamed red with promise. With each apple he took a pair of secateurs and cut each stalk to the same neat length, then took the soft green apple-paper and wrapped it back round the fruit like a nest. One by one he placed them on the wooden shelf, a perfect slope of apple-green and red.

As he looked up he saw the black dress, the long full skirt pulled into the waist, the ample bosom above. Black. The sign of an old woman. Or a widow. Her long auburn hair was pulled up under her hat, a few strands fallen, a touch of grey, tangled from the wind.

'Good day,' he said.

She looked up from the vegetables, managed a tired smile. 'Good day,' she said.

He was surprised. Her voice was deeper than expected. 'Carrot velly good. Velly flesh. Sweet.'

'Are they?' she asked. She looked again at the cabbages and selected the largest half from the stack.

He picked up an apple, one he had already polished, took the paring knife from the shelf behind the counter and cut them both a wedge. 'Apple velly good,' he said, biting into his slice. 'Help yourself.'

She hesitated. At last took small bites, chewed slowly, deliberately,

50

as if trying the fruit for the first time, and he thought he saw her eyes close for a moment and her lips lift in a slight smile, but she did not pick up the remains of the apple or the knife he had left for her.

She bought the half cabbage, a bundle of carrots tied with flax, and three spotty apples from the marked-down bin. She did not look at his face and he understood that she was embarrassed that she had not bought any of the good apples he had offered.

He wrapped the cabbage, then the carrots in newspaper, put the fruit into a brown paper bag and quickly, without fuss, added the rest of the good apple and one other. He saw the look of surprise, then a brief searching of his face. There were dark shadows under her sad, green eyes. She thanked him and he watched her walk into the street, the strands of her hair teased by the wind.

She came into the shop every Monday and Thursday. Each time she was very courteous. Sometimes she would smile, and he would see the fine lines about her eyes and across the freckles of her nose. Her white teeth.

One afternoon after she'd walked out the door Mrs Paterson tsk tsked. 'She buys day-old bread too, you know. Poor wee thing. You know the place with the peeling-off paint? The broken fence and the falling-down gate? She's got two children and obviously not enough to feed them. Such a pity about her husband. Donald McKechnie was such an attractive man.'

And so, when his brother couldn't see him, Yung added one good piece of fruit to the speckled or bruised ones Mrs McKechnie selected. If she chose three overripe pears, he added one shiny crisp apple. If she chose three speckled bananas, he added one juicy sweet orange. He would take the paring knife and offer her a taste of any new fruit that had come in, and even if some was already cut and left by a previous customer, he always gave her a new whole piece. When he passed her the vegetables and fruit, he said, 'Good day, Mrs McKechnie,' and he smiled, hoping that today would be the beginning of good fortune.

51

THE PURLIEUS OF HAINING STREET

Under a loose floorboard in his room, Robbie stored a small mound of coins – tiny farthings, threepences, large copper pennies – taken from the jar his mother hid in the pantry, or small amounts he kept back from his pay each week. He took one, two, at most three coins each week: quietly in the night, while she was outside hanging out the washing, when she went shopping.

Then every Friday he'd take a tram, each time choosing a different route, standing on the outer ledges with the men and the big boys. Every Saturday he'd buy a copy of *Truth* and take it to the Basin to read. There he'd lie back against the trunk of a cabbage tree and read the latest gossip.

He loved the colour of the words. They leapt from the page with the voice of his father. Stories of divorce and fallen women, the malodorous Chow and the Jew. Robbie didn't understand every word – what was *malodorous* and what about *purlieus . . . the purlieus of Haining Street*? – but he understood what was important. This was the world. The world of his father.

As Robbie chewed blades of grass and shared pages of *Truth* with Wally, he remembered his father at the Basin bowling a Chinaman, hitting a six as well as he could down a whisky. Sometimes on the longest days of summer they'd come down to watch the clubs practise or to have a few hits, or of a Saturday afternoon sit on the grassy slopes, his father smoking cigarettes, Robbie eating blackballs and peppermint rock, watching Wellington play Canterbury or Otago, and once even New Zealand play Australia.

Wally couldn't bowl (or bat) if his life depended on it, and even reading *Truth* made him bored. After a while Robbie put the paper down. 'Want some chuddy?' he asked.

They picked themselves up and ran along the winding paths, past the picket fences and wooden turnstiles, past Mr Strong's white horse – the one that pulled the giant roller on the grounds – and out the gate to the street.

In Fitchett's grocery Wally bought a packet of gum for a ha'penny and a small wooden box of sherbet. In the sherbet, wrapped in tissue, he found a tiny gadget made of tin. He reached into his pocket, pulled out his whistle and fitted it to his find. Then blew it. It sounded bonzer.

Mrs Fitchett frowned.

Robbie bought some bull's eyes and a lucky bag, rummaged through it hoping for a threepenny bit. Nothing but boiled lollies. He gave Wally a couple of bull's eyes; Wally gave Robbie some sherbet and a strip of chuddy.

They wandered across the grounds of the barracks, round the huge brick walls, into Buckle Street and down Taranaki. Past Haining Street, Frederick, Ingestre and Jessie. *The purlieus of . . .* Robbie did not turn his head. He crunched on a lolly and looked straight down Taranaki, at the butcher boys racing their horses, at the trams rolling along the tracks, the trammies swinging along the outer footboards, at the hawkers and fishmongers and men in straw boaters.

Along the waterfront they passed queues of horses and carts, men whistling, shouting, loading wooden boxes, barrels, earthenware jars. They found a spot on the jetty and sat down, the taste of sugar, mint, salty air in their mouths, their legs hanging out over the water. A cool breeze swept the smell of fish into their faces; gulls hung in the sky, shifted then fell, swooping over the boats. A steamer of West Coast coal was being unloaded. They watched the huge cane baskets being winched into the hold, then back up full of coal, the black-dusted men trundling them down the gangways, tipping them into the carts, then trundling them back up again, a haze of coal dust floating in the air.

Robbie took a stick of gum from his pocket, put it in his mouth. 'What's *purlieus*?' he asked, his voice barely audible above the gulls. '*The purlieus of Haining Street.*'

Wally smiled. 'Why don't we go and take a look. You ever been down there? The opium's so strong you can cut the air with a knife. It makes your skin creep, all them Chows – but you have bonzer dreams.'

Robbie stopped chewing. 'Dad said if you ever went down Haining Street you got kidnapped and boiled in a copper and made into preserved ginger.'

Wally laughed. 'You're scared, aren't you? C'mon, I dare you.' He looked across at Robbie out of the corner of his eye. Smiled. 'I'll go too – make sure you do it.'

They walked back along the waterfront, up Taranaki, past the greengroceries, laundries and pawn shops, past Ghuznee, Ingestre and Frederick. Then stood on the corner, looking down the narrow, dusty street. On each side there were small wooden houses, some two-storey, some only one, some with wooden fences, some without. 'Filthy cesspits,' Robbie's father had said, 'dirty slums.' The houses didn't seem much different from any of the others in Te Aro. They had the same red roofs and sash windows. No sign of the rats and open sewers he'd been warned about.

Outside one of the houses, two boys were crouched, bending over something.

'You ready?' said Wally. 'Get set . . . GO!'

And they were off, running as fast as they could, straight down the middle of the empty road, hardly daring to look around. The boys on the footpath looked up, and Robbie realised they were playing marbles. He could feel their eyes on the back of his head, their yellow faces watching. And he was running, running, leaving Wally further and further behind. He could smell something strange. Food cooking, meat and vegetables, sour and sweet and salty smells. It made him feel hungry and sick and hungry all at the same time. But he kept on running, dust pounding up from the road, his eyes straight ahead, running.

At the end of the street, he waited, panting, watching Wally huffing towards him.

'Did you (*huff*) smell the (*huff*) opium?' Wally asked, as he came to a stop.

'Yeah,' Robbie lied.

'It was coming from those houses with no windows. Did you see them? They were all boarded up.'

'Sure,' he said, looking back down the street. He wasn't sure whether he could see them or not. 'But did you have any dreams?' he asked.

'No, did you?'

'Nah, ran too fast. But you were in there longer. You might have them tonight.'

'That's what *purlieus* means.' Wally smiled. 'That's them dreams you get from all that opium.'

As they walked up Adelaide Road on the way home, Robbie took the purple mass of gum out of his mouth. It had lost all flavour – now it was only good for leaving on Edie's chair or for sticking things to or making into bullets. Wong Chung Bros was coming up on the right. He took the slingshot out of his pocket and aimed it at the window. There. A purple blob on the glass. From a distance, it looked like a piece of bruised plum, staring from the window amongst the shiny red apples, oranges, bananas.

Wally laughed. 'Shot.' He picked up a stone. 'Here,' he said.

Robbie hesitated.

'Come on, Robbie. Show 'em how it's done.'

Robbie looked at the gum stuck to the window. This was the shop his mother went to. He hadn't been inside, didn't know what the Chinks looked like, but he'd seen her go in and out. Sometimes as a treat, instead of parsnips or potatoes or spotty pears, she brought back a banana without a mark on it, or a glossy red apple that looked like it had been polished with Brasso. She would cut the good fruit, the beautiful, sweet fruit, in half, and give one half to him and the other to Edie, while she cut the rottenness out of the bad fruit for herself. Edie protested, saying the good fruit should be cut into three, and when their mother ignored her, neither of them would finish their share, each leaving half for their mother. 'We're full,' they would say, trying to hide their craving, until at last she started cutting everything into three.

'Robbie?'

Robbie looked into Wally's eager face. His outstretched hand. He took the stone – it felt heavy, too heavy – pulled back the sling.

'Bull's eye!' yelled Wally, laughing, whooping.

Robbie heard the crack, the tinkle of glass, a jagged, stone-sized, amplified hole in the window.

A Chinaman ran out of the shop, still wearing his white apron, looking up, then down the street. Shouting ugly words that see-sawed and rang in the air, swearing, shaking his fist. And they were running, past Fraser's milk cart, through the horse shit, past Sutcliffe's grocery, running. Just running.

Outside the house Wally bent, hands on knees, his laughter ragged from the effort of breathing. 'Did ya . . . see . . . the look . . . on his face?' he gasped. 'Marvellous . . . Blimmin'. . . . marvellous.'

'Blimmin' hilarious, if you ask me,' said Robbie as he lifted the broken gate. Pushed it open.

'Wait . . . the bugger's . . . given me . . . stitch . . .'

Robbie was already bounding up the few steps towards the front door. 'You reckon that's what those chinkies get up to? I mean you don't see any women, do you? You reckon they just . . .' He laughed, made crude thrusts with his body.

'You boys better watch out. You know Mum doesn't like swearing.'

Robbie turned. He hadn't seen Edie crouched by the fence. Probably digging in the dirt, playing with worms or chopping up spiders or whatever it was she did. Tell-tale. He gave her the fingers. 'Bitch!'

'Robert McKechnie!' His mother stood in the doorway, basket under her arm, obviously on her way out to do some shopping. 'One more foul word and I'll wash your mouth out with soap and water! Now apologise to your sister!'

Edie poked out her tongue.

Robbie glanced at Wally, who smiled. He smiled back. 'I'm *really* sorry, Edie, that I called you a BITCH . . .'

All he saw was Edie's smirk before a hand grabbed the back of his collar, an arm lifted him off his feet and he was half-carried, half-dragged into the house. *What the . . .?* He swung his arms and legs hard, twisted and wrenched himself free. But when he looked around Wally was nowhere to be seen. He poked his tongue out at Edie, but for once she didn't respond. Her face was pale, her jaw dropped.

He turned. His mother had collapsed on the doorstep, her hand over her eyes. For a moment he didn't move, unable to comprehend what had happened. Then he noticed a shudder. 'Mum?' He ran towards her.

He wrapped his arms around her, felt her hold onto him, felt the sobs buried within her. He looked up. Edie was standing beside them, her hand gently rubbing their mother's back, small cooing sounds coming from her mouth, sounds he remembered their mother making when he fell down the stairs, when she'd gently picked him up and cradled him in her arms.

IF THE WIND CHANGES

Katherine made the children's lunches – slices of bread spread with jam or dripping, broken biscuits, half an apple – and placed them in brown paper bags on the kitchen table. She set the table for breakfast, left out bread, jam, dripping, then climbed the stairs to bed.

She lay awake listening to Edie sleep beside her, listening to her own heartbeat, to the hours as they drained slowly from her. She woke head thick, limbs heavy, every movement as if through water. Some mornings she rose and made the children porridge and sprinkled it with sugar; some mornings the children came up to her bed and kissed her before they left for school.

Sometimes she did not rise till early afternoon, when she forced herself out of bed and down Adelaide Road. *If she could bring herself to*, she'd look for work. Other times she looked in shop windows, coveting the things she could not afford. She might go into Paterson's for day-old bread. Not that she liked Mrs Paterson especially – the old biddy seemed to like Donald more than seemed decent – but she was well meaning enough and at least she was someone to talk to.

Katherine'd had a few good friends at school. But she'd lost touch with Matilda Mulroney when her family moved to Melbourne. Then there was Minnie Ferguson, but she'd married a farmer and moved to the Waikato. At Gilbys, Katherine studied stenography, typing and book-keeping with Felicity Baker, and they'd certainly had fun together, but Felicity had married an accountant and moved to Wanganui.

Sometimes for want of something better to do, Katherine wandered into Wong Chung Bros. People said Chinamen all looked alike, but there was no mistaking these two. One was younger, more her own age. And he was tall. Unusually tall for a Chinaman. His hair was cut short in the western style, and he had straight white teeth – nothing like the buck-toothed caricatures you saw in the newspapers. Katherine had nothing against the other Mr Wong, but he never smiled, at least not in a way that seemed like he meant it; and even if, on the rare occasion she paid full price, sometimes the fruit he gave her softened into decay in just a few days.

The younger Mr Wong had a warm, generous smile that half closed and softened his eyes. And he liked to linger in conversation. She'd come into the shop to find him chatting with Mr or Mrs Paterson or with Mr Krupp from the pharmacy across the road. It seemed anyone with a friendly face was fair game. His accent was strong and his English limited, but he liked to gesticulate, laugh, commiserate. And not just about the wind and the weather, which in Wellington was always a likely topic of conversation.

One day he pointed at a photograph in the newspaper. 'Who this man?' he asked. 'People talking.'

She looked at the man in his motorcar, read the caption. 'He's the first to drive all around the North Island,' she said. 'In a motorcar.'

He grinned. 'You drive motorcar?'

'Me?' She laughed. 'You're joking!'

'Joking?'

'You make me laugh.'

He looked her in the eyes, and his face crinkled into a smile. 'You sit motorcar?'

'No.' She laughed again. 'I've never sat in a motorcar.'

'Motorcar good,' he said as he wrapped her cabbage. 'I like drive motorcar.'

'You've driven a motorcar?' How many were there in Wellington? You could probably count on your fingers.

'One day,' he said as he handed her the vegetables.

She walked out into the southerly. She could see him with his big grin, slender fingers around the steering wheel. How long had it been since she'd laughed? Her mother always said if the wind changed she'd be stuck like that, with that same stupid look on her face. She laughed again.

Let the wind change. For once, let it change.

A WOMAN OF INDEPENDENT MEANS

Katherine walked to Sutcliffe's, placed one penny on the counter and carried the *Post* home. Then over a milky tea she examined the *Wanted* column:

Wanted, lady willing to give corporal punishment to widower's four girls. Good salary. State age and experience.

Maid required for light duties by respectable gentleman. No Irish need apply.

Assistant required for woman of independent means.

After she'd graduated from Gilbys, Katherine had taken a job in the office of Kirkcaldie & Stains and had taken her own money home every week. But married women did not have careers. They gave up their jobs to younger unmarried girls, or to men who had families to support. It would have been shameful for Donald if he could not provide.

Now Katherine did not feel capable of anything, let alone taking on the role of an assistant. Yet some people had dreams. For a moment she saw Mr Wong's grinning face, his fingers wrapped around a steering wheel. She laid her head on the table, staring at the blurred page. A *woman of independent means*. The words conjured up a strange new world, a world that could only be realised once you walked through a doorway.

The house was on Wellington Terrace, a huge, new, two-storey bay villa with a first-floor balcony, turret and flagpole. The maid showed Katherine past the magnificent kauri staircase and into the study.

Mrs Margaret Newman, wife of Alexander Newman, Member of the House of Representatives for Lambton, only daughter of the late Sir Harold Salmond QC, sat facing the door. She motioned for Katherine to sit opposite her, and offered her tea.

Flames leapt in the fireplace. The brightly coloured flowers, leaves and tendrils of the carpet; the dark, wood-turned furniture; the bamboo and palms positioned about the room formed crazy patterns in Katherine's eyes. It was not cold, not inside, and yet Katherine could feel her hands shaking. She held them in her lap, unable to lift the teacup to her lips.

'It must be difficult for you,' Mrs Newman said, 'since your husband died. Tell me, how old are the children?'

She was in her late forties, a slim woman with grey streaking her chestnut hair. For the first time, Katherine looked her fully in the face. She had strong, handsome features with prominent cheekbones, and grey eyes that seemed very firm yet also not without kindness.

Mrs Newman talked about destitute women and children. Widows or women abandoned by scoundrels. Women who could not afford to leave their violent, beer-addled husbands. In her youth, Mrs Newman had been in the women's movement, campaigning alongside Kate Sheppard and Lily Atkinson, writing letters to the papers and politicians. Was Katherine registered for the vote?

'Yes,' Katherine said. And yet once it wouldn't have been as easy. Donald had thought women's franchise a ridiculous idea. He supported Seddon on that, just as he did on almost every one of his policies. But even the Premier could not withstand pressure from within his own party. By the next election Donald had changed his mind. Yes, of course Katherine should vote. Then there would be two votes for the Liberals.

Mrs Newman smiled, took a sip of her tea. 'A piece of cake?' she said.

Katherine's throat felt so tight she could barely talk. How could she eat cake also? She tried to decline gracefully.

'You worked in the office of Kirkcaldie & Stains? I just bought this bodice and skirt from Kirkcaldie's the other week. Why, thank you. Though if you want the very latest in European fashion, Sydney is far better. I go every winter to visit my sister.'

The warmer, drier climate was better for Mrs Newman's asthma and also for the ache she'd begun to feel in her fingers. She always went for several weeks, and during that time Katherine would need to work for at most a couple of hours each day. Just enough time to open the mail, skim the newspapers and telegraph her if there was anything urgent. Katherine would remain on full pay, of course, £3 a week, she wouldn't need to worry about the bills . . .

Katherine was stunned. That was as much as Donald had earned. She would work far fewer hours and still be able to buy meat every day, and butter and oranges. They could move to a bigger house with hot running water and a painted picket fence and a gate that did not fall over.

'You can take a holiday,' Mrs Newman was saying. 'Visit your mother in Masterton, perhaps.'

Katherine nodded. She didn't mention she never visited her mother for more than a few days. Her constant nagging and pronouncements on the sad death of Donald always made her desperate to escape home to Wellington. Thank God her mother had remarried and moved away.

Mrs Newman put down her teacup. 'Bring your daughter around after school to play the piano. I shall pay for lessons. A young lady should be able to play with facility. Of course, if your son is interested he is also welcome.' She stood up. 'Would you like to start next week?'

Margaret Newman stood at the bay window and watched as Katherine shut the iron gate and walked down the hill. She should probably have found a more experienced and capable assistant, but then she could never resist organising and bettering other people's lives. She considered it a form of patronage, her own experiment in eugenics. Better to pay Katherine well, even if it was more than her qualifications warranted, than abandon her to charity. After all, she was the same age her own daughter would have been. And there were children to consider. Katherine's daughter – now she sounded interesting.

At first Katherine walked around the house stiffly, keeping as far from the walls and the tables and sideboards as possible. Mrs Newman said the watercolour of the Maori above the piano was by Dorothy Kate Richmond and the oil of Wellington harbour was by Jimmy Nairn. And those were by Isabel Field and Frances Hodgkins – they were sisters, you know. The furniture was so highly polished Katherine was afraid she'd scratch it, or even leave her fingerprints on it. She was afraid she'd type too slowly, make errors with her spelling, file documents in the wrong folder, but Mrs Newman was surprisingly patient. She showed Katherine step by step what she expected, and gave her time to fall into a pattern.

Mrs Newman read all the major newspapers. 'Katherine, look at this,' she might say, roaring with laughter. Katherine laughed also – sometimes not so much because the story or cartoon was so amusing but because of Mrs Newman herself. How could such a dignified woman produce a sound that resembled a donkey braying, even, occasionally, a pig snorting?

Katherine woke in the mornings excited to go to work, pleased that at last someone appreciated her efforts, that the work she was doing was helping the cause of women and children.

Edie looked forward to playing the piano and borrowing books from Mrs Newman's library. But no matter how much Katherine cajoled him, all Robbie wanted was to run around with Billy and Wally and play cricket at the Basin.

Katherine started to enjoy the house, to take an interest in its gorgeous furnishings. Her favourite piece of furniture was the Ashford table in the hallway. She always stopped to admire it when she arrived at work and then again when she left several hours later. It was black marble inlaid with blooms of morning glory, poppies and irises. The flowers glowed, and Katherine marvelled at how the colours turned subtly from one shade to another.

Lapis lazuli, jasper, carnelian, agate, marble. These were magic words. They conjured other worlds, worlds where flowers never wilted, where nothing ever died. Katherine liked the table's roundness: no sharp edges, just a sense of completion. And there was something else Katherine liked, something she had not at first noticed: the table had a fine crack in it. Actually, two. One that ran from the edge of the marble right up to the inlaid flowers, and then another on the other side, right out to the opposing edge. She liked the cracks because everything else in the house seemed so perfect.

Once Katherine asked Mrs Newman about the cracks, and she saw her employer's face darken with anger. It was all the fault of one of the maids. Mrs Newman didn't know at the time, but every day the maid had polished the table with oil. Oil, for goodness sake! On a marble table! The girl was lucky she wasn't dismissed. Dismissed!

Mrs Newman sighed. It wasn't easy to get good help these days.

Katherine moved to a two-storey, three-bedroom cottage further down Adelaide Road. They had a bedroom each, a bathroom with running water and a gate that did not fall off its hinges. And in the backyard, surprisingly, there was an old rata, a remnant of native bush that had somehow escaped being cut for firewood. Robbie nailed battens to its trunk and took to climbing up and sitting on an overhanging branch. Sometimes when she called him for dinner Katherine would find him there, sitting on that branch, dangling his legs, reading a penny dreadful or spying on the neighbours' backyards.

A week after they moved in, Katherine woke early. It was barely light, but wind buffeted the house and she could not sleep. She rose and put on her housecoat, raised the blind. The children were still sleeping.

She pulled a box out from under her bed. She had packed it after Donald died, before they first moved, and had never unpacked it. She opened the newspaper-wrapped parcels one by one – four framed butterflies that had once hung in the parlour. She had forgotten their names. All except the *Doxocopa cherubina*. She turned each frame over, opened the back, unpinned the butterflies and laid them on the bed. They were beautiful lying on the white bedspread. They made her feel very sad.

She went to the window, pushed it up as far as it would go. The wind blew the lace curtains, her hair, across her face. Even rolled up, the wooden blind banged against the window frame. She pushed the curtains aside, took a deep cold breath and walked back to the bed. The butterflies had scattered like the petals of dying flowers. She picked them up and, taking care not to touch their wings, carried them to the window. Watched them fly. Wildly. Without thought or fear. Her hair, lace flew about her and she did not see where the wind took them or where they fell.

She closed the window and went back to the box. There was just one thing left.

She wiped her hand over the leather. Every week she had passed a cloth over it in the bookcase, but she had touched it only once, months after Donald's death, when she had packed it to move. Now she sat on the bed, laid the book on her lap. Fingered the gold lettering,

66

the dirty shine of its gilt-edged pages.

She opened it and stared at the columns of words, pushed her thumb into the bottom right-hand corner, lifted and turned another wad of pages. Frowned.

Here and there whole entries – words, their various meanings and derivations – had been obliterated with black ink. Why? Why some words and not others? She turned back in the book, searching for a link. Why, for instance, was *Enascent* intact, and *Enate*, but not the word in between?

Who had done this? Not Donald, surely. The dictionary had been his sacred text, and he the high priest. When he was alive she had almost been afraid to pass the cloth over its surfaces.

Suddenly, she laughed. Covered her mouth. She held the dictionary to her chest and shook with silent laughter. There was only one person clever enough to remember all those words. Words stored up from years of dinnertime interrogations and then obliterated in one fell swoop.

Katherine wiped tears from her eyes, stood up and carried the dictionary downstairs to the kitchen. Tore out pages, scrunched them and placed them in the range. Lit a match. She tore out more and fed the flames, which flared with such intensity, consuming *his* words. Her face, fingers, the front of her body felt hot, golden light reflecting on her skin, all around a great halo of heat. She added twigs, thin branches, a small log, and still she fed the flames, watching pages wrinkle and burn, turn thick with heat into old brown cloth, grey velvet. She stirred dark fragments – words, thoughts, memories – their edges of fire falling into ash, till she held nothing but the leather cover, its sad, empty spine. She did not want to smell the animal burning, to see its poor skin blacken and curl.

She carried it outside and dug under the rata, leaves swirling about her. Placed the leather in the damp earth and covered it again, tamping down with the spade. When flowers fell at the end of summer, they would mix red with the earth, with the poor animal soul, its dead skin.

She would buy a new dictionary. Something without Donald's history. A gift to herself. She would place it on the bookshelf in *her* parlour.

She went back into the house. The children were coming down the stairs. She put her hands on their warm cheeks and kissed their foreheads. 'Mum!' Robbie complained, but he did not pull away. 'Your hands are cold!' Edie said. 'What have you been doing?' She looked out towards the back garden.

Katherine smiled. She asked Edie to start the porridge, Robbie to set the table, walked up the stairs to her room.

She put on a bright blue dress, the first time since Donald's death that she hadn't worn black; looked in the dresser mirror, hugged herself and laughed. She went to the window, pushed it up and leaned into brightness. She felt like a poplar - orange leaves rustling in a dazzling blue sky.

THE UNEQUAL YOKE

Edie went to Mrs Newman's most days after school and practised the piano furiously.

'Slow down. Control,' her teacher would tell her as she played the beginning of *Für Elise*.

'But I don't like tinkly water music,' Edie complained. She liked the second part better. Not for her delightful minuets. She wanted grand music. Complicated music. She wanted to play Rachmaninov.

Sometimes Edie helped her mother with the filing or she'd curl up with books from the extensive library. Mrs Newman gave her *The White Ribbon* to read, Susie Mactier's *The Unequal Yoke: A New Zealand Story,* and *Mary Liddiard* by William Kingston.

But on the day her mother stopped wearing black, Edie did not go to Mrs Newman's. She ran home, desperate to get there before Robbie, who'd wandered off with his mates. She dropped her bag on the kitchen floor and went out to the backyard.

She'd watched her mother from her bedroom window. She'd seen her in the garden.

When Robbie came home, he didn't kick a ball down the hallway or try to annoy Edie. He went straight to his room, opened the dresser and took out his father's pocket-watch. He sat on his bed, fingering the gold chain, its greenstone amulets. Then propped a large hardcover book against his raised knees and pressed pen to paper.

'Why don't you come after school too?' Edie asked, standing in the doorway.

'That'll be the day! Bet you can't even come up with three good reasons.' He continued writing.

'Mrs Newman has paintings just like in a museum, and she has books you can't get from the library.'

'I said *good* reasons and anyway that was only two. Why would I want some stupid old lady telling me what to do? Mrs Newman says this. Mrs Newman says that. You're starting to sound just like her the way you talk.'

'We have madeira cake and shortbread and cold lemonade.'

Robbie looked up. 'Bring me back some. If you can hide Brussels sprouts in your pockets . . .'

'I do not! You're the one who doesn't eat your vegetables.'

'Who's the smart one now, eh?'

Edie bit her lip. 'Who are you writing to?' she asked after a while.

'None of your blinking business. Just because *you* don't have any friends. Blimey charley, if Dad could see you now . . .'

Edie's face flushed with tears.

Robbie looked down at his letter. He knew he was Dad's favourite; he didn't need to rub it in. But it was too late now. 'Go to Mrs Newman's and eat your cake,' he said at last. 'I don't care. And shut the blimmin' door!'

BLUE

When Mrs McKechnie walked into the shop after work, Yung forgot to greet her. He had never seen her in anything but black and now, in the brightness of her blue dress, she seemed younger. More alive.

When he'd cut his hair and donned western garb, his brother had scowled and muttered under his breath, 'You can't go back home now – the authorities could execute you.' Yung had smiled. To hell with the Dowager. He felt marvellously free.

Now he gazed at Mrs McKechnie and recognised a similar transformation. She held herself upright and had a new spring in her step, almost as if – if music started, if she let herself – she might dance across the shop floor. She smiled and he noticed her eyes. The colour of her dress made them seem very bright, more blue than green. They were strangely beautiful.

Yung did not know what to say. He'd had questions stored up – articles, photographs, illustrations from the newspaper, why this world was full of curiosities – but suddenly he could not remember.

It was she who started the conversation.

'Where's the other man?' she asked. 'I haven't seen him for weeks.'

'My brother?' He flipped the bag of apples to twist and seal the corners. 'He go home.'

'When does he come back?'

'A few month . . .' Yung bit his lip. 'He come back with . . . wife.'

'Oh . . . It must be lonely without family.'

He wrapped her cauliflower, tried to smile as he said good day, but did not look into her eyes. He watched her walk out the door, the copper of her hair bright against the blue of her dress.

He walked out the back, asked Cousin Gok-nam, who was washing carrots, to mind the shop. He walked up the stairs to his room, opened the sandalwood box on the dresser and took out the top letter. Read it slowly.

He lay back on the bed and stared at the ceiling, listening to the trams and horse-carts as they passed by on the street below, watching light fade.

He rose and picked up a bamboo flute. He'd made it lovingly – the way his father taught him when he was a child, digging out the inner sections, cutting holes along its length, whittling a piece of cork to plug the open end. Sometimes on a Sunday, or at night after the shop closed, if his brother did not thump on the door and tell him to sleep, he'd sit on his bed and play. Sometimes the flute, sometimes the haunting notes of the *erh hu*, the Chinese violin. He'd play a song about love, or perhaps about leaving home, about travelling thousands of *lei*, about waking at night alone.

The letter lay open on the bed. He held the flute, light in his hands, felt the sadness of its thin body. Pressed it to his lips.

SHADOWS

After his brother came back, whenever he was not needed in the shop, Yung went out. There was always someone to talk to, to be with, in *Tongyangai*.

He might visit a cook-shop with Fong-man and eat wontons or home-made noodles, or call into one of the gambling joints for heated debate or merely the latest gossip. He'd take the teapot from the padded basket by the door and pour himself a cup, then sit on the bench with the other men, back against the wall, sipping hot tea and watching *gweilo* and *Tongyan* alike come and go, buying and checking *pakapoo* tickets.

On warm summer evenings he'd join Cousin Gok-nam, whoever happened to be sitting outside their homes. They'd sit for hours on their haunches, smoking, bragging like *blowing bulls*, till all they could see was the bright orange glow of cigarettes in darkness, their disembodied voices calling to each other across the narrow street.

Sometimes he'd walk to Fong-man's shop in Cuba Street to play cards and discuss politics or poetry.

'What's wrong?' Fong-man asked one night as he dealt their hands. 'By now you should be telling me what your cousin Hung-seng's up to. Lecturing me on the latest from the *People's Newspaper*. Sun says this. Liang says that. You can be boring-to-death, but believe it or not

73

I've got used to it.'

Yung ignored him. It was strangely quiet. Only the flick as cards hit the wooden table.

'You sure you want to throw down that card? Definitely something wrong when you're letting me win . . .' Fong-man laid down his hand, looked Yung in the face. 'Your brother's woman, I hear she's pretty . . .'

Yung threw down his cards and stood up.

The trams had stopped for the night, the streets peopled only by shadows. He walked past blind shop fronts towards water.

His own wife had been pretty too . . . But how did *gweilo* say? *More than pretty face?*

He gazed at the darkness of Kelburne and the western hills, over the oily blackness of the harbour and across to Oriental Bay.

What was the word Mrs McKechnie used? How had she described it? This emptiness, this hungry space about him. If only he could express it in a foreign tongue, perhaps it would no longer belong to him.

LITTLE HEARTS

As Katherine walked into the shop she heard a young woman singing. Perhaps because of the woman's gusto and perhaps because of the tram that rattled past at the same moment, no one heard her steps on the linoleum. No one came through to serve her. Katherine stood in the middle of the shop, surrounded by stacks of copper-skinned onions, newly washed potatoes, cabbages, cauliflowers, carrots with feathery green foliage. She did not ring the bell on the counter; instead she listened. The voice was very high and thin, and the melody completely familiar, if a little off-key, but to Katherine's unpractised ear the words sounded like bubbles of music, popping one after the other. She listened, fascinated by the sound of a language she did not recognise and yet whose meaning she could understand. She felt like a child who has been sent to bed and yet who comes out again to hide behind the door listening. What songs had she heard in another tongue? She smiled. This was a weird and foreign language; it was *Jesus loves me this I know,* and then she couldn't stop singing *for the Bible tells me so*, and it was all in Chinese.

Mei-lin did not have any particular interest in Jesus-Son-of-God but she did like to sing. Mrs Mary Anne Wong, Annie for short, wife of the

Chinese Missioner, came visiting every fortnight, and in a city where there were so few Chinese women, and nowhere to go and nothing to do except work and cook and clean and look after the children, a visit by any one of them was always welcome. That is, apart from Cousin Gok-nam's wife, who talked as relentlessly as a tram. Mei-lin never got a word in, even to say she needed to go, and so she learned to walk away and let her cousin follow, even outside and into the yard before closing the toilet door behind her.

Annie Wong, on the other hand, Mei-lin adored. She liked Annie's soft eyes and face, the way she listened and laughed and helped her with anything. Down Frederick Street, at the Anglican Mission, Annie was upheld as a shining example of Christian womanhood, but all Chinese knew she was a very good Confucian. Annie knew how to live in barbarian lands – she was born in Australia. She spoke fluent Australian and she could read and write. And because she was coming to marry the Missioner, she was counted as clergy and didn't have to pay the poll tax. Annie showed Mei-lin where to buy the essentials that men never dreamed nor thought of; she translated documents and signs; she even taught Mei-lin some English; and on the rare occasion when Mei-lin got sick and Chinese herbs or the Haining Street doctor could do nothing, Annie took her to see Dr Bennett, a *gweilo* doctor, but nevertheless a kind one – and a woman.

Mei-lin would always make some delicacy in anticipation of Annie's visit: *siat kei ma*, fried noodles coated in syrup, and pressed and cut into squares; *bak dan gou*, steamed white sponge decorated with a cochineal design; or fried egg doughnuts rolled in sugar. They would sit down at the back of the shop while Mei-lin felt the child grow within her, while she watched through the doorway and listened for footsteps in the shop, for the bell on the counter to ring. They'd drink cups of Oolong tea and eat *little hearts* of sweet or savoury snacks. They'd talk and laugh and talk again, rubbing crumbs and oil or sticky sweetness from between their fingers. And while Annie helped Mei-lin with the ironing or the mending or scrubbing the floor, she'd teach her to sing.

And that's how Mei-lin learned so many new and fantastical songs, songs like *Stand Up, Stand Up For Jesus* and *Onward Christian Soldiers* that sounded majestic and bold and strong, the way Mei-lin felt inside (and not like a woman), or songs with catchy tunes that talked about Jesus and Jesus-love.

DOMINION

When Katherine arrived at work, Mrs Newman was seething. For a moment Katherine wondered whether she was late. Perhaps she'd made a mistake with the typing. But then her employer thrust the *Dominion* into her hands.

'Have you seen this?' she demanded, stabbing at the page.

If Mrs Newman hadn't been so angry, Katherine might have laughed out loud. Why waste a penny on a newspaper? Mrs Newman always told her anything of importance. Instead she read addresses given in Dunedin by Drs Ferdinand Batchelor and Truby King.

According to Dr Batchelor, from puberty, girls' education should be 'chiefly directed to domestic management, domestic economy, physiology and hygiene'.

'They're supposed to be pillars of the State, defenders of women and helpless babies, and look at what they do. He's an obstetrician, Katherine. Batchelor's *the* obstetrician. They teach at the medical school.'

Mrs Newman grabbed the paper. 'The average male, even the below-average male, becomes "useful and successful" while the brilliant female is lucky to attain mediocrity! Well, I wonder why. With men like him and King standing in the way, refusing women a foot in the door, what does he expect?

'Look at this. Look at what *Doctor* King says.' She almost spat the word out of her mouth, as if an insect had flown in and had to be expelled.

Katherine nearly stepped back – sometimes Mrs Newman was like a single-handed military operation – but she didn't want to seem rude.

'He says educating girls on similar lines to boys is "one of the most preposterous farces ever perpetuated". My sakes! They think educating girls is a defiance of nature!' She threw the newspaper down on the desk. 'And all the while they've got the churches and the House of Representatives and the medical establishment applauding. We've got to prepare a reply, Katherine, we need to get it in tomorrow's paper.'

Katherine watched a pencil knocked from the desktop fall towards the square of carpet. She watched Mrs Newman pacing the room, scratching at her wrist, at her forehead above her right eye. She always scratched when she was agitated. And where she scratched, the skin flared brown-red and turned dry and scaly.

How many times had Katherine fumed herself – at Donald, his mother, even her own mother? Their attitudes were only a window onto this greater world. She stared at the angry patches on Mrs Newman's skin. Even when the heart and mind were hidden, there were leakages – thoughts, feelings, desires seeping, erupting – within the sealed body.

'Well, what are you waiting for, Katherine? We've got a letter to write.'

Katherine quickly picked up the pencil. She folded the newspaper, sat down at her desk and pulled several sheets of paper from the drawer.

'SIR –' Mrs Newman began, '*I am appalled . . . yes . . . I am appalled at the addresses delivered yesterday by Drs Ferdinand Batchelor and Truby King . . .*

'*Who has the arrogance to declare, what Nature intends for Man and Woman? Once humankind believed . . .* What did we believe? Mmm . . . *Once we believed the earth and Man were the centre of the universe. But history and our evolution did not stop in the Dark Ages. The enlightened soul looks forward to a day when Man and Woman are accorded equal opportunity and value.*

'Is a child's intellectual capacity frozen at puberty? Why should it be the case for girls and not for boys?

'Surely if we value our families and our children, an intelligent woman who is the equal of her husband, and who can educate her children, is something to be prized. Is Man so insecure that his only pride is to have Woman by his side with the intellect of a vegetable?

'As our knowledge increases are we not to progress with it? An intelligent woman with an empty mind and little to do is an unhappy woman, driven to melancholy and despair. Yet a woman who is educated and stimulated by a fulfilling profession is interested and active in life, an asset to family and society . . . What do you think, Katherine? Read it out to me . . .

'Yes, that's good. Did you use capitals for Man and Woman? Like Nature. Yes, I think that will do. That will do well enough.'

Katherine took from the drawer thick cream paper monogrammed with the family crest and a sheet of plain white paper. She fed them into the typewriter with carbon in between, listening to the rollers turn, suddenly remembering a visit to the countryside she'd made with Mrs Newman only the week before – her first ride in a motorcar. Sitting with the wind blowing out her hair, she'd thought of Mr Wong, his lovely, ridiculous grin, and as the motorcar slowed and crossed the railway line, wheels rattling over the wooden bars of the cattlestop, she heard the sound of keys, the smooth black ovals with their white lettering, the feel of metal beneath her fingers, the rhythmic swish and clatter, the little bell, and the satisfaction of pulling the carriage across for the beginning of the next line.

As Katherine typed she did not think of pompous men in Dunedin – she was *so* tired of pompous men. She thought of the thrill of driving a motorcar; she thought of horses clipping the road, trams starting and stopping, trains clattering all the way to the beach at Plimmerton . . .

'Is it done, Katherine?' she heard Mrs Newman say. 'I'm going to take it down to the *Dominion* myself. Hand it to Mr Earle personally. Oh Katherine, before I go . . . please sit down.' She gestured to the chesterfield, sat down in the easy chair opposite.

And that was when she made Katherine promise that she wouldn't stand in her daughter's way. *But why would she? And even if she wanted to, how could she possibly stand before Mrs Newman's onslaught?*

'Do you realise how exceptional your daughter is?' Mrs Newman was saying. 'Over the years I have taken a number of girls under my wing and I can assure you, Katherine, that I have never come across a child as unusually curious or intelligent as Edie. She'll receive a university scholarship of course – that goes without saying. But that will only pay her fees and a small allowance, not enough to live on. Never mind, I'll provide an additional allowance. Edie will never be happy as a wife and mother, dedicated only to domestic duty . . . Well, were you happy, Katherine?'

What a question. And who could afford to think of it? Certainly not the unhappy. And those who were happy never needed to think of it.

No, Mrs Newman continued, Edie would follow in the footsteps of Emily Siedeberg or Dr Agnes Bennett. She'd prove that Batchelor and King were wrong. She'd have the chance to choose her own destiny.

200 MILLION

It was Mrs McKechnie who first told Yung of petitions for Lionel Terry's release. She pointed out articles in the newspapers, letters to the editor. Soon every Chinese in Wellington, in the whole damned country, knew. Yung organised a counter-petition. He wrote the Chinese version and got Annie Wong to translate it into English.

'This is the man who murdered one of us in Haining Street,' he told Mei-lin. 'He'll do it again without hesitation.'

'But I don't know how to write,' Mei-lin said. 'I don't even know how to sign my name.' Her hand rested on her pregnant belly.

'Make a mark like this,' Yung said, drawing a cross on the back of his hand. 'I'll write your name beside it.'

'Why ask her?' Shun said, as he walked past carrying a box of oranges.

'Shun Goh,' Yung said, 'does not Liang Ch'i-chao say if China's 200 million men are joined by 200 million women, then what can stand in our way? We are few in this land. How much more do we need our women?'

Shun shrugged and carried the box into the shop.

Mei-lin took the pen and made a wavering cross on the petition. She smiled at Yung, who did not meet her eyes. Yung could see why his brother bought her.

How many Chinese women were there in this town? Fifteen? Maybe not even that. Even when you included Mei-lin and Annie Wong and Cousin Gok-nam's wife and the babies and young girls.

There were *hundred men's women,* dirty uncouth *gweilo* women who sold their services, and a few of the men went to them, or the women came directly to the men. But who wanted to share his woman?

As Yung trimmed sack after sack of cauliflowers and cabbages, he sighed. Sometimes when he looked at Mei-lin, when he heard the softness of her voice, when he lay at night alone, he felt an ache. Of desolation.

THE LITTLE ORANGE BOOK

'So, do you play sport?' Katherine asked as he weighed her carrots. She mimed running, kicking a ball, bowling, then laughed at her own clumsiness. Just as well Robbie had plenty of friends to play with. The speed of his bowling terrified her.

Mr Wong laughed too. He admired her lack of embarrassment – she was so . . . unlike *Tongyan*. 'This Games, what do you call?' he asked.

'The Olympics,' she said again. 'Women are participating for the first time. Mrs Newman – my boss – she celebrated by giving me a glass of sherry and the rest of the day off.'

She giggled. (She didn't usually drink.) 'So, do you?'

He looked at her, puzzled.

'Do you play sport? And don't ask me to go through all that again!'

'No horley foe of moose,' he said, smiling.

She frowned.

He motioned for her to wait, went out the back of the shop and came back with a small orange book, *Glossary of English Phrases with Chinese Translations*, printed in Shanghai. He opened it and showed her.

Hoary foe of the Muse, the, she read. 'The Time, who is generally represented as an old man with hoary hair . . .' She burst out laughing, then saw the look on his face and stopped herself quickly. 'Just say, *I don't have time*,' she said. 'Keep it very simple.'

Now when she came into the shop he would ask her about this phrase or that and they would communicate with pidgin English, wild gestures, drawings on the unprinted edges of newspapers, even his loud Chinese that she never understood.

'Please *collect* talking,' he said. 'I want talking *ploper* English.' And he gave her such an earnest look, then such a mischievous grin, she laughed.

'All right,' she said. 'Speak slowly and try to say *rrrr. Prrroper* English. I want to speak *prrroper* English.'

'I want to speak *ploper* English.'

'*Prrroper* English.'

'*Plroper* English.'

'That's getting better. You need to *prrractice*. Say it over and over till you get it *rrright. Prrractice* makes *perrrfect*.'

'*Plactice* makes *perfect*.' He grinned. 'Look,' he said, opening his little orange book. '**Take at one's word**. Yes?'

Katherine nodded, her eyes slipping to the opposite page. **Take a shine to** – To take a fancy or liking to (S.); then there were strange markings she couldn't read, she presumed they were Chinese, and then the example: The coachman said he had *taken* quite *a shine to* the cook.

Katherine blushed. 'Yes,' she said, 'you can say that.'

He worked hard. Katherine could see it. Hear it. He remembered the phrases she taught him; his accent became less pronounced. When he took his time he could almost say, *Ernest Rutherford, Roderick the rat catcher, practice makes perfect.*

She noticed that when he moved across the shop floor she could not hear his footfalls, just the slightest ruffle of his clothing and her own shoes clipping the linoleum. His eyes were dark, so dark that after a time she found she could see her own reflection. This was unsettling, seeing herself in the eyes of another.

85

One day when she walked into the shop and Mr Wong, the elder, came out to serve her, she realised with dismay how disappointed she was. 'Good afternoon, Mr Wong,' she said, trying to smile, and at that moment she discovered she did not know their names, that she had no way to distinguish them except as young Mr Wong; tall Mr Wong; Mr Wong with the western hairstyle; Mr Wong and the little orange book; talking, laughing Mr Wong . . .

And then he came out also, carrying a box of spring carrots still with their leaves attached, and suddenly she could not help but smile.

'*Dang ngor lei la. Lei tau ha la,*' he said to his brother, and she did not understand a word, but the elder Mr Wong gave her a strange look and went back inside.

She chose three bananas, half a cauliflower and a small bag of potatoes. He smiled and picked out a bunch of carrots, told her they were very good, very fresh. He wrapped them with the leaves exposed and held them out to her with both hands. 'No money,' he said.

'Better to say, *No charge,*' she said. '*No money* means *you* have no money, not that I don't need to pay.'

She took the carrots, feeling as if the feathery tops spilling out of the newspaper were spring blooms. Why was she so light-headed? He was a Chinaman. A sallow-faced, squinty-eyed foreigner. The dregs of society. Heavens, he didn't even make it into society. And yet when she was with him she forgot who he was. After all, he had a strong, almost European nose. He was tall. He didn't *really* look Chinese.

Wong Chung-yung

THE DIABOLO

My heart is a string of firecrackers. It explodes at random: a mixed bag of Tom Thumbs, Double Happys, Mighty Cannons. Sky rockets whiz and flare, sparklers, Jumping Jacks head over heels. Not even Spring Festival, yet I hold all of this within me. I press my lips in a crooked smile, try to stop a songburst, a whoop, a torrent of blessings and curses.

I cannot understand this.

All for a devil woman. A devil woman.

Her nose is too big, and her breasts, and her feet. She doesn't walk like a woman. She has red devil hair. And yet she has kind, sad, beautiful blue-green eyes and full, luscious lips – and she calls me by name. Mr Wong, she says, as if I am a man and not a Chinaman.

Firecrackers are to frighten away devils. But she walks into the shop, and these explosions go off inside me, and she does not run away.

Today she comes with her daughter. I show them the best apples. 'Red Delicious nice and red but what is taste? No taste *la*! Red Delicious soft, like old wet cake. But Jonathan, crisp and juicy. Good taste. Try some *la*, please try.'

I cut off slices and wait for them to smile, to nod in agreement. She turns and calls to her son. Only then do I see him. He loiters by the doorway and does not want to come in. She insists. Taste apple, she tells him. Come and choose fruit.

I hold open the brown paper bag and let her daughter choose four, five, six apples, weighing them on the scales. 'One and threepence,' I say, adding one more apple to the bag, swinging it round, twisting the corners like cat's ears.

'Robbie,' she is calling. And at last he comes, holding a diabolo his father gave him. 'This was a craze,' she says, 'everyone played it.' But she doesn't know how.

'We play in China,' I say. 'Uncle bring from Peking.' And I'm crazy, *going crazy* – I show her.

I flick the string and send the wooden reel spinning into the air.

When I was a boy I could throw the diabolo high, do a cartwheel, a somersault or a backward flip, and then I'd catch it again. But now my body moves this much more slowly. I can still throw it in the air and catch it behind me, I know I can. But this shop is small and the ceiling low: the reel would plummet – a bird struck by stone.

The boy stares at me with a curled lip, a lip you could rest an oil bottle on. He holds one hand in his pocket, and now I know what it is. I have seen this boy. With his fatboy friend. They run behind horses and scoop up horse shit with iron shovels. 'Penny a bucket! Penny a bucket!' they shout. 'Do yer garden good!' I know this boy. I know what he hides in his pocket.

A grey day, brown dust, the gust of a northerly. Fraser's milk cart, the tired old horse pulling the steel urns. The rock came out of nowhere. The houses across the street, the horses, and kicked-up, blown-up dust. My beautiful window with the best polished fruit: the apples turned to show the reddest cheeks, the oranges, bananas and pears. My shatter-webbed window, my gorgeous fruit, sliced with glass. I ran out and there he was, smirking, running away, slingshot in his hand.

'Thank you, Mr Wong,' she says. 'Say thank you, Edie, Robbie.'

The girl hesitates, says thank you. I give the diabolo to her.

Mrs McKechnie. Kind-heart, bad-luck woman. Mother of a redhead, bad-heart boy. Wife of a dead man.

THE SHADOW

Edie was sure Robbie had taken her teddy bear. Where had he hidden it? Had he ripped off his head like the porcelain doll Nana gave her? Not that she particularly cared for Minnie, apart from as the recipient of imaginary lifesaving operations. When Robbie fractured her skull there was no blood or white or grey matter, no interesting convolutions of the frontal lobe, only shards of painted china and a disappointing hollowness.

But Teddy was different. Everybody who was anybody had their own teddy. Even Mrs Newman had one – she took him to the opera. Mrs Newman told her he was named for the US President.

While Robbie was out with Billy, Edie searched his room. Under his bed amid dirty shoes, cricket balls, wickets, marbles, a football and dead spider, she found three very smelly socks in varying shades of brown and black, which she picked up between the tips of her thumb and forefinger and placed under his pillow. She washed her hands, came back and searched his wardrobe. At the back, under cricket pads, gloves, a slingshot, train set and old jersey, she found a cardboard box marked in large black capitals:

R. D. MCKECHNIE
PRIVATE AND CONFIDENTIAL
KEEP OUT!

Inside were two slim soft-covered booklets – *The Shadow* and *God or Mammon?* – and a collection of tracts, home-made cards and letters:

Sunnyside Lunatic Asylum,
29 August 1909

Dear Robbie, – Thanks for yours of the 19 August. I remember your father well and was sad to hear of his passing. I still recall his hospitality and excellent conversation. You must not let this loss set you back, as would be the case of lesser mortals. Your father was a true Briton and you would do well to follow his example.

   I enclose my books and a card which I have made for your instruction.

   With every good wish,
   Yours as ever,
   Lionel Terry.

The Shadow had a watercolour on its cover, all black and grey and off-whites. In the top left corner, a man with mad, pinprick eyes flew in the air, holding a scimitar high over his head, ready to sweep down from the clouds and strike. Below, only spires, domed roofs and crosses were visible. Inside were the words:

To
my Brother Britons
I Dedicate this Work
L. T.
July, 1904

then a prayer, an introduction which continued for eleven pages, and a long rhyming poem full of words like *vile traducer, plague-fraught offal of the earth* and *stinking swamp of black iniquity*.

   A card read:

Many fools have many moods,
And follies great and small,

But the fools who swallow foreign foods,
Are the biggest fools of all!

Another:

The patriot is governed by his brain, the traitor by his stomach.

Edie put the cards, letters, everything back in the box in exactly the same order. Replaced the box in the wardrobe.

That night she found Teddy. He was in the top drawer of her dresser, one of her own stockings pulled over his head.

PART II

KWANGTUNG, CHINA TO WELLINGTON

1907-1915

Oi Harn Goong, the founding ancestor of the Wong clan in Melon Ridge, named the village 'hoping his new home would endow him with prolific offspring like proverbial melons on the vines'.

Edmon Wong, Zengcheng New Zealanders

Ridge: *(agriculture) one of a set of raised strips separated by furrows; (gardening) raised hotbed for melons, etc.*

The Oxford Illustrated Dictionary, Second Edition

Chung-yung's Wife

RED SILK

My father was a shipbuilder, and his father before him. They built the large riverboats that plied the Pearl River with their cargoes of salt, and the seafaring junks that sailed from Canton to Amoy and Formosa. Father had three hundred men who worked in his yards, and we lived in a red-columned mansion in the eastern hills of Canton.

Father was an enlightened man. Although I was only a daughter, he made sure I was educated, almost like a son. We had a private tutor who taught us calligraphy, painting and poetry. I read the *Five Classics*, the *Four Books*, the *Book of Filial Piety*. And I dreamed of Mu-lan, the daughter who dressed as a man and saved her father from battle.

But I never wore the clothes of a man. I could not go out like my brothers to watch the street theatre, or sit in tea-houses with pearl-faced women – the red dust of their cheeks, their lips painted rosebud vermilion. Sometimes I'd go out in a sedan chair and watch the world from behind its curtains, but mostly I stayed at home, reading *The Dream of the Red Chamber*, *Journey to the West*, or doing needlework.

I was a good girl, respectable. Until I was fifteen, no one outside of the family knew of my existence. Then Father's elder sister arranged my marriage. She inquired after all the good families with eligible sons. There was the eldest son of Magistrate Chew, but although his father was known as a fair man, the son was renowned for his foul temper and lack of respect for the ancestors. There was the second son of the Lees, the wealthiest family in Canton – ah, but he was a spendthrift and a gambler. There was the third son of the Kwoks, who had a thriving silk business, but he was born with not enough breath – they say he had beautiful blue-white skin, a gentle man waiting to expire. ___

It was then that my aunt heard of my husband. A man from the neighbouring village of my father. A man whose older brother lived in the New Gold Mountain and had made enough money to send for him. His name was Wong Chung-yung. He was eighteen, and being a Gold Mountain man he had prospects. I did not know whether he was tall or handsome or kind, or whether he could quote from the classics or write a good couplet, but there did not seem to be any history of madness or of leprosy or tuberculosis – or of excessive opium or gambling. And our horoscopes were favourable: there would be plenty of sons and a life of good fortune.

Mother was First Wife. She gave birth to two sons and me, the only daughter. No one spoke of these things, but I know Mother did not want Father – it was she who found Second Wife for him. Over the years there followed a third wife, and then the fourth. Fourth Wife was barely older than I was, uneducated but wily. She had large phoenix eyes and fine white skin, paled with the application of crushed pearl cream. She was, after all, educated in pleasing men.

Mother could order Second, Third or Fourth Wife to do her bidding, and I had precedence over all their daughters. This is the way things are: the first has power; the last has none – unless by stealth and deception. Fourth Wife fed Second Wife opium-laced dumplings, and she died – though nothing, of course, was proven.

Now I would become a wife also. Unlike Mother, I hoped there would be no others.

✤

On the day selected according to the almanac, Father and Eldest Brother carried me to the sedan chair. As we came outside, a chaperone hired from my father's village opened an umbrella; another threw a handful of rice to feed and distract the spirits. Everything was red – red silk, red satin and brocade – red as happiness and the mark on a bed sheet. They took me to my husband's house to the pounding of gongs, hoping not to meet any pregnant cats or dogs, or indeed any four-legged things. I heard my husband outside the sedan chair – he kicked in the door and carried me inside.

This was the place Father-in-law had rented: two rooms on the south side of a courtyard that was shared with three other families. Still in the eastern suburbs, where the Gold Mountain men buy when they come home with their riches.

There I learned to steam rice covered with half a finger of water. I learned how to hold a live chicken and a cleaver – how to pull the skin tight and pluck out the feathers of the throat. Bare pocked skin stretching over the windpipe, the way the eyes close in like a blade. I could pour the blood into a rice bowl, plunge the body into scalding water and strip off the feathers. One cut to pull down the warm entrails.

I learned to wash clothes, my hands stinging with the cold water of winter, callused from the smooth wooden stick, from beating a man's trousers on stone.

And I went shopping in the market – the first time I had walked the dusty streets, the first time I had been out alone. I did not know how to carry the bottles of pickles and fish, the vegetables and the flour. Many times I dropped them and had to go back to buy all that I had broken.

My husband stayed with me six months, enough time to fill me with a son. Then he sailed for the New Gold Mountain and I came to his village. To the house of his mother and father and his older brother's wife.

I wept for three days. Mother-in-law scolded, 'Do you want your son to bear the mark of your tears?' And so I tried to forget my husband – a man who made me laugh and cry and consider wondrous possibilities. I washed my face and closed my heart. And when my time came, I gave birth to twin boys.

This was a comfort to me. My husband's older brother's wife had no children, only daughters. The first was saved, the second smothered by ashes when she turned her face to suckle, and only after much weeping the third was left by the roadside. No one knows whether she was taken as a slave girl or eaten by dogs.

But I gave birth to sons, the first who looked like my mother and the second who took after his father. This was a double happiness, a blessing of the goddess Kuan Yin.

It was Sister-in-law's envy that cursed us – that, and the ghosts of her daughters.

The day before their fifth birthday, my sons came down with fever. I boiled ten different herbs, fed my sons the bitter black tea; I took a coin and scraped their foreheads, the backs of their arms and along their spines; I went to the temple, lit incense and prayed to Buddha and Kuan Yin.

It was on the fourth day, the number of death, that the one like my mother died. Only the one like my husband survived.

Now I look at my son whom I love – I see the straightness of his nose, the fullness of his lips, a certain way of lifting his head when lost in contemplation – this is the shape, the space left behind by my husband.

Chung-yung's Wife

TILE KILN

Every woman has two faces. One a fine white porcelain – a slipping smoothness, carefully shaped, dressed for the eye. The other big and raw and strong, ingrained with the hardness of life.

I do not speak these things; I cannot think in daylight. Only at night when all is quiet, when the only sounds are those of frogs calling and Father-in-law's sporadic snoring. When I lie awake in this room barely big enough for the beds and the wooden barrel toilet.

I listen to Mother-in-law swear and push Father-in-law onto his side, his snort and snuffle and ease into breathing. I hear Sister-in-law cry out in her sleep, and I hold and kiss my son; smell the small boy smell of him, the mud and grass and lychee trees and play by the river.

My sons. My memory of their births and the aftermath is fragmented. Here, and not here, like reading a book where one central chapter has been reworked at random – here a full paragraph, there a full whitespace, here the end of a sentence with no beginning, there a beginning with no end.

I remember my body, squeezed by the hand of God, my innards pressed together, so that all I could do was stop breathing. I heard deep groaning. Tearing pain. The sound of boiling water, and far away Mother-in-law crying out, 'His backside, it's his backside.'

When I woke, Mother-in-law was screaming. I could not open my right eye. The pain in my head, in my body.

Then my left eye closed over.

The midwife called out, 'It's a boy, it's a boy,' but I could not see. My face was thick with pain – my forehead, my eyes, my ear.

Mother-in-law screaming at Sister-in-law. The midwife quietly saying, 'There's another.'

Later, Sister-in-law said she had done it to waken me. I had fainted with the pain of labour. So she had picked up the lid from the pot of boiling water and put it down on my forehead.

The heat of the metal burned into me, and when she pulled it away she took my skin also.

I could not open my eyes for nearly two days. Mother-in-law told me that my face swelled the way dried fish stomach puffs up when put into a slow fire. My right ear stuck out from my swollen head. My lips were fatter than Father-in-law's fingers. I remember throbbing, the wound oozing into my hair and down my face, lying in bed shivering with cold, my bedclothes soaked with sweat. And I remember my sons – their thin cries like the mewls of two kittens.

I did not go out of the house for six months, and even then Mother-in-law would not let me stay in the sun. I did not wash clothes or gather firewood or shop in the market while my face and my body healed.

I have no right eyebrow now, no hair where the pot lid touched my face – just a raised, widened forehead, a sweeping arc of skin like a gibbous moon, pale and puckered, knotty, as if afflicted by tiny, colourless varicose veins. My right eye is pulled upwards, the whole of my face drawn tight by the scar.

My husband does not know – I am the only one who knows how to write.

There is an old saying: Never marry a woman from Tile Kiln. We live in a small village and theirs is large. When the sweet potato harvest is good, they come in the night, and by morning nothing remains. Never pick a fight with a man or woman from Tile Kiln, they say. Their brothers and uncles and cousins are too numerous.

Chung-shun's Wife

THE DEAD

The earth's full of the dead. They hold up the land and wander the streets. Come to the door, pretend they are beggars.

Alone. I hear knock-knocking, strange voices.

I am very still. Silent.

The New Gold Mountain is full of devils. They have red hair and big noses. They all look alike.

Husband went to the New Gold Mountain twenty-two years ago. Devils made him pay to get off the ship. He paid for the ship and then he still had to pay. All the money. Because we are *Tongyan*, he said. White devils don't have to pay and black devils don't have to pay, only people from the Middle Kingdom. This is the poll tax, he said, this is why I could not go with him.

I waited twenty-one years and he came back. Bought concubine. Bitch concubine that men go *nerve-sick* over. Her father gambled *fantan* and *pakapoo* and smoked up the money. Ha! Then he sold her to buy opium.

Husband took her to Canton. Paid for her to learn to read devil language so she could pass the devil test. He took her with him. *Fuck her grandmother.* She was first woman to see the New Gold Mountain.

102

Husband is Number One Son, I am Wife. Every day I get up first. Use rice stalks to light the stove, boil the water, steep tea. Feed the fire with sticks from lychee orchard. Feed Mother- and Father-in-law.

Every day I get water from the river. Carry two big pails, swing my hips, swing the pails on the shoulder pole. Every day do what Mother-in-law says.

Husband has brother: Number Two Son. He left wife here too; went to be with Husband in the New Gold Mountain. Sister-in-law has small feet like rich man's wife, so does not work in the field.

She writes the red scrolls, so we do not pay a scroll-writer. Around the door she writes, *In and out of the house, walk in peace.* She writes above the fireplace to protect us while cooking. On both sides of window, she writes. She writes the red paper scrolls with long curling black ink, so devils and ghosts do not come.

She writes the letters to my husband. I say, Tell him I am good wife – do everything Mother-in-law says. Tell him, Send plenty of money. Tell him, Come back. She tells him I am useless, no-good wife – I know. She tells him, Get concubine. Don't come back. She reads Husband's letters. Says concubine has a son.

Ghosts everywhere. On graves: dirt-hills with turf for head. There are no names. Where are the ancestors? Who can remember? The dead get dug up, their bones put in urns. Lychee orchard is full of urns. No lids, so dead can get out.

I do not go to lychee orchard. I tell Sister-in-law, Go get sticks for fire.

River is full, too. Full of drowned ghosts. Girl babies and bad women and boy babies who got sick and died. I tell Sister-in-law, Go wash the clothes in river, but she has small feet – I still have to bring back the water.

Long time ago Husband looks at me and says, 'Stupid woman, scared of ghosts. That's no ghost, just dirty beggar.' He drinks wine, tells me ghost story . . . *Night-time, raining hard. He walking home on built-up earth of rice paddy. Drunk and cannot walk straight. Terrible ghost comes, coming to him. He's running; ghost coming. He runs faster, faster, ghost light still coming, tumbling over rice paddy. He falls in rice paddy; ghost still coming, big shiny ball, rolling, tumbling to him. Cannot get up, ghost coming.*

'What happens, what happens?' I hide my head in my hands.

Husband laughs. 'Ghost afraid, just like stupid woman,' he says. 'Ghost come closer, closer, then gone. Just rain on rice paddy.'

Night-time. Raining. I cannot sleep. Ghosts come. They stand over my bed. I see heads but no body. They all have girl faces.

Husband says the New Gold Mountain is full of white devils. They smell like sheep-meat and butter; they don't like *Tongyan*. But not many ghosts in the New Gold Mountain. Not so many kill themselves or get killed. Husband says you hear someone outside door in the New Gold Mountain, this is not ghost, this is *Tongyan* or *gweilo*. No ghosts on raining night. He says, in the New Gold Mountain all ghosts are ghosts, you know.

I say, 'Know, don't know, don't like ghosts.'

When I die, Mother- and Father-in-law dead, Husband in New Gold Mountain. Who burns paper money and incense and puts out food? Who looks after me?

THE CONCUBINE'S STORY

Mei-lin sat in the back of the shop, cutting sheets of paper from a huge roll, folding and pasting brown paper bags – ½, 1, 2, up to 5lb sizes. Wai-wai lay beside her in his apple-box crib. Every so often she would smile at him, make soft noises with her tongue and lips, and when her hands were tired she would stoop down and touch his face, let him grasp her little finger.

Shun tied bananas into bundles – each banana fastened by its stem, half an inch apart, a yellow staircase of fruit, string and slip-knots. As he finished he hung each bundle above the layers of polished fruit in the front window.

Mei-lin heard the nasal voice of the postman. She picked up Wai-wai and walked through the doorway into the shop. She knew, as Shun tore the envelope open, as he unfolded the yellow paper, that the letter was from the Wife. She watched his face, the slight crinkle of skin on his forehead, his eyes reading the words again. He refolded the paper precisely on its crease lines, replaced it in the envelope and slipped it into his inside jacket pocket.

'She wants the boy,' he said, without looking at her.

The baby gurgled. Curdled milk spilled on his gown, across her breast, a dark stain spreading over the blue fabric of her dress. She wiped his face with the hem of his gown, turned, walked back through the doorway, up the stairs to the bedroom. Closed the door.

She was pouring water from a porcelain jug into the basin on the dresser when Shun came in. He reached out to touch her arm, but her body stiffened and his hand fell to his side.

'She's the Wife,' he said quietly. 'She has no sons.'

Mei-lin unbuttoned Wai-wai's gown, eased his arms out of the sleeves. She took a white muslin cloth, dipped it in the basin and squeezed it out. Gently she wiped his face and chest.

Shun put his hand on her shoulder.

Turtle egg, she thought. *Bastard.* She swung round on him, saw his eyes flicker wide, his hands lift as he stumbled backwards. She stopped, turned back to the baby.

She had always spoken carefully, her words liquid, a fragrant oil.

Pig. Raised by a dog.

He stood away from her, just a little further than a hand could reach. 'We have each other,' he said. 'What does she have?'

Fart talk. She pulled a towel from the end of the bed, wrapped Wai-wai in it. Turned to face him, holding her son against her shoulder.

'Where are we? China? You are the Husband!'

Wai-wai started to cry. She jiggled the boy in her arms, made soft clicking noises with her tongue.

'He's the oldest son, we have to send him home, how will he get an education—'

'When he's old enough, of course, send him home, but why now? He's only a baby!'

Shun looked away, said nothing.

'If you have any feeling for me, then find it in your liver . . .' She tried to reach out to him, but he pulled away.

'She knows Cousin Gok-nam is going home, maybe the year after next.' Shun stopped, looked across at her. 'His wife could look after the boy on the ship.'

That night Mei-lin cooked rice, and pork-bone and puha soup: nothing else. She set out two pairs of chopsticks, two china spoons, two pale green rice bowls. She served the father of her son and his brother, then sat down away from the table, holding Wai-wai on her knees. She sat watching them as they sucked the fat marrow, the gelatinous gristle, as they flicked the soft grey meat off with their tongues, leaving clean ribs and knuckles on the table. A tide line on the wooden surface.

Hours later, as she lay in bed, she heard Shun climbing the stairs – the creak of the fifth step from the top, the way he leaned more onto his right leg than his left. She turned away from the door, pulled the spun-cotton quilt over the back of her head. The door opened, clicked shut. She heard the metal of his braces hitting the floorboards, felt the shift in the mattress as he climbed into bed. The smell of cigarettes. Ng Ga Pei wine.

She had never refused him. Every night she had massaged his feet, kissed his cock, told him little lies. Their room was a *tent of hibiscus*: when they weren't lying together like clouds and rain, she would rub his shoulders and neck, ease him into sleep. He had paid 500 *man* for her. But she had made him love her.

He lifted her pyjama top, slid his cracked hands down her pants, scratched over her buttocks, her hips, across her breasts. She tried to turn, to push him away, but he held her, pushed hard into her. At the window lace curtains lifted and fell. She could see clouds in a small rectangle of sky, ghost lit, moving, moving away, and she couldn't breathe, couldn't open her mouth or twist herself free. She heard a cry she did not recognise, a wrenching, her nails clawing across his cheeks.

'Bitch!' He punched her hard in the face. Got up, grabbed at his clothes.

107

She heard the door slam, stumbling down the stairs, cursing, leaving by the back door. Wai-wai screaming. She lay on the bed shaking, cradling her bloodied face, her body curled, closed like a fist.

SLICES OF CROW

It was after midnight. The northerly had freshened and Shun shivered. He had left the house blindly, wearing only his crumpled shirt and trousers, his slippers. A fine mist of rain settled on his hair and skin, dampness in his head.

That evening he had closed the shop early, before ten o'clock, and had sat alone in the kitchen long after Yung had gone to bed. 'Market in the morning,' his brother had said, 'I'll go.' He'd said it a little too loudly, with an edge of brightness, and Shun had watched him, and watched him walk up the stairs, and thought about Mei-lin and Wai-wai lying in bed asleep, about his wife back home in China.

He finished the bottle of rice wine in the cupboard, the one Mei-lin used for cooking, and then opened another. He was hot and knew his face had the redness of a non-drinker. He poured the burnt-orange liquid into his glass; it smelled of rind mixed with strong alcohol. His lips stretched into a thin smile. '*Gon booi*,' he said, *dry the cup*, raising his glass to the empty chairs, to the kettle growing cold on the range.

He wanted to shut down his mind, like Ah Wing who spent all his money on *pakapoo* and *hundred men's women*, and never sent remittances home. But Ah Wing was cursed, cursed by his mother and cursed by his father: a man who would die and never find rest, destined to wander with no one to lay out food for him, no one to burn paper money and paper clothes and houses. A hungry beggar.

Shun felt inside his jacket but couldn't find the pocket, then realised he was looking on the wrong side. There – in the lining, a crinkle of paper. He pulled out the envelope and read the words slowly – this was his name, this was his address. In this no man's land, even his name had become something he did not understand.

Wong Chung-shun.

Husband.

Wife.

Mother of his Son.

He lifted his glass. In the light the liquor flashed orange, gold, polished tortoiseshell, like the comb Mei-lin wore in her black, oiled hair. He pushed back his chair, left the envelope, the full glass of wine on the table, and lurched to the stairs. His leg ached; his limp was always more pronounced when he was tired. He wanted – desperately.

He'd watched her at night pull combs from her hair, watched it slowly uncoil and fall down her back as if alive. When she came to him as he lay on the bed, her hair fell loose over him, entangled him, and he imagined she had come from water, her hair thick, shiny as black seaweed.

He liked the small gasps she made when he entered her, again and again. He liked the smallness of her, the way he could lift and move her like a doll. He'd known when he first saw her, when her father let him see her from behind the curtain. He'd wanted to take her. To come from behind and pull her into darkness, before she saw his face. Before she knew his name. He knew from that moment he would fuck her. Own her.

As he pulled off her underwear he knew he could break her if he wasn't careful. If he wanted.

110

Fish in water, that's what they were – what they had been. But now he was cast out onto the wet streets with nothing left to draw him back in. He walked not knowing his destination, the act of walking having its own purpose, an act of meditation. Around the Basin, past cabbage trees shaking their black, spiky heads across the empty fields; up Buckle Street towards the barracks; right into Tory, past the bell-tower of Mount Cook School; left into Haining.

It was dark, quiet; some of the houses seemed unoccupied, their windows shuttered like black faces without eyes, the eyelids grown over. Shun stopped outside Number 34. He walked past the front door where Ah Wing lived in one small room, then into the narrow alley.

'*Hoi moon,* he shouted at an upstairs window, *open up*, then waited by the side door. It was steel clad, with no latch, no doorknob.

A faint, familiar smell, sweet and earthy, drifted in the cool air.

Upstairs someone pulled a rope. Shun entered, and the piece of timber at the bottom of the door pivoted to relock it. Now he stood in a cubicle facing another steel-sheathed door.

'*Hoi moon.*'

It unlocked and he walked along the hallway, up the stairs, through ever stronger fumes, his slippers flip-flapping on the wooden boards.

At the top the trapdoor was open, a metal cover lying beside it. Thick smoke and hot, fuggy air made Shun draw back and hold his breath. One side of Ah Keung's mouth lifted in recognition but his eyes did not smile.

In the centre of the room a small lamp gave out the only light, its flame burning through the top of the bell-shaped glass. Two men gathered on grass mats around it, their bird-faces caught in sharp relief. One prepared his pipe, dipping a long needle into the flame; the other lay on his side, propped by a wooden pillow, shoulders and back hunched, sucking a bamboo pipe, drinking the smoke in one long pull. Against the far wall the shadows of three, maybe four other men lay on wooden benches.

Shun had smoked *slices of crow* two or three times, reluctantly, just after the accident when the pain in his leg had been too much to bear. Now all he wanted was release – for his tired muscles and his mind to be smoothed from within.

He watched Ah Keung dip a long hatpin into a sachet of dark toffee, turning it to coat the end. He warmed it over the flame and dipped it again, twirling and lifting the pin, twirling and lifting till the substance formed a cone-shaped bead. He roasted the bead till it started to bubble, then pressed it into the bowl of a bamboo pipe, pushing the pin through the hole, pulling it out.

Shun took the pipe. *Ah foo yung, hibiscus,* he thought; *ah foo wing, take prisoner for ever.* He lay down on a grass mat, his head and neck resting against a wooden pillow, put the bowl to the flame, the pipe to his mouth, his body curled like a drawn bow.

Close your eyes now and listen, for this is a story passed down through the ages, a once-upon-a-time story about a girl who longed for a husband, yet none could be found for her. Despairing, she sought lovers, but all drew back in horror, for her skin was deeply pockmarked.

At last unable to bear her loneliness any longer, she drank poison, and as she lay dying she called down a curse upon every man who had spurned her. 'In my lifetime you scorned me,' she said, 'but in my death you shall give all that you have, and more, so shall you desire me.'

After her death each of the men succumbed to a curious sickness. Doctors searched far and wide for a cure but none could be found. Then one day a herbalist came upon an unusual plant growing by the girl's graveside. It was tall, with flamboyant red flowers, each with four large petals. When the petals fell, they left a large green boll. The herbalist cut one of the bolls and collected the thick, milky liquid. He mixed it with rice wine and gave it to one of the men.

Instantly he recovered.

Each of the men drank the liquid. Pain and anxiety left their bodies and they were filled with a calm they had never known. Their senses sharpened, their minds opened, a beautiful woman with fine white skin beckoned to them.

Then disappeared.

The men became sick again. They longed for release but could not find it. And so they took the liquid again.

Their bodies settled, as if into sleep, their minds budded, branched and flowed. The woman called to them, and disappeared.

And so the men grew sick, their bodies, their minds wracked with desire and despair. Each time they drank the liquid, they became well, but each time the woman disappeared, they fell sicker than ever.

VINEGAR

Shun came home two days later reeking of that sweet, suffocating smell, his pupils tiny dots in the dark of his eyes. Mei-lin held her breath. *He was the same age as her father.* She watched him climb the stairs and sleep for another day.

Until he had woken and washed the stink from his skin, his hair, his mouth, until she had erased the stench from his clothes and bedclothes in boiling soapy water, she took a quilt and slept on the floor, holding Wai-wai in her arms.

Afterwards, she returned to his bed, but always retired early, turning her back to the door when she heard him climb the stairs, never turning, even onto her back, until she heard his deepening breath, his slide into oblivion.

Sunday, as soon as they'd finished breakfast and cleaned the shop, Shun went with Yung to Haining Street as usual. He did not stop with his brother to drink tea. Instead he walked to Ah Chong's.

He smelled the roast pork even as he walked down the alley to the backyard. He asked for a lean cut of rump and inspected it carefully. Was the skin crispy? Was there just the right lacing of tender fat and meat? He walked to other kitchens and bought dim sum, home-made noodles and little custard tarts. He went straight home.

Mei-lin held Wai-wai across her body, looked at her favourite

114

foods – and refused to eat them.

That night Shun engaged his brother in a game of cards, half-heartedly arguing about imperialist powers, the imminent fall of the Dynasty, the hope of the new Republic. Yung quoted Liang Ch'i-chao: 'If you want to keep the old complete, you have to make something new every day.' But Shun didn't understand. He didn't care. The world had become a moving picture, voiceless, devoid of colour, a series of unnatural movements punctuated by the sound of a frenzied piano.

He watched as days and nights passed before him. He watched the mother of his son, watched the silence settle over them.

They argued again. Only once. 'No one sends a baby home without his mother,' Mei-lin said, 'even with another woman. What about dysentery? And even when the ship arrives, how long does it take to get back to the village? What about bandits? What about floods? What about famine?'

He avoided her eyes.

'What's wrong with you? Are you mad? Or are you a coward?'

He almost hit her, but the look on her face stopped him. The hard, steady gaze, the set of her mouth against him.

'All day she *eats vinegar*,' Mei-lin said. 'She's a tiger. Why are you doing this? What hold has she got over you?'

It was a long time ago, before Shun and his wife were born or even conceived. It had been raining for weeks. Shun's father heard cries from the swollen river. He dropped his shoulder pole and did not notice the vegetables scatter. He leapt into the water and pulled the drowning man onto the riverbank.

Afterwards, the man pledged his first daughter.

Shun was fourteen, his wife three years older, when they met on their wedding day. After the whole roast pig and the wine and firecrackers, he lifted her red head-dress. And looked away.

Her face was wide. It was pocked and dimpled, her mouth like a twist on a steamed *cha siu* bun. He went to bed with her and pretended to sleep.

She worked hard. She collected water from the river. She scrubbed the barrel toilet clean. On special occasions she cooked his, his parents' favourite foods – crispy-skinned chicken, steamed whole fish, sweet soup of snow-ear fungus.

She was like a bossy older sister. *As noisy and annoying as a devil.*

He grew up. He made up ghost stories that she always believed. He learned to laugh at her.

He drank, closed his ears and eyes – and went to bed with her.

She bore daughters and wailed when the second and third were taken from her. Her mouth set fast in her crooked face; her eyes hardened to small pieces of obsidian.

She complained. She raged. She *spilled pepper.*

Shun left for the New Gold Mountain.

When he came back, he barely recognised her. Her skin was dark and wrinkled like poor man's leather. Her back had the beginnings of a stoop. Only the twist of her mouth was familiar, her obsidian eyes.

How could she object to a concubine? She had not produced a son. She offered her maid. A child she could control, completely.

And then she saw Mei-lin, saw his utter bewitchment. 'Give me a son,' she pleaded. 'Give me a son.'

He looked at her and shook his head in disbelief. How could she even hope to conceive?

How he pitied her.

In darkness he lay, desperately thinking of Mei-lin. But when he touched her coarse skin, smelt the foul breath of her rotted teeth – the years of spitting sugar cane – his penis softened.

Shun woke. He gazed in half-light at Mei-lin's hair against the pillow, the paleness of her skin, her rosebud lips.

He lay on his side of the bed and felt old, shrivelled. His *ch'i* was drying up, his flesh turning to bone.

SLAVE GIRL

Mei-lin felt the hand on her arm and turned. Wai-wai had crept up behind her as she sat on an apple box, darning a sock and waiting for customers, and now his face pushed into her belly. She put down the needle and picked him up. He snuggled into her, his tiny fingers holding her breast, sniffing her skin just as she too would bury her face in him, breathe him in. '*Ho dak yi*,' he whispered, *adorable, good-to-kiss.* Then more loudly, 'You good-for-nothing slave girl!'

Mei-lin laughed. She had whispered endearments to him, then called out loudly, 'Good-for-nothing slave girl!' so the spirits would believe he was just a worthless girl and wouldn't steal him away. And he had remembered every word she had spoken, the exact tone, the love and the desperation, and had echoed them back to her. The words bubbled in her liver, warm and light, until she realised what he'd said, a baby speaking without comprehension. She held him close, felt the smoothness of his skin against her face, smelt his milk-drunk smell. But now he was struggling, wanting to go and play with apple boxes and newspapers, with the cricket his father had placed with fruit peelings in a glass preserving jar. She let him down and watched him toddle away.

Every week in rotation, whenever the father of her son could spare her in the shop, she went calling. On another woman's kitchen; on greengrocery, laundry, Chinese grocery. She'd drink tea and gossip about affairs back home – who had borne a son or who only a daughter, whose house had been swept away in the floods or whose rice harvest had been plundered by bandits. And as they ate and drank and talked, she'd remember the instructions of the father of her son.

'What hope do we have,' she'd say, 'unless we are free from Imperial corruption. The new Emperor is only three years old and the Regent is weak and dominated by foreign powers. Why do you think the *gweilo* treat us with such contempt? Do they treat the dwarves from the east like this? No, Japan is counted among the imperialist powers, just as hungry for our land and our blood.'

She'd pause, trying again to remember the way his brother put it, because Yung knew better how to present an argument; because if she thought too long about the father of her son, his words, his face, his hands, she wanted to spit, she wanted to scream, she wanted to . . .

'Our motherland needs us,' she'd say. 'But what can we do? We have to overthrow the Dowager. We aren't Manchus, we're people of the *Tong* dynasty, not the *Ch'ing*. We must bring China into the modern age. Speak to your husbands. Persuade them to give to the founding of the Republic. Persuade them to be generous. Sun Yat-sen is one of us. He speaks our language. He has lived overseas. He has trained overseas. He knows our plight. He alone knows how to make China strong again. Only then will we lift our heads high and meet the barbarians eye to eye.'

And so Mei-lin supported the work of Yung – and of the father of her son. And the cause of *Tongyan* and women, because in modern China she hoped women would also be educated, just like the wife of Sun Yat-sen and her sisters. Think of the women of the French Revolution who dared to seize their own destinies, Yung had said. Mei-lin remembered every word of the brother of the father of her son, a

119

man who showed her respect by speaking to her openly, intelligently about the cause.

Most of the women Mei-lin visited, and their husbands, treated her with respect. They knew she worked hard, that she earned her right to be here. Not like the wives left behind who had maids and remittance money. Here every woman worked night and day. And she as much as any of them. Only some of *his* family looked down on her.

Not three months before, when she'd visited Cousin Gok-nam's wife (because Cousin Gok-nam had so far pledged only £5), the stupid woman had jabbered about the planned trip home.

'Now don't you be worried about Wai-wai, it's for his own good, you don't want him to grow up like the *gweilo la*? *Aaaiyaa*. Big Mother will spoil him rotten, she'll love him to death, he's such a lovely boy, and don't you worry, I'll look after him on the voyage like one of my own and when he comes back you won't know him, he'll be so grown up and clever, just like his uncle . . .'

Mei-lin wanted to slap her. This woman knew exactly how she felt about Big Mother, about Wai-wai leaving, and yet here she was rubbing her face in it.

'What would you know?' she said, looking hard at her cousin. 'It's not as if you have any sons.'

'*Aaaiyaa*. Big Mother has her right *la*, after all you *are* only a . . .' Her eyes narrowed. 'I hear he paid 500 *man* for you, quite a sum considering your father was . . . you're lucky you're pretty, otherwise you could have ended up a slave girl sleeping on the floor in some rich man's house *la*, and then what do you think they would have done to you, if not the master, then the sons and the men servants . . .'

'Bitch! I may not be a wife, but I've given him a son. What have you done *la*? Why do you think he wants to go back? He'll leave you behind to serve his mother and father, and how do you think they'll treat you? If your mother-in-law beats you, who will pity you? It really won't matter if you live or die. Regardless, he'll tell the authorities you died in China and he'll bring out another wife. A younger and prettier wife. One who will give him a son.'

Mei-lin hadn't gone back, and neither had Cousin Gok-nam's wife come visiting. Usually she came at least once a week, to chatter about who was going home or who had won money playing *fantan* or *pakapoo*, and to eat Mei-lin's steamed white sponge, which had a reputation as the best in Wellington. Shun had asked Mei-lin once or twice whether she'd spoken to her. Cousin Gok-nam still hadn't given more money.

But suddenly it didn't matter. Cousin Gok-nam had lost everything playing *pakapoo* and now he couldn't go back home, let alone give to the Revolution. When Shun told her, Mei-lin excused herself quickly and ran upstairs. She closed the door to their room and burst out laughing. She threw herself on the bed and wiped tears from her eyes, her body shaking and shaking as if something very hard, bound tight inside her, had suddenly sprung free.

A small, slimy hand touched her wrist. 'Eat *la*, eat *la*.' Wai-wai was pushing a soggy, half-eaten biscuit at her, wet crumbs stuck to his lips, right cheek, chin, pieces stuck to his shirt.

Mei-lin smiled. Was that the biscuit she'd given him yesterday? Where had the rascal hidden it? 'Thank you, good boy.' She pushed the crumbling biscuit back at him. 'Eat *la*,' she said softly, wiping the back of her hand across the corner of her eye, gathering him up in her arms.

THE CABLE CAR

Sundays were always a luxury: the day of the week when everyone slept at least half an hour longer. Mei-lin rose at six. Lit the coal range and boiled the water, opened the tin of Oolong tea and sniffed the dark smoky leaves. She loved that smell, the almost muskiness of it. After her father had gambled everything away, before he had sold her, there had been no tea, only cups of hot water. She put a scant teaspoon into the porcelain teapot, added boiling water, watched the leaves expand and unfurl, the lighter twigs floating on the surface of the colouring water. She put on the lid and replaced the pot in its padded wicker basket. Then she started on the rice gruel. She washed the rice, added pork bones marinated and roasted in garlic, ginger, rice wine, sugar and soy, put the pot on the range, two-thirds filled it with water, added several more slices of ginger, and tilted the lid just a little so it wouldn't boil over.

The brothers rose at 6.30. *Jo san, early morning,* they said to each other as they met on the stairs. They drank their tea, then Shun scrubbed out the shop with soda, soap and hot water. He wiped the shelving and benches, the cash register and the scales. He scrubbed the floor. He brought the soft ripe fruit in from the window and replaced it with the freshest, the rosiest fruit. And once, he paused for a moment, looking out through the glass at the empty street, at the dark shop

122

windows – Mackenzie's Butchery, Wilson's Drapery, Krupp's Pharmacy – at the clear blue sky.

Out the back, Yung arranged a line of upright apple boxes. He lit a kerosene lamp, then went into the banana ripening room. He stared for a moment in the semi-darkness, breathing in the gas, then came out again, blinking at the brightness, carrying a case of bananas which he placed on top of an apple box. He brought in three empty banana cases from the stack outside the back door and placed them on either side of the full one. Then he sorted the bananas into three groups – green, semi-ripe, ripe – carefully arranging them in the appropriate case. As he worked he sang arias from Cantonese operas, folk songs, ditties he made up as he went along, bringing case after case out of the gaseous twilight of the banana room. When he had brought out and sorted all the bananas, he put the unripe ones back, the semi-ripe closest to the door, then took the ripe ones into the shop. Any spotty or overripe fruit on the shelves – apples or pears with smooth depressions of brown rot, or bananas blighted with freckles or bruises rising though the yellow skin – he put into the marked-down bins for stewing or baking or frying. Salad bananas. He didn't understand English – the language, like the people, kept changing the rules. They cooked a banana and called it salad; they ate raw lettuce and called it salad. He shook his head and smiled. On special occasions, when he boiled lettuce and poured oyster sauce-flavoured mushrooms on top, did this make it salad also?

At 7.45, Mei-lin called them for breakfast. They washed their hands and came to the table.

'It's a good day,' said Yung, as he sprinkled spring onion on his gruel. 'Warm and not too windy.' He slurped happily. 'Today, I was thinking of doing something different.'

Every Sunday the men went down Haining Street to eat and drink and gossip with their village cousins and others from their county –

with any Chinese, in fact: the accents might be different, sometimes even difficult to understand, but here in the New Gold Mountain they were all brothers. Mei-lin stayed home with Wai-wai, or sometimes took him to visit the few other women and children.

But *sai yan*, westerners, took outings on Sundays. In summer time they might go to the Basin Reserve or take the ferry to Days Bay or go for a swim along Oriental Parade. Even the women did it. Yung had seen some of them. There had been a crowd (mostly men) watching, enjoying the daring of the latest attire. Their costumes exposed their arms and shoulders, the tops of their chests and a V of flesh on their backs; they even exposed their thighs. Where the wet fabric covered them, it clung to every curve, leaving little for the imagination.

Mrs McKechnie had told him about the cable car, how there was a tram at the top and one at the bottom, how one slid up while the other slid down, passing in the middle, stopping at each station with a ring of the bell. She told him about the grand Kiosk at the top where the young gentlemen took the young ladies to have tea and cakes for sixpence.

'It goes up the hill to Kelburne,' Yung said, 'and you look out at the hills and houses and the harbour. You can come back down on it again or walk through the botanical gardens. I think I'll take a tram and then the cable car. I can take Wai-wai too. It won't cost anything for him and he'll love the engines.'

Shun raised his eyebrows. They'd never been on a tram, let alone the cable car. Trams cost a penny so they walked everywhere.

'The cable car only costs a penny for a return ticket,' Yung said. 'Won't it be fun, Wai-wai?'

Wai-wai began to plead louder and louder with his father. Shun always found it hard to say no to him, and he did not like the idea of his son knowing and experiencing more than him. He would go too. He looked across the kitchen table, through the wisps of steam rising from the bowls of gruel, and saw the disappointment on Mei-lin's face.

Why not, he thought and smiled at her. 'Wai-wai's mother can come too.'

Mei-lin could feel the beginning of tears at the back of her eyes. She blinked, willed them away. She had never been on an outing, never ridden a tram or cable car. She looked across at the father of her son. It had been months and she had barely spoken to him.

That night, Shun woke with Mei-lin in his arms. Why hadn't he done it earlier? He brushed the hair from her eyes, told her he would arrange an adoption. If they could not find a suitable boy in Melon Ridge, then they would look for a Wong from White Stone or Sand Head villages. They would find a number two son for his wife back in China.

FIELD

It seemed the strangest question to ask after they'd known each other for so long, perhaps the hardest, because it seemed so intimate. If it had been anyone else, Katherine would have known – she knew the baker next door was George, even though she only ever called him Mr Paterson. Everyone knew. (George's pies were famous in Newtown, in all of Wellington by the way people talked.) But no one knew the names of the Chinese. Occasionally someone might say Mr – Mr Wong or Mr Choy. But usually it was the Chinaman next door to Paterson's or the John on the corner of Tory and Webb. They were all called John, the Chinese. And even if anyone bothered to find out, who could remember? Their names were like birds that never came in to land.

Katherine was afraid to ask. Afraid he would speak his name and it would hover close to her ear, her cheek, her tongue, then fly away from her. How could she ask him? Again and again. As if his name was unimportant. As if he merely provided a service for which she paid and dismissed him.

He was wrapping turnips in a page of the *Evening Post* and she'd expected him to open his full, wide lips. Without realising, she had turned her face a little, still looking intently at his dark eyes, his mouth, straining her ears as if spreading a net. But instead he'd leaned in closer, held out his left hand for her to see. She did not understand, yet she'd looked into his palm, as if to read his life line, his heart line, the lines of the number of his children. And then he lifted his right index finger like a pen, and wrote stroke upon stroke on his hand.

'*Wong*,' he said, and started over, slowly, kindly, as if to a child. 'My name has grass on top,' he said, drawing a short horizontal line on his skin and then two small ones down through it. Then a longer horizontal line underneath.

A name, she thought, has a sound which disappears, and now also a physical presence, a shape on skin, an apparition.

'The belly of my name is a field,' he said, drawing a grid like a window dissected into four small panes. How strange, she thought, the way the Chinese draw windows, how they draw three sides of the frame, then the two bars within and only last the bottom sill, as if there is no need for closure unless there is something of importance to close. No, a field, she thought again, not a window on the future, but something more earthy. Now two strokes underneath, like two short legs dancing, holding his name up to the world.

She watched him write his Christian name (but what does that mean, the word Christian?). '*Chung*,' he was saying, and she was lost, somewhere after the symbol for China, the centre of all things, and three strokes of a heart beating. 'Faithful,' he was saying, 'loyal,' and she thought about faith, about loyalty and what might be true. '*Yung*,' he was saying, 'courageous,' and she thought about courage, about what she had always been afraid to do, what she'd always been afraid to be.

She thought about how his surname came first, how his family had the ultimate priority. Katherine came first for her. Not McKechnie, which was only her husband's name; not even Lachlan, her father's name. Only Katherine. Whatever she could count on for herself.

127

She watched his finger move across the skin - this strange intimacy of language - and asked him without thinking for a Chinese name, an opening into his language, a window into his world.

GHOSTS, DREAMS

It was 4.30 when she came in on her way home from work. She said he looked tired. He remembered smiling weakly. He'd been up at six to go to the market, spent all day unloading the cart, washing and trimming vegetables. Another six hours to go, bringing in the cauliflowers, cabbages, onions, shutting the shop, tidying up.

She was surprised. Did he always have to work such long hours? What about his brother? Of course they took turns: he finished early on Mondays, Thursdays and Saturdays, at about seven when they had dinner and his brother took over. And what did he do then? He might have said that he went down *Tongyangai* and met up with friends like Fong-man, occasionally played a game of dominoes or cards, mostly drank tea and argued about politics, but then he looked at her again and remembered Haining Street was a swear word in English, something like bastard or whore, a place that *gweilo* used at night to frighten their children. He remembered she knew nothing of China, or Sun Yat-sen and the Revolution, and maybe – probably – she didn't care. He felt a nervous laugh rising in his throat.

'Do you like knitting?' she asked. 'I hear that sea captains enjoy knitting. It's supposed to be good when there's nothing else to do.'

'Nitting?'

129

She mimed some kind of action with her hands, but he didn't understand.

'Don't worry, just kidding.' She saw his bewilderment. 'Joking. I was only joking.'

He saw the twinkle in her eyes. He was still curious – what was this *nitting* she joked about, and what was the other word, did she say *kidding*? – but he did not ask again. Sometimes he'd sidetrack her with his questions and they'd forget what they'd been talking about. Sometimes he was too plain tired.

'So what do you do when you're not working?' she asked again.

'I walk,' he said. Already he'd forgotten the new words. Instead he was swallowed by night, the rocking of one foot in front of the other, everything full of shadow and half-light – moon, star, lamplight – the streets emptied of people and filled with ghosts, dreams, strange possibilities.

'I like walking too,' she said, and he was surprised, and didn't know what he'd told her and what he'd only thought, because there was always a gap between thought and its expression, especially in another language. 'It's a good time to think,' he heard her say, and he looked up from the cauliflower he'd chosen because it was the biggest and freshest and whitest, and he asked her where she liked to walk.

'Sometimes we walk to Oriental Parade or even down to the beach at Island Bay. If it's fine, that is. The children like to play in the water.

'Robbie kicks a ball or if there are other boys down there he'll join them for cricket . . . Edie makes elaborate – big – sandcastles . . . Sometimes we just go to the Basin. It's so much closer . . .'

She sighed. 'Sometimes I think I need time to myself. Away from Mrs Newman telling me what to do. Away from the children . . .' She smiled.

He nodded. He needed time away from the shop too. Away from his brother. But perhaps he had too much time. Alone.

There was silence, just the crinkling and rustling of newspaper. As he handed the wrapped cauliflower to her, the small bag of Brussels

130

sprouts, he told her about the place at the Basin, under the cabbage trees, where he liked to lie down and think and look at the night sky.

The next evening, Thursday, he did not go down Haining Street or Frederick or Taranaki. He walked to the Basin. There was no one under the pine or cabbage trees. He walked a circuit, then another, and another. Then he lay down under a tree and looked up at the moonless sky, at the stars shining out of darkness.

It was different here. The stars made unrecognisable pictures; they told other stories.

He could feel the damp coming through his clothes from the grass underneath, even from the air. His mother would scold. *Cold-to-death,* she'd call. *Rice bucket,* is that all you can do? Eat rice and nothing else? Your brother can't read but is he so stupid?

Yung laughed and gazed at the stars, which glowed larger and more wondrously fuzzy because of myopia.

He thought about how far away they were. He thought about the cowherd and spinning-maid, of whom the heavens disapproved because passion interfered with their work – two lovers whom the Jade Emperor turned into stars, whose paths crossed only once every year, on the seventh day of the seventh month.

He sighed. Who could understand women and their complicated thinking – especially a foreign woman. He could feel the damp moving through his clothes, through his skin, even through his flesh to the marrow at the heart of his bones, when he heard her voice.

'Hello,' she called from a distance.

He lifted his head and saw her silhouette. 'Hello,' he said, and realising that she might not be sure whether it was him, he stood up and tipped his hat in the manner of a *gweilo* to a lady. 'Mrs McKechnie,' he said.

STROKE UPON STROKE

He'd looked into her eyes as he told her about moonlight, starlight, the place under the cabbage trees at the Basin. Katherine blushed and left the shop quickly.

But she couldn't stop thinking. As she cooked dinner, as she sent the children to bed. She couldn't sleep.

The next day she gazed at the black typewriter keys and thought of his hair, his eyes, the gentle, husky sound of his voice. What had Mrs Newman just said? What was she supposed to be doing?

She passed by the shop on the way home, saw his brother stacking pumpkins. Did not go in.

Her stomach felt tight. At dinner, she could not eat.

'Are you all right, Mum?' Edie asked.

'What? Yes, I'm fine. Just got a stomach-ache.' She put down her fork.

'Brussels sprouts give me stomach-ache too,' Robbie said, pushing his plate away.

Katherine could see him looking at her, waiting for her to argue with him, waiting for her to make him eat, but for once she said nothing.

The children went to bed and the house fell silent.

Katherine opened a book and closed it. She picked up her knitting and put it down again. She looked in at the children. Came back downstairs and paced from room to room. Not a sound from upstairs. Not a sound.

She put on her coat and walked out the back door.

It was a new moon; she could barely make out his silhouette under the cabbage trees. 'Mrs McKechnie,' he said, as if he'd been waiting.

How did he know it was her? How *could* he be waiting?

She was suddenly afraid. She'd made a terrible mistake with Donald. And now, what in God's name was she doing?

He stood up and walked towards her, and she didn't know what to say. She had to say something.

'You haven't given me a name,' she blurted out. 'I asked you over a month ago and you still haven't given me a name.' She wanted to cry. What a stupid thing to say. As if she'd come all this way – as if she'd left her children asleep in bed – just because he'd forgotten. What had come over her? It had been a stupid, stupid thing to ask of him, even then. And now . . .

A tram rattled past, turning out of Adelaide Road, into Rugby and along Sussex; another travelled along Kent Terrace. A drunk called out as he stumbled out of the Caledonian, the clip-clop of a horse-cart, the ragged sound of a motorcar.

What was he saying? Was he laughing? Not his usual gravelly laugh but something quieter, more hesitant.

The leaves of a cabbage tree shook above them.

Her face felt hot. She was shaking. She wanted to run, but her legs felt weak, as if her bones had softened, as if she were falling. 'I . . . I have to go . . .' she whispered.

But then he moved closer, took her in his arms as if to still her shaking.

He turned her hand and slowly traced onto her palm with his finger. She could hardly see, only movements of darkness within darkness,

133

but she could smell ginger and aniseed, the smell of a man's fresh sweat, and she could feel the shape of her name, the sensation of skin against skin.

'*Lai*,' he said. 'This is Chinese family name, not name we give foreigners, not name like English. You put this name with word for bright and this is sun come out of night. You have all these colours.' She could hear his breathing, feel her own short breaths. '*Bik-yuk*,' he was saying. 'This is Christian name. It means jade.' And he was writing again, stroking her palm with her name. '*Bik*,' he was saying. 'This is word for king and this is white. Under is rock. *Yuk*. This is three jades,' he was drawing horizontal lines, 'and this string hold them together. Many woman have name like beautiful or flower but you are pure and clear . . .'

She heard a tram swing through her silence into Adelaide Road, felt him touch her hair, her cheek, brush her lips, which parted and left a line of moisture on his fingers.

A THOUSAND MILES

You take one step, two, you open your eyes – and you've travelled a thousand miles.

What is she doing?

She avoided him for days. There were no more vegetables. No bananas or oranges to give the children for their lunches. She wondered about walking further, finding a different fruiterer.

She walked past without turning to look. She could still feel his fingers, his lips . . . She wanted to scream. She wanted the earth to swallow her . . .

She walked but could not enter another greengrocery. She walked. And turned back.

She entered and felt his eyes move over her face, down her body.

'I need vegetables – and fruit,' she said, her voice quivering. 'For the children.' She had no strength. She could not choose.

He unhooked a bundle of bananas from above the window, selected oranges and carrots, cauliflower and onions. Potatoes. As he gave them to her, his fingers brushed across her hand.

'Tonight,' he said softly. 'Where no one see us.'

LANTERN

Katherine sent the children to bed at nine o'clock. Edie seemed to fall almost immediately into sleep, her face as clear and calm as the moon. Robbie complained. He was twelve, after all, and not a child. Surely he could stay up till at least 9.30. She let him read for fifteen minutes only, then came and turned off the light and went back downstairs. There was mending to do. A sock of Robbie's where his big hungry toe had eaten its way through the wool, a pair of trousers that had split at the knee. He was so hard on his clothes – running around kicking balls, climbing trees, forgetting to cut his toenails; these were only a couple of months old.

She used to grumble at Donald because he never gave enough for housekeeping. Now she had enough and still she was doing the mending. She smiled sadly. Then, unhappiness had coloured everything; now, it was merely the habits of a lifetime. 'But Katie,' her mother would say, 'they're perfectly good. All you need to do is apply a little thread and elbow grease.'

Katherine stared at her sewing basket. She did not want to think of her mother. She rose and went into the kitchen, filled the kettle and put it on the range. She walked up and down, her shoes ringing on the wooden floorboards. She made tea and sat at the table, holding the hot cup in her hands. It grew cold and she poured it away. She swept the floor. After ten minutes she realised she had been scattering coal dust, walking through it, spreading dust from one pile into many. She put the broom away. Sat down at the table. Stood up, started pacing again. Stopped. She climbed the stairs quietly and looked in at the children.

Edie lay, arms tossed up as if softly under arrest, but Robbie looked like he'd been running, fighting; he'd tangled himself in the bedding as if caught in a spider's web. She'd untangled him so many times, ever since he was a wee boy. She picked his pillow up from the floor and placed it under his head, pulled the sheets and eiderdown gently, and tucked him in again as if he were still her baby, as if he were still four years old. She closed the door behind her and did not see his eyes flicker open.

Downstairs, she stared again at the mending. Surely there was more to life than elbow grease.

She put on her coat, pulled her biggest hat – the green one with the orange flowers – well down over her face, and secured it with a hatpin. She put a box of matches in her pocket, picked up the lantern, unlit, then stepped out the back door.

The cool of night enveloped her. A clouded sky. She stood there, almost walked back into the kitchen and closed the door again. Why was she doing this? She was crazy. She knew she was crazy.

She listened. The children were asleep.

She walked down the side of the house, through the gate, then over the road. She turned and stared at the darkness of the upstairs windows. She had to either walk straight back across the road or go on. She could feel his lips on her hair, her throat . . . with every step it seemed to get a little easier, her heart beating in her mouth.

She walked down Adelaide Road towards the shops. Everything was closed – except for the Tramways Hotel, which spilled gloomy yellow light and laughter onto the footpath. And the greengrocery. No, not him, but his brother carrying shelves of fruit and vegetables inside. She walked, holding the unlit lantern, knowing no one in the little wooden cottages saw her in the darkness, hoping no one she knew would stumble across her in the street. Opposite the Basin Reserve she turned right, quickly, away from the pale light of the street lamp, up the driveway to the College. Lights off in the dormitories, all those boys – some not much older than Robbie – lying in their beds whispering, sighing, dreaming. Past the big kitchens where servants still washed supper dishes and prepared the next day's breakfast. Through the grounds of the school, up to the town belt.

Among the trees she hesitated. Long pine trunks, branches swayed and sang above her. She used to play here when she was a girl – as soon as he described it, she knew where he was meaning – but she'd never come at night. She paused to let her eyes adjust to the darkness, took a deep breath and walked slowly, feeling each step along the ground before she put her full weight on it. She could see shadows, degrees of black and black. At last, when she thought no one would see her through the pines, she fumbled with the matches and lit the lantern. Light escaped from just one glass side. Now she saw the earth rise and fall away, tree roots, ridges and valleys, carpets of pine needles, broken glass, pine cones, empty bottles. What was more frightening: blindness or the shadows cast by the flame?

She walked tentatively, searching for the tree, the only one half-burnt by lightning . . . there . . . she caught hold of the trunk and walked behind it straight into . . . she gasped and fell back, but hands caught her, pulled her up. She held on as if drowning in air, the lantern swinging, sending light zigzagging over branch and trunk and root. Across his sleeve, collar, face. She could smell him: soap, ginger and garlic, a man smell. Her feet found steady ground; she let go, and then he let go also, their bodies so close she could feel him breathing. She looked up and the brim of her hat swept across his face.

They fell back. She was apologising and he was saying something she could not understand. He was laughing, and laughter rose from her like a small skein of wool unravelling. Then silence: just the rustle

138

of pine needles, the call of a morepork, the distant clatter of trams. 'I suppose I should take it off,' she said.

He said nothing.

She put down the lantern, suddenly wishing she'd blown out the flame. The hatpin. Her fingers felt thick, clumsy. She was pulling the pin from her hair, feeling that this was an extreme act of intimacy, like taking off one's clothes, petticoat by petticoat, like being caught in moonlight naked. She dropped the hat, her hair falling over the back of her neck, over her face, felt his lips on her forehead, his hand cup and lift her chin, her mouth towards him . . .

Afterwards, she climbed into the coldness of her bed, felt the thin layer of sweat on her skin, stared at the ghost of a street lamp through her window.

She listened to the sounds of darkness, closed her eyes. Her mother's face slipped under her eyelids, her voice through the ears she tried to squeeze shut: *Why do you always bring home stray dogs and cats? What's wrong with you? People will think I didn't bring you up right.*

It hadn't been men. She hadn't had any men before Donald – and anyway, even now her mother was still under Donald's spell. It was Matilda Mulroney, who didn't have any friends because she was dirty and had a vague off-putting smell but whose wicked sense of humour Katherine adored. It was the three-legged dog that followed her home.

If she was honest – and oh, honesty was a taskmaster it was easier to avoid – Katherine had noticed the Chinese.

Why, for instance, were they almost exclusively men? And why did people call them celestials? Because they were aliens? Because no one knew anything about them? Apart from Haining Street, that is. Apart from opium and gambling.

Katherine noticed as they walked down the street or when she went into their greengroceries. Once, almost all of them had a long plait that fell down their back, that they sometimes coiled up under their hats, their foreheads shaved right up the scalp. But more and more were cutting their hair.

There were stories of danger and iniquity that seemed ludicrous if compelling. Yet most Chinamen seemed so thin and small. So polite and unassuming.

If they had not spoken such halting English, if their accent had not been so difficult, if they had not looked so out of place, so very foreign, perhaps she would not have noticed the Chinese at all.

It reminded her of the way she had been with Donald . . .

Yet this Chinaman was different. Chinamen were aberrations, and he, an aberration amongst them . . . She smiled. He had, she realised, Matilda's mischievous grin.

She knew it was madness.

She would not go to him again. He would wait and wait and she would not come.

It was a dream – a beautiful, discomfortable dream. She would wake up. Of course, it was only a dream.

But she could still feel him inside her, the ache of him like a bruise.

It hadn't been like this with Donald.

It was the tenderness.

He entered and she wept. Silently. She was not crying. It's just that tears slipped from her eyes and she did not know why.

When he touched her it felt like wholeness. She forgot who he was. He was a man, he was *this* man, and now there was no other reason for being. Except for him to fill her. And fill her.

The intensity of their bodies filling the world.

Yung rose early. He could not keep still. He felt as if he had boundless energy. He walked to the markets composing short poems in his head, reciting them to himself, whistling old love ballads. His body no longer belonged to himself; it seemed so light, he felt like he could run up walls, perform miraculous feats of endurance.

Bidding hadn't started yet. He walked through the cavernous buildings, past the auctioneers with their clipboards; through the throng of other buyers; past the huge concrete pillars and the timber-painted signs nailed to the walls or hanging from the ceiling – Sandy Pope, George Thomas, Leary, Thompson Bros, Townsend & Paul, D. Bowie, Market Gardeners; past the lines of produce, here a line of cauliflowers, there a line of cabbages, here lettuces, there apples or pears; past the stacks of wooden cases and jute super-sacks with the name of the grower written on paper tags. He hummed as he walked, only after some time realising what he was humming – a bawdy folk song about a bridegroom waiting with his friends for the bride. He laughed and kept humming, hunting out the produce from the best growers, calling out to his fellow clansmen, 'Have you eaten yet?' then smiling, 'Yes, yes, I have eaten,' even though he had eaten nothing since the night before; his shoes sounding out on the damp wooden floorboards, somewhere just above the hum of excited conversation, the yelling, the banging of wooden boxes, the clip-clop of horses on the road outside. Jonquils. He stood in Market Gardeners, smelling jonquils. He laughed. Today he would buy flowers.

Why did she meet him? Why? She knew she had to save herself.

She wanted to bury her face in his skin. She longed for his caresses, his fullness, his hardness pushing into her, through her. She longed for his desperation, the shudder of him, the gentleness of their fall into sleep.

She could not sleep. She could not eat.

'Are you all right?' Mrs Newman asked. 'You look so tired and pale. Take the day off and go to bed. And don't come back till you're feeling better.'

She met him, fell into his arms. He entered and she cried out. She
wanted to cry out *I love you*.

Sometimes in the early hours while the city slept and the only sounds
were those of the lion and monkeys carried on the night air from the
zoo, he accompanied her along the darkest side streets towards home,
picking up and handing to her small mementos – a fragrant rambling
rose stolen from Mrs Farrell's garden, its colour only truly known once
she'd brought it home and examined it in the light of her hallway. It
was a game they played – pink, yellow, orange, red: 'You say pink, I say
yellow, no tricking, tomorrow you tell me yellow, yes?'

Once she plucked from the gutter a broken stone shaped like a
heart and gave it to him. He turned it in his fingers, looked at her
sideways, one eyebrow raised. 'It's a heart,' she exclaimed, but still
he did not understand. 'Heart,' she said, making a fist with her hand,
beating her chest. Did he not know about the heart? About love?

'Heart,' he said, the word blooming in his mind. *Sum, sum gon,*
my heart and liver. He held the stone in his palm, placed it his breast
pocket. In truth, it looked nothing like a heart, nothing like two love
knots intertwined, but now he understood what she was giving him.

He reached into a mass of foliage tumbling from a wooden fence.
'In China,' he said, 'we have *fa cha*, flower tea. It tastes like this.' He
held the tiny flowers to her face and she inhaled deeply. Star-flowers,
she thought, as if intoxicated.

Katherine examined the flowers in the light of her bedroom. A few
were still slender pink buds, but others had opened delicate creamy
petals. She laid them beside her pillow, and all night, and for several
nights after, the fragrance filled the dark air and coloured the world
of her dreams.

BOILING WATER

'These smell nice, Mum. What are they?'

Katherine looked up from the potatoes she was peeling. Edie held the flowers in her outstretched hand.

For a moment Katherine didn't know what to say. She gazed at her daughter's palm, at the delicate petals now wrinkled and edged with brown.

'They . . . they're called jasmine,' she said.

'Where did you get them from?'

Katherine shifted her weight from one foot to another, carried on peeling, tried to sound casual. 'Haven't you seen them before? They grow over fences, well, anywhere.'

'Is that where you go at night?'

Katherine dropped the paring knife, just missed her foot. *Damn!* 'Edie, can you pick it up?'

Edie picked up the knife and ran it under the tap. She handed it to her mother and waited.

'I . . . I like to get some fresh air. Sometimes I need time to myself . . .' Katherine chopped the potato in half, into quarters, dropped the pieces – too quickly – into the pot on the range. Boiling water splashed up and caught the back of her hand. *Hell's bells.* She ran her hand under cold running water.

'Are you all right, Mum?'

Katherine turned and gazed at her daughter. She had looked so like Edie at the same age, yet how different their lives were. Katherine had had to look after all her younger brothers and sisters. With her parents out or working, she'd be left to care for the 'babies'.

Robbie would be thirteen in January and even Edie was older than she'd been.

She blushed. Her mother was not . . .

But it was never more than a couple of hours, was it? She had to remember to take her watch. She had to make sure she was away for no more than an hour – no, that wasn't enough, not by the time she walked there and back – one and a half, two: surely the children would be all right for an hour and a half? Wouldn't they?

'Mum? Are you all right?'

'Yes, I'm fine . . . You have to be careful with boiling water. Best to slip the vegetables in very gently . . .' She turned off the tap and dried her hands, carried on peeling potatoes.

'Mum?'

'Yes?'

'You didn't used to.'

'Didn't used to what?' She chopped and carried the potatoes on the wooden board to the pot. *Carefully now. Don't do it again.*

'You didn't used to go out at night.'

Katherine stared at the boiling, thickening water. She could feel Edie staring. She did not look up.

Robbie would pretend he was asleep when his mother came into his room. He wanted to throw his arms around her, to beg her to stay.

He listened to her footsteps descend the staircase, heard the back door open and click shut, his ears so finely tuned he could imagine her footsteps, the gate opening and closing, the sound of her breathing, the way it drifted further and still further away in the night air.

One night, before the moon rose, he put his coat on over his nightgown, pulled on his shoes and crept out behind her, following her down Adelaide Road. Once she stopped and turned, looked back as if she knew someone was there. She looked for one long moment, past the telegraph pole, past wood and wool, skin and bone, now joined as one creature; she looked into thin air, then turned and continued walking.

He followed, careful to make no sound, turning into the College grounds, watching her walk up into the town belt. He followed a little way in but couldn't see, worried that she'd hear the crackle of branches or broken bottles, worried that he'd trip and call out as he fell. And then in the distance he saw the lighted lamp, her silhouette, a man reach out towards her.

Edie heard Robbie slip out at night. She watched him from the darkness of their mother's upstairs window, the bed still made from the morning, too neat, too cold. Empty. She looked over the street, watched the flicker of movement as he walked down Adelaide Road, then disappeared.

She lay in bed unable to sleep, listening.

Once, when she heard him climb back up the stairs, she went out to him. 'Where have you been?' she asked. 'Where's Mum?'

He looked at her and said nothing. He went into his room and closed the door.

PUPPET SHOW

When Yung opened the shop, the stink repelled him. Someone had urinated over the door during the night. A drunk making his way from the Tramways, he thought, as he washed it down with a solution of carbolic acid and hot water.

It kept happening. Yung spoke to Mrs Paterson, Mr Mackenzie, Mr Wilson, Mr Krupp. No one else had a problem.

One morning it was faeces smeared in arcs over the front window. Afterwards Yung washed with soap and hot water, smelling his hands, then washing them again and again until his skin felt tight and pale and papery. Mei-lin offered him oil to rub in.

When they woke each morning, as they descended the stairs, each of them felt a certain dread. Even the relief of finding nothing never set them fully at ease.

Yung wanted to see Katherine every night, could tell by the way she held him and held him before they parted that she wanted this too. But she would not meet him more than two, perhaps three nights a week. The children, she said.

He sighed. She had changed his mindset. His vocabulary. He stopped himself now when he went to say *gweilo*; stopped himself mid-sentence and said, *sai yan*, westerner, instead.

There on the shop floor, surrounded by apples and pears and bananas, he'd spoken in his halting English and Katherine had listened. She'd spoken slowly, simply, choosing her words carefully, and he'd listened. He'd listened intensely, as if to music or a teacher who spoke an unfamiliar dialect. There were words he didn't understand, words she didn't understand. They would try to explain, their hands moving in the air like figures in a puppet show, their voices raised as if their lack of comprehension were the fault of a special kind of deafness. Yet over the years he had become more fluent.

And now, now that they met at night, now that they touched, everything had changed. She would come into the shop on her way back from work and they'd speak a little coolly, look at each other and try not to look, aware of other customers, even passersby on the footpath outside. He would hand her a paper bag of apples or a wrapped cabbage, and sometimes his hand would brush hers.

And all he could think of was the bed he made for her under the destroyed tree, the intense warmth as he came down on her. As he entered.

Better Than a Dog

'How long have you been working for me, Katherine? I've never seen you looking so good.

'Do you remember what you were like? A lost puppy. You were! And now look at you. Mr Newman was saying to me the other day, "That Katherine McKechnie, she's lost ten years off that pretty face of hers." He says I've done you a world of good.'

Mrs Newman laughed. She put her pen down and clasped her hands in front of her. 'So who is he, Katherine?

'Come on, Katherine, I know that look – you're like a blushing bride. I swear if I didn't know better, you'd break into song as you typed my letters. You're in love, Katherine. Who is he?

'No, I haven't heard any rumours. You've obviously been careful, but you used to be so punctual. No, I'm not concerned if now and then you're five or ten minutes late. Though love can be injurious to one's health if one doesn't get enough sleep . . .

'I'm not going to tell anyone, Katherine, not even Mr Newman. I understand the life of a widow with children is hardly conducive to romantic entanglements. What man wants a used chalice, as they say, let alone another man's children?

'Is he married? No?

'Oh.

'Well, you certainly are full of surprises.'

Mrs Newman picked up her pen, wrote a few words. Crossed them out.

'You should be careful . . .

'Katherine. I have nothing against the Chinese. They're a hard-working race, they keep pretty much to themselves, and they don't deserve the vilification granted them in the newspapers. But—

'Katherine, listen. What does your fellow Briton see, the one who struggles to put bread and dripping on the table? The Chinamen undercut us with prices that would put a decent working man in the poorhouse. They take work away from impoverished laundrywomen. They suck the country dry and then return to the Flowery Land with everything that is rightfully ours. That's what people say, and you know it.

'Katherine, don't look at me like that, I'm only trying to open your eyes. At least you should be careful of your reputation.

'Yes, I realise you're being careful. Otherwise I'm sure I would have heard about this a long time ago . . .

'But Katherine, make sure you're doubly careful. You may be a widow, but your husband was a respected member of the community . . .'

Mrs Newman burst into donkey-like laughter. She convulsed, ending in a loud snort. 'Oh, Katherine you are a party! Of course I know women aren't just appendages of their husbands! But, seriously Katherine, you must realise that it's only the lowest class of women who consort with Chinamen. Those who have nothing to lose.

'All right, so there might be a few respectable women who marry Chinamen. Ladies who play the piano at church and fall in love while working for the Lord among the heathen. These are the kind of women who answer the call of God to the darkest heart of Africa or China and die in childbirth or of some unspeakable tropical disease.

'Katherine, listen to me. Did you know that if you marry an alien, you lose your British citizenship? No, I didn't think so. A woman gets married and she might as well be an infant or a lunatic or an idiot. I wish I was joking. You marry a Chinaman and you lose the right to vote, you won't get the old-age pension, Katherine, you lose everything. And if you're thinking of living in sin, God forbid, you must have heard of the cases that have gone through the court? Doesn't *Truth* love to report such cases? Low-class women living with Chinamen. I've heard it said that they're better treated by the John than their drunken husbands, but Katherine, the police have picked up women from Haining Street and charged them with vagrancy and being without means of support. They've taken British children away from their mothers – despite the mothers protesting that the children are well cared for – because the house was frequented by Chinamen!

'He doesn't live in Haining Street? Katherine, it's a matter of appearances. He's a Chinaman. That makes him worse than a Jew and maybe a little better than a dog. Maybe. Do you think they'd pick up a woman who was living with a white man, even a drunkard, and charge her with vagrancy? Do you think they'd take away her children?

'Katherine, I'm telling you this for your own good. Everything you do or don't do has its consequences. Just make sure you are prepared for them.'

AS THE EARTH TURNS SILVER

What was it? He wanted to know why she held back. Why she did not respond to his kisses.

She did not know what to say. She could hear Mrs Newman's words but could not tell him. 'The children know I come out at night,' she said.

For a moment there was silence. Then he drew her to him, kissed her hair. 'Come,' he said, taking her by the hand, leading her out from the cover of trees, back through the College grounds, down to the city.

It was a clear night. A full moon. She was afraid with such bright moonlight even at ghost hour, as he called it, when the living slept and only the dead walked the streets. What if someone saw them?

But he was wearing a hat, he said. If someone came, he would look down or away. She could do the talking. No one would see he was Chinese.

She asked where they were going. She was anxious about leaving the children for too long. And what about the police? Didn't they patrol the streets at night? What if a constable stopped them? But he put his finger to her lips and led her down the promenade – the path through gardens and trees – between Cambridge and Kent Terraces. They walked through stillness, through shadow and moonlit brightness, the statue of Queen Victoria looming ever closer before them. Katherine stopped and placed her hand on the granite pedestal, looked up at the great bronze figure. She looked old, hard, and yet she'd loved her Albert.

'Come,' he said again, and they walked past the Zealandia Hotel, past the City Destructor chimneys, to the silent boats, the empty baths, the sweep of the harbour along Oriental Parade.

He laughed at the name; told her this was his street, not Adelaide Road, not Haining Street, not Frederick or Taranaki or Tory. He told her to look at the moon and street lights reflected in black water. Had she ever seen it like this at night? The most beautiful street in Wellington. This Chinese street where no Chinese lived.

He came from behind and held her in his arms, told her to look again at earth and sky and water. Could she see how the world turned silver? People died, he told her, because they were afraid. They did not go out at night on dangerous water. They did not see the earth as it turned overnight to silver.

She gazed at the ripples of light on blackness. But people died in dangerous water. She turned to face him, told him it didn't even have to be dangerous. Her husband fell drunk into the harbour one night. They pulled him out in the morning.

He was silent for a while. Then he told her there were two ways to die. One was . . . he looked at her, uncertain how to express it in English.

'Inevitable?' she said. 'It comes to everyone?'

'Yes,' he said. 'Yes'. The corners of his mouth lifted. But then he looked at her intently. The other way, he said, this inside death, was not . . . inevitable. People took it in their hands, they held it and would not let go. Some people did this and did not know. Some people knew what they were doing.

He kissed her eyelid. Told her they were born for dangerous water.

She looked up at him. Shivered.

'You're cold,' he said. He put his coat over her shoulders, and they turned and walked back along the harbour, past the bereft boats, back towards the city and home.

MORE THAN HORSES

'She's taking your soul away.'

Yung looked up from the tub where he was washing excess soil from the potatoes. He did not reply.

'Nothing good can come from this. You should stop it now.' When his brother still gave no response, Shun said, 'If a woman is married to a rooster, she is married to him all her life.'

In his mind, Yung completed the proverb: If a woman is married to a dog, she is married to him all her life; if she is married to a washing stick, she must carry it all her life. He kept scrubbing the potatoes. 'In the New Gold Mountain,' he said, 'a virtuous woman is widowed and may marry again.'

His brother spat into the cabbage trimmings. 'And what luck is this, to take a dead man's wife? You want the bad luck too?' He waved the trimming knife in his hand. 'You think the piss on the door's a coincidence?'

Yung did not look up.

'I don't know what you see in her. Your wife was a beauty.'

Yung remembered his wife's pale, clear skin, her small hands with their long fingers, the way she walked on her tiny feet like a light wind blowing through willow. Now his memories were like a dream, or perhaps a vision of what might have been. This he remembered: his wife laughed like bamboo yielding, like its leaves rustling in the wind. Her figure was slender and her feet like tender bamboo shoots. And yet what he'd treasured most was talking with her. Sometimes she argued with him. About poetry. He chuckled, remembering her furrowed brow, the intensity in a woman who was usually so compliant. He preferred Tu Fu, but she loved Li Po because there was so much space, she said, so much room for the spirit and the imagination. Like a chapter from *A Floating Life*, they had a game where they composed couplets, one after the other, until their rhymes degenerated from works of beauty into foolishness and laughter.

Mrs McKechnie – Katherine's skin was freckled and her mouth large. She wore large black boots like other western women and did not sway as she walked. She knew nothing of Chinese poetry, and sometimes even simple communication was fraught with mis-understanding.

Once in the early days when he delivered her vegetables, she'd offered him a cup of tea and he, being polite, declined, as is the custom. But she had taken him at his word and did not offer again, and then again. In hindsight he realised this was not rudeness, or even a lack of generosity. It was the foreigner's way. He had to bite his lip and receive quickly, or not at all.

Yung looked across at his brother, who had a little wife to share his bed each night. He looked down at the dark, brown water. His hands were cold, the skin ingrained with dirt like the patterns on bamboo, like the ripples of waves on sand.

Mrs McKechnie. Yes, she bore a dead man's name; yes, she was a big-nosed, red-haired foreigner; and yet the words of Po Lo came to him now: 'To find a good horse,' he said, 'you look at its shape, you look at its muscle and bone, but to find a great horse, you forget all these things.'

Shun had never read Lieh Tzu, and at times like now he envied, no, resented his brother's learning – learning that he, by hard toil, had paid for. But Yung didn't look up, didn't see his brother's anger. He continued oblivious. 'When you look at a horse,' he said, 'there are more important things than horses.'

Shun sighed. It was never easy to talk to his brother. To admonish or advise him. Yung always quoted from the classics or some revolutionary like Liang Ch'i-chao or Sung Chiao-jen or Sun Yat-sen, or else he came out with brilliant, sickening words of his own.

Shun tried again. 'Look at Yue Jackson,' he said. 'Do you think it is easy for him? Do you think the *gweilo* treat him like one of their own? Do you think it was easy for him in China? Or for his mother?'

Yung thought about the English Secretary at the Consulate, the son of a Scottish mother and a Sei Yap father. He would see him at community meetings or when they met new arrivals off the ships. And these days he would see him each Sunday afternoon at the Consulate.

Yung had had difficulty choosing which class to go to: with his brother to the English class taught by Yue Jackson or the Chinese class taught by Consul Kwei. Of course he wanted to improve his English, but now did he not have Katherine? Really, what he longed for was his own language. His own literature, history, philosophy – to have Consul Kwei write the first line of a couplet so that he could complete it.

Yung looked at his older brother, the strands of black hair now mixed with white, his tired, bloodshot eyes. Shun Goh did not understand poetry. Yes, he wanted the overthrow of the Manchus too, just like every patriotic Chinese, but he did not love to play with words or ideas, to play with life.

Yung thought about the paleness of Yue Jackson's skin, the lightness of his hair, his Chinese eyes – and wondered what a child borne with Katherine would be like. A child falling between two worlds. A child belonging nowhere . . .

When Shun saw he could not persuade his brother, he told him to bring Katherine back at night. It was dangerous to wander about late.

'Remember Joe Kum-yung,' he said. 'Winter is coming. What if you get pneumonia? Do you expect me to hire that Cousin Gok-nam? Useless ghost! Do we have to have his wife making trouble in this house? What if you die of cold? What will I say to Mother and Father?

'Tell her to come here at night. Take her to your room. I don't want to see her.'

YELLOW FLOWERS HILL

Sometimes as he waited Yung imagined entering her bedroom, watching her let down and brush her hair, the long, slow strokes through red-brown waves. He imagined lying between her sheets, surrounded by the smell of her, his face upon her pillow. Sometimes an ache grew from the centre of his being – a shiver of pain that threatened to overwhelm him.

He understood about her children. The judgements of *gweilo* society. Yet deep within he recognised her shame. And he felt the heat of it move through his face and take his whole body.

What had brought them together? What did they share?

They had walked at night and gazed at the bright flare in the sky. She'd told him the same comet appeared in 1066, just before a battle he'd never heard of. 'Some people say they signal the end of the world,' she said, hunching into her coat.

He gazed at her profile as they passed under a street lamp, the illumination of her nose, cheek, the fullness of her lips, the drift into darkness, the slow drift back into light.

Yes, he thought. Not the word itself, because there is nothing as simple as a universal yes or no in Chinese, in their stead a multiplicity of expressions, each turned to its purpose. Yes, Chinese astrologers also believed this – that a comet foretold disaster – and yet there was another meaning.

'What is this?' he asked. It was 1 a.m. and there he was standing in a pale pool of lamplight, as if gripping something in his hands, making short pushing, pulling motions in front of him, from side to side.

Katherine frowned. 'You mean sweeping?' she asked. 'With a broom?'

'Yes, yes.' He was smiling now. He pointed at the patch of brightness in the sky, like the straw head of a broom set on fire. 'Broom stars,' he said. 'We call broom stars.'

He wanted, tried to tell her, that a comet in the south swept away the old and introduced a new order. He wanted to tell her many things. But sometimes in English the words caught in his throat, thickened on his tongue.

They were lying in his bed, her face tucked into his shoulder, when Katherine asked why the long face.

'Long face?' He was puzzled.

'Sad,' she said. 'Why are you so sad?'

He did not know what to say. He stroked the hair from her face. How could he tell her about Hung-seng? How could he even begin to explain?

They had played on the bank near the bend of the stream, just outside the entrance to the village – Hung-seng and Yung and the other children. There were banana palms, and trees they climbed, sunlight filtering through the branches. They gathered seed pods that fell to the ground, crushed them with stone and dipped the ends of long grass stalks into the sticky liquid. They caught dragonflies, waiting for them to come in to land, creeping up and touching the wings – there – with the sticky ends. He and Hung-seng and the others.

159

Hung-seng was four years younger. A village cousin, like a little brother. Yung had shown him how to skip stones in the stream. At low tide they waded into the mud and lifted broken crockery, trying to catch shrimp before they darted away. They caught crickets for fighting and kept them in tobacco tins that old men brought back from the New Gold Mountain. How different the vision of a child – a small street back then seemed large; a man not ten years older than Yung had seemed old.

After his marriage, Yung moved to Canton, then on to the New Gold Mountain. He and Hung-seng wrote. They exchanged poetry, debated how best to modernise China. Hung-seng, with a growing number of young people, went to Japan for study. And stayed. He met Sun Yat-sen and helped found the *People's Newspaper*, the journal of Sun's Alliance Society. He sent Yung every edition. And despite the rivalry, he also sent Liang Ch'i-chao's *New People's Miscellany*. 'So that we can have informed debate,' he'd written. 'Liang may be conservative, but he also wants reform. I think he's right that we should study the strengths of other nations and so create a new culture.'

And then Hung-seng returned to Canton. His letters suggested something was planned. Nothing specific.

The letters stopped. Until today, when a letter had come from Hung-seng's brother. Hung-seng had been one of over a hundred killed in a failed uprising. The government had left the bodies in the street. As warning. Days later his brother risked his life to help gather up the dead. They found seventy-two and buried them together at Yellow Flowers Hill.

Hung-seng was never found.

Yung looked at Katherine, her long copper hair swept over his pillow, and didn't know what to tell her. How could he speak of foreign domination – Manchu, British, French, German, Russian, Japanese –

160

the struggle for liberty – with a foreigner?

'My friend died,' he said at last. 'He was like my brother.'

When she asked how, he stared up at the ceiling. The pansies, violas, polyanthus he'd stolen from night-time gardens and placed in a bowl on the dresser cast flickering shadows on the pale plaster sky as the candle burned down.

The comet had come a year too soon. He thought of words he'd looked up in his Chinese-English dictionary and on nights when he'd lain alone spoken into darkness, practising the feel on his tongue, the sound of a foreign language.

'Liberty, equality, fraternity,' he said. And he knew she didn't understand.

Months later bombs exploded in Hankow. In Wuchang a soldier killed his commanding officer. The Revolution had begun.

Yung could not help but laugh, words of explanation spilling out, drenching Katherine with a heady mix of English and Cantonese.

Province after province declared its independence from Manchu rule. Negotiations began. Finally the Empress Dowager abdicated and Sun Yat-sen was declared the first President.

In Wellington, in Sydney, around the world there were fireworks, banquets, myriad celebrations. Yung gave a rousing speech and raised his glass to the new Republic; he cracked jokes and told long and twisted tales that had everyone holding their bellies in raucous laughter. And yet something, someone, was missing.

They had come to send remittances home. To return as wealthy men. Yet always wealth eluded them. Now, back home, there was so much to be done. Hung-seng had died for this, but what had *he* done except debate with his countrymen and raise money for Sun and the Revolution?

Wasn't this the time to go home?

Shun Goh would not understand. How could they go home?

he'd say. Where was the money? There were carrots to be washed, cauliflowers to be trimmed, debts to be repaid.

When she came to his door, he pulled her into his body, his face in her hair. He knew Chinese hair – smooth and black and strong – its gift for spiking the eye at intimate moments, but even now Katherine's surprised him – soft baby hair tickling his nose, so full of air.

He knew he *loved* her. Though he could never utter that word. It was not that *Tongyan* didn't feel affection, need, desire – something more than duty, which seemed to flow with the breast milk. But love was a word that only *gweilo* spoke. Something you might feel but never utter.

As he held her in his arms, he did not know what to choose – the homeland he had waited for, worked for, prayed for; or this never-ending ache, this last sigh of breath at the end of the world.

A CHILDREN'S ATLAS

'You know where she goes, don't you?'

Robbie looked up, stared at Edie in the doorway and went back to writing.

'If you don't tell me, I'll tell Mum who you're writing to.'

'So who am I writing to?'

'Isn't it obvious?'

Robbie stabbed at the letter with his pen, swore under his breath. The nib had gone through the paper, and now a blot of ink seeped into the cover of the book underneath: Whitcombe & Tombs' *Children's Atlas*. His mother would be furious.

'If you're so smart, then why don't you know where she goes at night? Isn't it obvious?'

'She visits someone, doesn't she?'

Robbie stared at her.

'But why does it have to be a secret?'

'Because it's disgusting, that's why!'

In one movement he hurled the book, letter, pen - an arc of ink drops - through the air. The book smashed against the wall and slumped to the floor, the pen left an ink stain on the wallpaper, rolled back and hit the mat. A torn sheet of paper drifted down.

'If Dad was here this would never have happened!' Robbie burst into tears.

The only time Edie remembered him crying was when their father died. If he was still here . . . if their father was still here, how different would it be?

Edie felt the urge to stroke Robbie's back, his hair, but he seemed so far away, so very far away, the distance between them unsurpassable.

She stared at his shaking body, felt tears form in her own eyes. She did not know who she was crying for. She turned and walked into their mother's room, looked out the window at the street below. She should start dinner. Peel potatoes and carrots, chop cabbage. Their mother would be home.

Soon.

THE FUTURE OF HUMANKIND

Edie did not remember raised voices, just as she did not remember small signs of tenderness. Even as a six-year-old she noticed the tension in her mother's face, the way she'd held herself separate from her father.

Every time Mrs Newman opened a newspaper, pointed out interesting articles and encouraged her to read them, even when she heard a paper boy standing on a street corner calling out his wares, Edie remembered her father: the smells of whisky, tobacco, ink, the smudgy shadows on his hands and once-white cuffs, on his cheek or jaw or the side of his nose, his inky hands thrown in the air in the midst of heated conversation. Her father. A man who could have devised some of the problems she faced at school:

A man leaves £4000 to each of three sons and £1500 to each of two daughters, what is his estate? Or: *Divide £100 between two men and two women so that each man may get twice the share of a woman.*

These are the things she remembered later, after Mrs Newman had held out an envelope and asked her, 'What does this say, Edie?'

Edie was puzzled. 'Mrs Alexander Newman, 215 . . .'

'Yes, yes. Now tell me, what's wrong with it?' Mrs Newman had looked at her intently, peering over the top of her spectacles.

Edie stared at the plain white envelope, postmarked Wellington.

Nothing especially interesting about the handwriting. No spelling mistakes. 'Um . . . I don't know,' she said at last.

'What is my name, Edie? Is it Alexander? What does this say about the standing – or not – of the married woman? Do I belong to my husband like his Ford, for instance? Something to be cranked up to do his bidding?'

Edie wanted to laugh. She couldn't imagine Mr Newman having much success. Mrs Newman could crank herself up on her own, thank you very much. Or did he delight in provoking her?

'Can you imagine my husband being addressed as Mr Margaret Newman or even Mr Margaret Salmond?' she was saying, and Edie mused about Mr Newman. Was he like a certain Mr Bennet she'd read of and loved? A man who could laugh at his wife without her even knowing?

But Mrs Newman had moved on. Had Edie met Dr Bennett? she asked, and for a moment Edie was confused, lost in the connection between a Jane Austen novel and a pioneer of women in medicine.

'A remarkable woman,' Mrs Newman was saying. What would she do without the likes of Dr Agnes Bennett and Mrs Grace Neill. Standing up to the likes of Ferdinand Batchelor and Truby King.

'Surely you've heard of Dr Bennett? I met her years ago in Sydney when she came to attend my sister. It's a crying shame. Did you know, before she came to New Zealand no one wanted a lady doctor? And look at her now – superintendent of St Helen's. Who would have dreamed even ten years ago – a woman in charge of a hospital!'

Mrs Newman smiled at Edie. 'I really must introduce you to Dr Bennett, my dear. Doctors hold lives, destinies, the future of humankind in their hands. And our Dr Bennett is at the forefront.'

The first time Edie saw the pulleys attached to the roof in the garage, she laughed out loud. Dr Bennett was using them to raise the huge cover on her motorcar.

'Yes, it is a bit of a rigmarole, isn't it? But being prone to catarrh makes travelling in an open motorcar quite inadvisable, and of course you should always, always take the advice of your doctor.' Dr Bennett glanced at Edie and grinned. 'Especially when that doctor happens to be yourself.'

Edie laughed again. The motorcar, with its high removable roof and sides, had been specially built for Dr Bennett. It was nicknamed the 'Pill-box' and was almost as famous as the good doctor herself. Dr Bennett was the first woman to drive a motorcar in Wellington; she was entirely self-taught. Edie noticed that everyone always gave the Pill-box a very wide berth.

They went into the house, where Dr Bennett made tea. 'I hear from Mrs Newman that you have a curious mind.

'Not many people understand this in a girl. They say *ladies* shouldn't ask too many questions. They think we want to know too much.' Dr Bennett smiled – a small, sad smile. She poured boiling water over the leaves in the teapot and carried the laden tray out to the parlour. 'Don't let this dampen your spirits,' she said.

Dr Bennett offered shortbread. 'I hear you aren't especially close to your brother. When I was a girl I played with my brothers all the time. I was what you might call a tomboy, romping about in the paddocks and the bush and the beach. I think those were the happiest days of my life.'

She was quiet for a while, and Edie wondered about Dr Bennett's life in Australia and England. Mrs Newman had told her Dr Bennett's mother died when she was very young.

They drank tea, discussed sedimentary rocks, Lister's discovery of antiseptics, Dr Bennett's days at Sydney University and at Medical School in Edinburgh. Late afternoon light faded.

'I'll drive you home, Edie. Your mother must be wondering what has happened to you.'

Edie didn't say she didn't want to go home.

As Dr Bennett drove, she said, 'Books can be very good friends, Edie, especially when you are lonely. But don't neglect physical exercise. Learn to walk – and to run – not just with the intellect but also with the heart and the body. Social interaction, fresh air and physical activity will sustain you through many a trial and tribulation.'

Edie watched Dr Bennett drive away. She watched street lamps blink into life. She opened the gate and walked up to the door.

THE NEW FRECKLED WONDER

Edie was supposed to be so smart, but for all her highfalutin talk a train could run over her and she'd have no blinking idea. How could she be so stupid! Robbie scowled and bowled yet another wide.

'What's yer problem, dolt?' Billy called. 'Wal, get that ball!'

'Who're ya calling dolt? Ya idiot!'

'Whoa. What's going on?'

'Where'd the ball go?' Wally called.

'Under that tree, dolt!'

Robbie broke into a grin. 'Yeah, under the tree, dolt!'

He ran forward, put out his hand and the ball landed clean in his palm. He polished it on his trousers as he walked back, took a run up and bowled. The ball slipped between bat and thigh, sliced through the stumps. Robbie threw his hands in the air. 'Hooya!'

Billy smiled. 'Your bat.'

Billy was all right. Not as good as Robbie's dad, of course, but all right. Robbie stood in the crease, thumping his bat against the summer-scorched grass. His dad had always told him to take his time when he first went out. Get your eye in, he'd say. Don't go for the big shot and get out for a duck.

But today he didn't care. He cut the ball on the offside and sent it past Wally for a four.

'Crikey Rob, I'm doggo!'

'If you were a decent keeper . . .'

'Who're you calling indecent?'

Robbie laughed. 'Do you good to go for a run, mate.'

Wally straightened his shoulders, sucked in his belly. 'They say I'm not half the man I was.'

'Wal, you're a real ladies' man.'

Wally blew on his fingers. 'Like to think so.'

Billy laughed. 'You should both come down to the gym sometime. That'll sort you out, Wal. Went with me cousin the other day and we joined up. Charlie O'Donnell, he trained with the Great Sandow. He's marvellous.'

'Why don't we go down now?' Robbie said. 'Have a look around.'

As they walked out onto Buckle Street, he asked, 'You got my ball, Wal?'

Wally was still breathing heavily. He pulled the ball out of his pocket, tossed it over.

Robbie heard steel wheels on the track, the sound of a bell. A Toast Rack was rounding the bend. 'Let's get a tram,' he yelled. He tucked his bat under his arm, threw the ball in the air, caught it as he ran.

They climbed aboard and sat open to the weather, the blast of the northerly shaking out their hair. Toast Rack made sense, but why did people call them Hong Kong cars?

'Because they originally came from Hong Kong, dolt!' said Billy.

Robbie grinned. As the trammie swung along the outer footboards collecting fares and Wal wiped sweat from his face with a handkerchief, he nudged Billy. 'What d'ya reckon are the chances of him hitting the centre pole? Or falling off and killing himself like that poor blighter in Oriental Bay?'

He laughed. He wouldn't mind a bit of excitement. Mac was all right, and Robbie had moved on now from butcher boy delivering meat to apprentice. It wasn't so bad, learning how to chop carcasses, cut chops and steaks and all that, but the danger of swinging along the footboards or, even better, driving a tram – now that would be the life.

As if he'd read his mind, Billy said, 'You know, after that poor blighter maybe they're down on numbers. Maybe I can con my way into a job, eh?'

Robbie glanced at Billy. That was the one thing he hated about Billy. He was only eighteen months older, but he looked like he was three or even four. He got away with all kinds of things Robbie could only dream of.

'We're there!' Billy rang the bell and they leapt off in Cuba Street.

Even before they entered, they heard skipping ropes whipping the air, hitting the floorboards, the sound of leather against leather. As the door swung open, they were hit with the stink of horse liniment and sweat.

Two men danced and dodged and threw punches in the ring. A man shadow-boxed in front of an enormous mirror. Others pounded heavy bags, pummelled speed balls, lifted dumb-bells. Two boys wrestled on a canvas mat. Others did press-ups or sit-ups or chin-ups from a bar.

The words BREATHE MORE AIR AND HAVE RICHER BLOOD were painted on the wall, alongside posters of Eugen Sandow flexing his muscles. What I wouldn't give to look like that! Robbie thought.

'What d'ya reckon Edie'd think of this?' Billy yelled. He leapt and grabbed rings hanging from the ceiling, pulled himself up shakily.

'You've got to be joking, mate! You've got to do better than that!' Robbie eyed his friend. 'What're you saying, anyway? Are you keen on my sister?'

Billy jumped down. 'Dunno, Rob. She can be a bit weird, but you've got to admit she's cute.'

'Edie?' Wally laughed. 'You're interested in that stuck-up bitch?'

Robbie turned and slammed his fist into Wally's face.

'Ow. What'd you do that for?'

Robbie shook out his hand, stared embarrassed at Wal on the floor. 'Look, mate,' he said at last, 'I can say what I like - she's my sister after all - but that doesn't give you the right.'

'We get real bad press for our tempers, don't we?'

Robbie turned.

A man with thinning red hair and a broken nose grinned at him. 'No need to fuel the flames, eh?' The man winked. 'What's your name, son? Rob, eh? My name's Charlie. Charlie O'Donnell. For a skinny fella you sure have a fine right hook. A young Ruby Robert, if I say so myself.' The man laughed. 'Billy, show our new Freckled Wonder the ropes. See what we can do with him.'

SILENCE

Edie often came after school to Mrs Newman's, but Katherine hardly saw Robbie. Every afternoon when she arrived home from work he was at the gym. He'd come home for dinner and then go straight back out with Billy again. It made her wonder about this Charlie O'Donnell. Still it kept Robbie off the streets and out of trouble, and it stopped him talking endlessly about Donald. *Dad this* and *Dad that*. Not that she could blame him. A boy needed a man in his life – Charlie O'Donnell would do just fine.

'Robbie is hardly ever home these days,' she said as she climbed into Yung's bed. 'I don't know who he is any more.'

Yung didn't answer. He held her in his arms but did not want to make love.

'What is it?' she asked. 'What's the matter?'

He was silent, and when she kissed his cheek it was wet.

Wong Chung-yung

MELON RIDGE

There are no hills, no mountainous ridges in Melon Ridge, only the round tombs of generations lying stretched to the east, their faces looking out over the water. Over the river that winds through a thousand villages on its way from the Pearl, past ten thousand villages on its way to the sea. There are no melons in Melon Ridge, only long leaves of rice that ruffle fields green in spring and autumn, and lush groves of lychees yielding their fruit in summer.

This is our village, famous throughout all of Kwangtung. They say the lychees of Melon Ridge are the best in China. Just break the crisp, red shell and inside the membrane is dry – a translucent skin filled with green-white flesh, juicy and sweet, fragrant of flowers and full of meat, and at its heart the smallest brown stone, smooth as jade flicked by the tongue. This is the story we tell, the story we have told for generations.

I still remember the flowers, the small cream heads among the dark green leaves. In springtime you can smell them everywhere, and in summer when the fruit is ripening on the branches the *gau pei dan* come – the *dog fart bullets* – red insects like cockroaches, with their brown spots and their stinking beating wings. I used to sit in the trees eating the smooth white fruit, and they would be there also, sucking out the juice and biting young boys. My mother would scold me for the pain – *rice bucket*, is that all you can eat, rice and lychees? – as she spread knobs of ointment as long as her uncut thumbnails on the great red swellings.

They say the 'dog farts' like the taste of men who have been away – the sojourners whose blood is sweet and foreign. But I have never been back.

These are the things I remember: the lychee trees, the *gau pei dan*, the grassy smell of rice when it is ready to harvest.

I remember the mother of my son's smooth white skin and tender hands. The tiny silk slippers embroidered with flowers that she wore each night in bed.

She wrote about my son – my Number Two Son – who was born after my return here. The resemblance is unmistakable. Look in the mirror, she said, and there you will see your son.

All I know is the letters, the envelopes coming back in my own handwriting, self-addressed, so that she cannot mistake this strange language: Wong Chung-yung, 100 Adelaide Road, Wellington, New Zealand. And inside her beautiful grass script (or sometimes his): Respectful Husband, The roof is leaking, please ask Elder Brother to send 20 *man* . . . The river has flooded again and the house has collapsed – should we rebuild with mud bricks or will you send money for fired ones which will not dissolve in water? . . . Cousin So-and-so has died and there are expenses . . . And sometimes there'd be the beginning line of a couplet, or a response to mine.

Now it is his writing that has come – a sheet of paper so thin I hold it to the light, almost read the black ink from the other side.

Excellent Father,
I am writing to tell you that Mother died of fever on the fourth day of the fourth month at two in the afternoon. She was sick for three days. I have arranged for her burial in the family plot on the eighth, as this is a favourable day according to the almanac. All the money will be used up to pay the monks and pall-bearers, and to buy the coffin, the bowls and chopsticks, the beef and fish and vegetables.
Your foolish son . . .

175

Every three months I have sent £5 home. I have educated my son and repaid our debt. I have saved £120 - £100 for the poll tax, almost the £22 for the ship (steerage class) - but now I have to repay funeral expenses, and prepare for his wedding . . .

How many years have we waited? And already she has been buried three weeks.

There are many hundreds of lychee trees in Melon Ridge. They cover the land across the river. They say the lychees are *ho sik*, the very best in China. Yes, there are hundreds of trees, but there is only one - half withered, half alive - that bears the gorgeous fruit, the fruit that is given to officials.

LONGEVITY

The boy was sitting at the kitchen table, chewing a pencil, staring at a sheet of figures. Yung had come through to set the kettle on the stove. 'Wai-wai,' he said.

His brother's son looked up at him longingly, dreaming of footballs and slingshots and climbing trees like *gweilo* children, not gluing paper bags or stacking fruit or sitting at the table doing homework.

Yung smiled. 'Here, I'll show you a trick.' He flourished his hands in the way of travelling tumblers and magicians, in the way he remembered of singers and performers at a market.

'Hold your hands like this.' He held his hands out alongside his nephew's, his long fingers extended.

'One times nine,' he said, bending the smallest finger of his left hand down. 'You see, bend the first finger and the answer is the number of fingers to the right. How many? That's nine fingers to the right, so one times nine is nine.

'Now, two times nine. Bend the second finger from the left. You have one finger to the left; this is the number of tens. And you have eight fingers to the right; this is the number of ones. That's eighteen. So, two times nine is eighteen.

'Three times nine. Bend the third finger and what do you have? Two fingers to the left and seven to the right. Yes, that's twenty-seven.

So, three times nine is twenty-seven.

'Let me see you do four times nine. Yes. Three tens and six ones. Thirty-six. Keep going. Do this right up to ten times nine.

'No, you can't do this with the three times table.' He laughed. He looked at the boy's homework and remembered how young he was. 'You can't do this with any of the other times tables. That would make it too easy, wouldn't it? And, of course, you can only do it up to ten.'

The kettle whistled on the stove. Yung opened the padded wicker basket on the bench, took out the porcelain teapot and poured in boiling water. 'Nine is an important number,' he said. 'It means eternity. Long life. Like the long noodles we eat at New Year.'

He poured five cups of tea, gave one to Wai-wai. 'Drink tea,' he said. 'It will clear your mind. Help you think.'

The boy had his father's strong, wide face but something of his mother's intense, sad eyes. Yung patted him on the head. 'As you grow up you will learn the nine considerations,' he said. 'How to be a good man. How to live a good, long life.'

He took a cup of tea to his brother, who was taking the trimmings out for the pig man from Lower Hutt. Shun Goh motioned to leave it inside.

He took a cup to Mei-lin, who was sewing a patch over the knee of Wai-wai's trousers. He held the tea out to her with two hands.

She looked up at him. 'Thank you,' she said as she received the cup with both hands, and he saw the trace of a tear in her eyes.

He took his own cup into the shop, then a box of oranges. He pulled the fruit from their tissue, placing the soft paper into a bag to be used in the outhouse, then, two in each hand, he stacked the oranges row by glowing row on the wooden shelf. He could keep bringing in boxes, keep stacking them and stacking them till they spilled over and tumbled beyond the confines of wood and linoleum and glass – nine times ten, nine times twenty, nine times thirty – hundreds, thousands, tens of thousands of glowing orbs burning in his liver . . . he could live and breathe and die forever beyond his ten fingers, beyond the colour of his skin, his small imagination . . .

He looked at the stack of oranges, their round dimpled skin, each so alike in their fieriness and yet, upon examination, so individual. He looked at the empty box and realised it was the simple things that counted – a single cup of tea held with both hands.

He tried to picture his own son, whom everyone said had grown in his image. What would he say to him? How would they speak?

He saw him pouring tea, praying before a shrine to his mother. He saw him kowtowing before her photograph, a bowl of oranges or mandarins, the white smoke of incense wrinkling the air.

WHITE

He made her angry. For telling her what to do. What not to do. For lying to her.

They had been in bed together when she told him about Donald, how he'd taken her life, how he'd used language and power against her. She'd thought he'd just hold her in his arms, stroke her hair. Instead he sat upright, stared straight into her eyes and told her Donald hadn't stolen from her; she had given to him – freely.

'You think I like boys saying Ching Chong Chinaman, push over apples all bruised. Beat Fong-man?' Now he was angry. 'Brother says, no trouble, don't get trouble. Your Bible says, turn cheek. How many cheek I got? You give cheek, more cheek, no face left . . .'

He calmed down now, slowed his words, tried to put them together more carefully. 'Katherine, you don't belong to him. Language does not belong to him. You think bad but don't know China. How many Chinese women under man's foot? How many can read? How many man? English is your language. Your gift. Write your name on it. Language not good or bad. Your mouth good or bad. Donald is dead man. You alive . . .'

She yelled at him. She was sick of men, and not just men, telling her what to do. She burst into tears.

She knew he was right.

But now this . . .

He was wearing white. They were all wearing white, and she did not understand. This was how she first understood. That white was the colour of his wife. The colour of his new dead wife.

He'd never told her.

Did she ask?

But did not husbands live together with their wives, did they not share the marital bed? Did not his own brother have a wife here, had she not borne him a son? How many years had she known him, and when did he ever tell her – when did he ever say he had a wife?

She hit him. She was flailing her arms, her fists; she just wanted to hit him and hit him. But he grabbed hold of her, pulled her into his chest and held her. And when she could not struggle any more, when she looked into his face, his dark, dark eyes, all she could see was a deep and abiding sadness.

THE PHOTOGRAPH

Katherine asked to see.

'What is the use,' he said. 'Nineteen years I have not seen her. Let bygones be.' But she insisted.

Yung had one photograph. From before her disfigurement, from before the birth of their sons.

She had never told him, but when Cousin Gok-nam's wife came out she said, 'Such a pity, such beautiful eyes, such beautiful pale skin. Now people do not speak to her or serve her at the market. Of course, they don't want the bad luck to rub off on them.'

Yung remembered looking at Cousin Gok-nam's wife, at her squinty eyes and her dark, rough skin. He watched her take another slurp of tea and bite into a piece of Sister-in-law's steamed sponge. She smiled and he saw the pale cake crumbs in her mouth, coating her yellow teeth. And he disliked her.

He knew she was dead even before the letter arrived. It was the fourth day of the fourth month. Light was fading. Something fell upstairs. And when he went up, the sandalwood box lay on the floor – her letters scattered.

He knew there weren't many ghosts here. They didn't come to the door or meet him on the road on rainy nights. There were no stranger ghosts – they did not come across water. The only ghosts he saw were familiar.

Now he'd see her sitting there sometimes, watching him. She'd look at him through her pulled-back eye and say – nothing.

And so he burned paper money, paper clothes, and paper houses for her. He burned incense and laid out oranges so she would not go hungry.

He remembered her laughter when they lived alone in Canton. When he took her hands in his own, when she touched his cheek, her hands were the size of a child's.

He did not remember her like this. They took the photograph after he came here, after she moved in with Father, Mother and Sister-in-law. She did not smile. She did not laugh. Photographs were so pale, so colourless. They were portraits of the dead.

It was so long ago. Were it not for this photograph, he would not remember her face, yet now she came at night and he knew her.

Sometimes as he lay with Katherine, she'd come and sit in the chair in the corner of the room. He did not tell Katherine why his penis went soft, why he turned and buried his face in her hair, why he held her. And held her.

Katherine did not know why she felt so desperate to see, so desperate not to. Photographs were so unreal, so black and white, so unsmiling. She took the photograph of his wife in her hands and realised how different their worlds were. What did she have in common with this woman, except that once she breathed too, once they both bore children.

She was pretty, Katherine thought, though her hairstyle was unattractive. Not just the way the hair was oiled and pulled back from the face so tightly, but the forehead itself, which was so impossibly

183

deep and square. This could not be baldness – this was a young woman with only a thin, square helmet of hair.

'What happened to her?' Katherine asked, pointing at the forehead.

'They . . .' He was pulling, trying to show her.

'They pluck it out?'

'Yes, yes, when they get married.'

Katherine felt sickened. The woman lived and died – in the style of the severely married.

She stared at the photograph, wondering what the woman was thinking, gazing into the camera as if into the future, her long face captured in a perfect state of non-being. Her hands rested stiffly on her lap: bangles round her wrists, a ring on her finger, a white handkerchief. She sat in a huge wooden chair, her elbows turned out, barely touching the carved sides. It made her seem very small – a pale-skinned woman in loose silk. Across her chest, falling from the throat, silk thread butterflies fastened her tunic. And below the full silk trousers, impossibly small silk shoes.

His sister-in-law looked so different from this, with her long full skirts and bodice jackets, her unplucked hair pulled back so much more gently, wispy about the face.

'She was beautiful,' Katherine said as she passed the photograph back.

Yung looked across at her. 'Yes,' he said. 'Yes, she is.'

MOON

Katherine came to him in the most unexpected moments – even in the rolling 'r's of the man who bought two large parsnips and half a dozen carrots. 'Rrrr . . .' he said, 'rrrr . . .' as if speaking in code.

She came in the smell of lavender and vanilla. In the memory of pork pies.

It was she who had introduced him to them, understanding now the Chinese love of pork. 'They're very English,' she'd told him as she gave him the brown paper bag. Kuch's in Cuba Street made the best pork pies in town.

'Kuch's? Is this English name?' he'd asked, and she only smiled.

He loved the plump pink filling ringed with gelatine, the rich short pastry as full as a moon. They were as close as he got to moon cakes all year round, as if every night might be when the moon was fullest, when family came together to eat and gaze at its brightness.

Now, lying awake at 2 a.m., he watched moonlight at the end of his bed. Suddenly he did not know where might be home.

PART III
WELLINGTON (& DUNEDIN)
1914–1916

But pleasures are like poppies spread,
You seize the flow'r, its bloom is shed;
Or like the snow falls in the river,
A moment white – then melts for ever . . .

Robert Burns, *Tam o'Shanter*

FOR KING AND COUNTRY

No one talked about anything else, whether customers coming into the shop to buy a string of saveloys or Mac weighing up kidneys and gravy beef or Mrs Mac wrapping trotters in white paper. The notices were everywhere – posted on lamp posts, walls, windows.

Long before three o'clock, shops started closing. Mac and Mrs Mackenzie, Robbie and the butcher boys were lucky to get onto an overcrowded tram, which travelled ever more slowly through the city, caught up in the streams of people moving through the streets to Parliament. Robbie wanted to get as close to the action as possible. He squeezed his way through – treading on toes, getting elbowed in the ribs and subjected to the odd curse – until finally he found Billy, slick in his trammie uniform, not five rows back from the vestibule. When the Governor, Prime Minister and Leader of the Opposition appeared, they joined twelve thousand voices as they broke into cheers.

The Governor stepped forward and silence fell, an expectation that made Robbie shiver, that prickled his skin, a living, growing, invisible organism cloaking the crowd.

'It's war,' Billy whispered. 'It's got to be war.'

They listened as the Governor read His Majesty's statement, then his own reply. 'Fellow subjects,' he continued as the applause subsided. 'Since I sent out that notice to you this morning, I have received another telegram: WAR HAS BROKEN OUT WITH GERMANY.'

Something wound tight in Rob's gut loosened and leapt from his mouth. He was shaking, his voice joining Billy's, the crowd's, in thunderous cheering. They cheered for the King, they cheered for the Governor, they sang *God Save the King*, thousands upon thousands of voices in unison. Robbie and Billy stood, arms about each other's shoulders, swaying. Robbie felt tears at the back of his eyes. He shook himself and sang louder, his voice rasping, cracking.

The Governor said he would send the following reply: 'The Empire will stand united, calm, resolute, trusting in God.'

When the applause died away, the Prime Minister came forward:

'. . . we shall be called upon to make sacrifices . . . but I am confident that those sacrifices will be met individually and willingly and in a manner worthy of the occasion and the highest traditions of the great race and Empire to which we belong . . . Keep cool, stand fast, do your duty to country and Empire.'

'We will do that!' Robbie called out. Heads turned and he blushed.

The Prime Minister looked him in the eye. 'I'm sure you will,' he said.

Billy thumped Robbie on the back. 'Always liked being the centre of attention, eh.'

At any other time he might have laughed and punched him back – after all, hadn't it always been Billy who stole the limelight? – but now the colour had drained from Robbie's face. The Leader of the Opposition started speaking, but Robbie hardly heard anything. All he could see was the Prime Minister's face looking into his own, his words echoing in his mind.

'There's no way they'll think you're twenty,' Billy laughed.

Robbie swore and threw a right hook, which Billy only just managed to duck.

'I'll never get a chance,' he told his mother later, his whole body slumped in misery. 'Everyone says it'll all be over by Christmas.'

'Thank God if it is,' she said. 'You're only sixteen, Robbie . . .'

'Mum! I'm nearly seventeen!' He could tell she was going to say something but then she looked into his eyes and stopped.

'No one knows how long it'll go for,' she said at last. 'Mrs Newman read in the *Dominion* that the bankers think it'll be over in six months. They say Germany hasn't got the money for any longer. But some commander in Europe thinks it'll take a good three years, God help us.'

At the Buckle Street Drill Hall the officer smiled. 'We're taking the Territorials first, young man, and we don't take 'em before twenty.'

Robbie scowled. Why didn't he have Billy's deep voice, his strong physique?

He started shaving morning and night. He drank twice as much milk: two glasses at breakfast, two when he got home, another two before bed. He hung from his doorway till his fingers went stiff and he almost couldn't feel the pain, till his vertebrae (and arm sockets) stretched and clicked and loosened and he felt longer, taller. And even as he lay in bed at night he practised, training his tenor voice to turn deeper, like a tunneller digging deeper, now deeper into the dark hillside.

Every day for months on end he went to the gym and punched the heavy bag as if his life depended on it, aiming for an imagined face on the leather. Sometimes it was the moustachioed face of the Kaiser; sometimes, when he thought of his mother, it was the squint-eyed face of the Chow. He lifted dumb-bells, did sit-ups, chin-ups, press-ups.

'Tighten those muscles! Do ya want me to kill ya?' Billy yelled as he dropped a medicine ball onto Robbie's stomach.

Afterwards they'd catch a tram together. 'Dave,' Billy'd say, or 'Jack,' or 'Ed, this is me mate Rob', and they'd both get on for free.

Lucky pig, Robbie would think. What I wouldn't give for a job like this.

'Why not?' Billy said. 'Rig the truth a bit. They wouldn't usually consider a bloke before nineteen, twenty, but these aren't usual times. There's a war going on. I'm joining up, mate. We're all joining up. There's sure to be jobs going. Go and see Kev. Tell him I sent you.'

Katherine never expected him to get it. After all, who had ever heard of a seventeen-year-old trammie. Everyone knew, even with the war on, that for every trammie job there were always six men chasing.

At the interview Rob convinced them with his brashness. Nineteen, he said, just to make sure he met the minimum age. He knew the timetables of trains, boats, service cars. He could point out all the beauty spots of Wellington city. Yes, he knew every shop, just about everyone who lived in Cuba Street, Manners, Lambton Quay. But was he self-controlled, patient? Did he have plenty of tact? He kept a straight face. Of course. He passed the medical, the examinations. His vision was perfect; his balance unshakable.

They gave him the instruction book and list of lost passes; a great-coat and freshly pressed uniform that smelt vaguely of turpentine, ammonia, gum arabic. Women admired the navy serge, the silver buttons, the flat peaked cap.

There was no time off for smoko but Robbie didn't care. He liked drinking his tea on the job, his teeth rattling against the enamel cup, steel wheels ringing as they rounded a bend.

Sometimes he'd see Wal, and when the inspectors weren't around he'd let him ride for free, but now all his spare time was spent at the gym. And there was no way Wal could be cajoled into training.

Billy went into camp at Trentham. It seemed pretty much like the only men left were those who were too old or obviously too young, or ones like Wal who had failed the medical.

Robbie trained harder, felt the slow muscular change. He had his dream job. There were only two other things he wanted. To make things right.

THE LEADEN CASKET

Edie did not want Dr Bennett to leave. They stood on the wharf as the wind blew salt into their faces, as gulls screeched their ugly goodbyes.

'We can't stay still, Edie,' Dr Bennett said, touching her arm. 'We must pursue every opportunity. Create it for ourselves. The New Zealand Army may not welcome women but the Croix Rouge does.'

Edie wanted to cry. What if she never came back?

Dr Bennett gave her a robust hug. 'Have you read *The Merchant of Venice?*' she asked. 'Bassanio chooses the leaden casket over the silver or gold. Do you know what is inside?'

Edie nodded. '*Who chooseth me must give and hazard all he hath.*'

Dr Bennett smiled. 'Yes.' She held Edie by the shoulders, looked at her intently. 'Never forget that, Edie. You must have the courage to give and hazard all. You must be prepared to withstand the deepest disappointment, frustration, exasperation . . .

'Oh, Edie, it's not as excruciating as it sounds. Not all the time!' She laughed. 'You are allowed fun too, you know, but,' and now she was very serious, 'intelligence of the brain is not enough. If you want to fulfil your dreams, you will have to work relentlessly. At least twice as hard as any man. You must find within yourself the necessary determination, the will and the wisdom. And you must also cultivate intelligence of the heart.

'Write to me, my dear, and I'll do my best to write back – though you must realise that mail at the Front can be unreliable.'

Dr Bennett gave Edie another hug. She held her, stroked her back. 'My mother died when I was very young, Edie. I felt so alone. But you have Mrs Newman. You still have your mother.'

Edie watched the ship slip its moorings and slowly move out into the harbour. From Sydney, Dr Bennett would sail through the Suez Canal and on to the Middle East. To who knows what? Who knows where?

How could she be so certain? So unafraid?

Edie watched the ship disappear. She remembered the caskets.

THE OATH

Robbie breathed in the dust that flew up as carts, trams, motorcars made their way along Taranaki Street. Men were heading for pubs, thinking about beer and whisky; men and women were walking home, thinking of Irish stew and roast dinners.

He smiled. He could see the huge double-storey brick building up ahead on the corner. He'd trained as a cadet in the firing ranges underneath, stood with the crowd on the night war was declared – Buckle Street one dense lane of boys, men, people cheering. It had been seventeen months since he'd been turned away, but now his training had yielded results. He'd grown three inches, gained fifteen pounds and sculpted his slender body till he could feel the hard contours of muscle through his dark blue uniform. He ran his hand over his jaw. He hadn't shaved for more than two days.

He paused just inside the vast hall, admired the steel trusses supporting the roof, remembered how as a boy he'd wagged school and watched the horses with block and tackle struggle to lift them into place. Late afternoon light fell through the skylights. Officers sat behind desks, filling out forms; men in suits, dungarees, workmen's clothes sat in front, rag-tag queues of one man here, two there.

Robbie studied the faces. If anyone recognised him, knew his age, he'd go elsewhere. There were drill halls up and down the country. He could take the train to Petone and sign up there. He could go further afield. He'd find an officer to take him.

When he sat down, the recruiting officer looked him over. But this was no longer 1914. Now there was a new vocabulary: Gallipoli, Anzac, Chunuk Bair. Each morning mothers, wives, fiancées opened the newspaper and turned immediately to the Roll of Honour, scanning the names under Killed in Action, Died of Wounds, Wounded Admitted to Hospital. *Evans, Rflmn, Harold William. Next-of-kin Mrs R. Evans, 126 Riddiford Street, Newtown (mother). Right foot and cheek.*

The officer studied Robbie's uniform. How many kids under twenty would even get a look-in on a job like that? He asked the questions and filled out the form: name – Robert Donald McKechnie; place of birth – Wellington; British subject – yes; date of birth . . . Robbie had rehearsed it over and over, until now even he almost believed it. The same birth date, just two years older.

The officer smiled. 'Happy birthday,' he said, and he passed Robbie the form to sign, then took him through the oath, sincerely promising and swearing to be faithful, to observe and obey, so help me God.

The doctor measured his height and weight, his chest both fully expanded and empty. He checked his vision, hearing, heart and lungs, the condition of his teeth. (Had he brushed them this morning?) The doctor made him turn his ankles and wrists in circles, bend and extend his arms and legs. He made him stand, legs apart, his hands on the white cotton sheet of the bed. This is what he'd heard of. What all the boys talked about. He held his breath as the doctor parted his buttocks and then reached between his legs and grasped his balls. 'That's fine,' the doctor said, then added, 'Now, what was your religion?' What's religion got to do with a medical? Robbie thought.

'Presbyterian?' the doctor asked, before he signed the certificate.

When Robbie came home and told his mother, she screamed at him. How dare he put her through this? Hadn't he seen the casualty lists in the newspapers each day? Mrs Dunn's son was killed at Gallipoli. Mrs Shirley's survived, but without a leg. 'You're only—'

'Eighteen today,' he said calmly. Defiantly. He could smell roast lamb, could tell his mother had gone to some trouble to cook his favourites. For a moment he felt a pang of guilt, and yet he could not help himself. 'Dad would have backed me up all the way,' he said.

'I don't give a damn about your father! He's been dead . . . nine years. *Nine* years, you hear me – and you're still bringing him up like a bad dinner!'

Tears rose suddenly at the back of Robbie's eyes. He shoved past her, stormed out the door. Slammed it behind him.

As Katherine and Edic ate, looking at Robbie's empty chair, Katherine knew that if she tried to stop him he could just as easily run away. He could join up in Napier or Wanganui or even Christchurch or Dunedin. He could join up under a false name. And all she would have left would be absence. Silence. A tomb she might search and search for and never find because it bore another boy's name.

THE LIONS

Anticipation made Edie flush with excitement. She'd never shown much interest in the usual womanly preoccupations, shopping included, but this was all part of the process of leaving, of making a life of her own. She needed woollen combinations, a navy woollen skirt, a new coat. A girl had to be prepared for snow – why, the modern woman had to be prepared for any eventuality.

As they came back up Adelaide Road, laden with bags and parcels, her mother said, 'We need vegetables for dinner.'

'Oh Mum, can't you get them tomorrow?' Edie couldn't wait to get home. She wanted to lay out her purchases, to organise her trunk.

'We used up all the cabbage last night; there're only two potatoes, one carrot and no onions.'

Edie groaned but followed her mother into the shop. She couldn't leave her to lug everything home.

Mr Wong came out and broke into a smile. 'Been shopping?'

'Yes!' Edie's mother grinned. 'Edie is going to Medical School in Dunedin.' She looked so proud that Edie squirmed, but Mr Wong seemed pleased.

'This is good,' he said. 'Helping people.' He cut a pear and gave each of them a generous slice.

'Mum, this is so sweet. Let's get some.'

Mr Wong handed Edie a brown paper bag. 'No, not that one,' he said. 'Too ripe. This one better. No bruise.'

He weighed the pears and added one more. Medicine was good, he was saying, but – he smiled sheepishly – Chinese medicine was better. He twisted the bag and handed it to Edie, talked about pulses – at least that's what she gathered from the way he demonstrated, pressing his fingers on the inside of his wrist. He talked about the healing power of food and Chinese herbal medicine. Something about hot and cold. She didn't understand.

'More pear?' he said, pointing at the knife, the cut fruit. 'Help yourself.'

Edie noticed his straight white teeth, the easy warmth of his smile.

'Sun Yat-sen,' he was saying, 'he is father of modern China. He studied medicine.'

Edie didn't know anything about China, but she understood the compliment.

Her mother beamed. 'We need vegetables,' she said.

He smiled and recommended the beans, silver beet, the new potatoes. And the plums were very good. Try one.

'Very cold in Dunedin,' he said. 'My cousin live there. Buy warm clothes. Don't want to go to hospital.'

Edie's mother laughed. 'That's what we've been doing. Anyway, she's going to be a doctor. Of course, she'll end up in a hospital!'

Mr Wong's eyes twinkled. 'Chinese people say you go to hospital, you die in hospital. Work in hospital good. Die in hospital no good.'

Edie looked at the brightness of her mother's face, at Mr Wong's impish grin. She blushed. She had never seen her mother like that with anyone.

Mr Wong asked them to wait, then disappeared out the back of the shop. When he returned, he was carrying two large soapstone ornaments.

'Lions,' he said. 'This is man lion,' he said, holding out the one with an ornamental ball under his left paw. 'And this is lady lion,' he said of the one with what looked like a cub under her right paw.

Edie had never seen anything like them. They had bulbous, mythical faces. In truth, they looked nothing like the lion at Wellington Zoo.

'In Dunedin,' Mr Wong said, 'you put man lion on right side of door and lady lion on left side. They will protect you. All right?'

Edie didn't know what to say. They were cumbersome, heavy, exactly not what she needed in her trunk. But she didn't want to be rude, especially not in front of her mother.

They walked out of the shop carrying a lion each, bags of clothes, the pears. 'He can be so impractical,' her mother said, and smiled.

Only when they got home did they realise they hadn't bought any vegetables. They hadn't even paid for the pears.

'Oh well,' her mother said, laughing like a young girl. 'I'll go in again tomorrow. We couldn't have carried any more anyway.'

Edie considered trying to smash the lions. She still couldn't believe it. No wonder Robbie had been so distraught. Her mother was not unattractive. Couldn't she find a respectable man?

And yet, when had she ever seen her mother like that?

Never with her father.

She studied the lions carefully. They were not unlike her insect collections - so ugly they were actually quite impressive. At the last moment she packed them.

All the way to Dunedin - to the boat, the railway station and eventually to St Margaret's - she struggled with her trunk and cursed him, had to accept the assistance of both kind and overbearing men - a skinny young one who seemed barely able to carry his own frame but whose pride would not allow him to accept defeat; a rather corpulent banker whose face broke out in a sweat and turned red as a post box; a stevedore who lifted its weight as if it were half empty.

All the girls at the hostel commented on them. She told them about the crazy Chinaman who gave them to her. Surely a bookmark, something light and compact, would have been more suitable, she said. They laughed. Over time she developed all number of tales about their exotic origins, their myriad magic powers.

TEA

Katherine wandered about the empty house. She walked into the children's rooms, ran her fingers over their pillows, smelled their sheets.

She would keep everything the same – Robbie's model trains dusted on the dresser, the aeroplanes he'd made from balsa wood, paper and string suspended from the ceiling, his boxing gloves hanging from the hook behind the door. He'd come back on leave, after all, at least for the few months before he sailed.

In Edie's room, Katherine examined the collections of bones and insects, classified in their trays; flicked through the scrapbooks filled with newspaper cuttings of disasters and drawings of body parts; fingered the mother-of-pearl cartouche on the rosewood jewellery box. Donald had given it to Katherine before they married, and after he died she had given it to Edie. Inside was a ring with a piece of cut glass stuck to it like a jewel, an amethyst brooch from Donald's mother, and two necklaces.

Katherine touched the blue velvet lining. Years ago, she had kept letters, postcards, special trinkets in the hidden side drawer. She lifted the pin . . . and gasped. Inside lay the *Doxocopa cherubina*, the iridescent blue of its torn wings brought out by the velvet lining.

Katherine did not go back into Edie's room except to wash the sheets and remake the bed, to let in air and dust the furniture. She did not open the drawers or any of Edie's things.

She wandered about the other rooms, considered rearrangements so that the house would seem different, perhaps not so empty. But after she'd moved the dining table from the middle of the room to under the window, she felt as if she had walked into a stranger's house and sat down in his still-warm chair to eat an abandoned dinner. When she looked in the pantry and meat safe, suddenly it seemed pointless to cook for one.

Yet she was grateful. Mrs Newman's brisk demands filled her day and kept her mind busy. *The devil finds work for idle hands*, her mother had said. And when she stopped by the fruit shop on her way home, when Yung's fingers brushed her hand as he gave her apples, Katherine realised she no longer had to rouse herself from his bed at one or two in the morning. She waited until Mrs Paterson had left with her carrots, then for the first time invited him to her home.

If he saw anyone on the street, Yung walked past her house and around the block. Only when he was sure no one saw him did he open the serviceman's gate. He quickly slipped off his shoes and, watching the neighbour's upstairs blinds, carried them silently down the side of the house to the backyard. He walked up the wooden steps, left his shoes in the porch and entered quietly, without knocking.

She offered him cake or a small sweet biscuit, and tea, which he drank weak and black. He watched her add milk and sugar to her cup and wondered if the paleness of her skin came from the milk she drank, her small sips.

He waited.

The first few times he waited for her to lead him to her room, because this was her house and if she did not take him there, then he would drink his tea and gaze at her face, the way she looked back at him, a gentleness about the eyes, and if she said nothing, did nothing,

203

then after a couple of hours he would leave again without having touched her. Yet always she took him out of the kitchen, along the hall and up the stairs. And he was always aware of the light and any shadows that might move across the blinds as he took her in his arms, as he came down on her.

After a while, after he understood the look in her eyes as he opened her door, sometimes he would not wait for tea or for any invitation. He would take her before she could speak. Wherever she was, he would take her – on the kitchen table, on the floor in the hall, walking her backwards or carrying her into the parlour, onto the sofa or up the stairs to her bed.

Sometimes she cried out, *I love you*. The words entered his skin. He breathed them in.

Like incense.

IF THE TIME HAS NOT COME

Yung was making *kau yuk*. This was an act of love. Just as sneezes in springtime come in threes, so he prepared the ingredients. First the belly pork, rich with skin and streaks of fat and meat, thick slices marinated in ginger, garlic, star anise, sugar and soy, then fried and marinated again. Beetroot, washed and peeled and sliced, purple-red juice entering his skin, its love stain on his fingers. And the egg, beaten with a little salt, fried into thin pancakes and cut into pieces.

This is how he assembled it. First a slice of pork, then a piece of beetroot and a slice of egg, now another slice of pork. Round the inside of the bowl he arranged the layers, packing them in a tight spiral. Then he tied string over it all like a package. In the afternoon he would steam it over the range till the fat meat glistened and melted in the mouth, till the gravy flowed. When everyone arrived, he'd lift the bowl out by the string, pour the soupy gravy into a pot and thicken it with starch. He'd serve fried noodles; and whole terakihi steamed with ginger and soy; crispy-skinned chicken; Chinese mushrooms with oyster sauce laid over a bed of boiled lettuce; stuffed bean curd; oyster sauce and hot oil poured over blanched and fried Chinese broccoli; and a rich pork soup, laced with gelatinous threads of shark's fin and strings of beaten egg. He would invert the *kau yuk* onto a plate of boiled spinach and pour the gravy over. He would sit down to eat with family and friends.

Not all of his family, his friends.

He did not know what to call her. He did not even know how to explain.

He put water in the steamer, placed the bowl of *kau yuk* inside and covered it with a lid. Tonight he would eat and drink and celebrate because Yuan Shih-k'ai, the dictator, the murderer, was dead.

Only six months before, Yuan had tried to proclaim himself Emperor. You didn't have to be a revolutionary to be outraged. A man who, with the cunning of a snake, had stolen the presidency from Sun, who'd sold off the country and left the treasury empty. The man who'd assassinated Sung Chiao-jen, the Republic's greatest hope, who step by calculated step had destroyed the Republic and massacred the people.

Then one Sunday night Consul Kwei called a meeting at the Association in Tory Street. Poor Consul Kwei. Never become an official if your conscience is heavier than duty. Everyone went, of course, all the men. They stood around or sat in their rows, smoking and talking about the price of Californian lemons, which had shot up from a few pence to a shilling; about Ah Lee who made a killing from accumulating large stores of rice before the price doubled. They sat about eating toasted watermelon seeds, cracking the shells with their teeth, flicking the husks onto the floor. They talked about Wong-Too who'd gone home for a visit and couldn't get back; about the shortage of labour because of the war. Then Consul Kwei stood up and thanked everyone for coming. He thanked them for supporting President Yuan. He urged them to support Emperor Yuan.

Someone turned out the light even as Kwei was speaking. Suddenly half the crowd were on their feet, shouting, 'Murderer! Turncoat! Beat him to death!' People started throwing chairs or anything else they could get their hands on. Yung caught a chair in mid-air, just before it hit Fong-man. Another hit him in the side. He looked for the Consul and found him under the table.

When it finally died down, Yung addressed the crowd. 'There are few of us here who support Yuan Shih-k'ai,' he said. 'In fact most of us curse the womb that bore him. But that's no excuse for this kind of behaviour.' Then together with Fong-man and Shun Goh, he escorted the Consul out of the building.

Things were not the same with the Chinese Association. Since that meeting, people had lost their unity. They talked about setting up their own county associations. It was all very ironic. Consul Kwei's son had told Yung he wanted to make a bomb. He wanted to blow up Yuan. Such is the foolishness of youth. Yung had advised him to be more circumspect, but now there was no need. Yuan was dead, a man broken by his own deeds. A rhyme came to Yung; it echoed down the alleys of his childhood:

Goodness begets goodness
Evil begets evil
Nothing is without its consequences
If the time has not come
Then the time will certainly come
For consequences.

SMALL MERCIES

Katherine could still hear the speeches on the steps of Parliament, still see Robbie's shining, upturned face.

Be thankful for small mercies. That's what her mother had taught her. And she was thankful. For this year Mrs Newman's visit to Sydney coincided with Robbie's embarkation. She'd only need to work an hour or two a day; she could take days off; she could cook pikelets and madeira cake and Robbie's favourite dinners. On the day he sailed she could follow the parade, wave him goodbye.

Small mercies.

Yung would come by four or five or six nights a week, but on the other nights when she went to bed early she still couldn't sleep. She lay awake for hours thinking about Robbie, his embarkation, the campaigns in Europe, whether or how he'd come home.

She carried a heaviness in her bones, a cough that lingered.

During Robbie's last, full leave, she asked Yung not to come. She'd call in at the shop on her way back from work – it was only a week after all, when her son slept at home. Then his leave would be reduced to a few half days and he'd have to be in camp by midnight. Yung could come by then, after Robbie had returned to Trentham. She kissed him, held his hand. 'He's my son,' she said.

Robbie spent hours riding the trams or going to the gym, came home for dinner, then went out again with his mates, coming back only to fall into bed smelling of beer. Katherine didn't mind. He was home. She hurried through her work at Mrs Newman's, called in at the shop, then spent her time shopping, cooking, washing and ironing Robbie's clothes, knitting socks, making Christmas cake and shortbread for him to take away.

She tried not to cough.

By the time Robbie's leave was down to half days, and Yung returned, Katherine's limbs ached, her skull felt stuffed with wet rags; she was using ten handkerchiefs a day, her nose red and chafed and sore.

On the last night of leave but one, after Robbie had gone, Yung placed a bag of lemons on the kitchen table. For her cold, he said. They sat, she drinking hot lemon and honey, he, weak black tea.

'He's only eighteen,' she said.

He was silent, then said, 'When I leave China, I am eighteen.'

Katherine looked into his dark, calm eyes. But he wasn't the one left behind. *He* was the one who left his wife and family. For *filthy lucre.* Suddenly she felt angry. How dare he compare *this* with Robbie going to war?

He reached across the table, but she pulled away her hand.

She could feel tears but closed her eyes. The room was warm from the coal range yet she was shaking. 'What if he doesn't come home? What if he comes back with no arms or . . .'

He said nothing for a long time. 'You lucky,' he said quietly. 'You have eighteen years with your son. I never . . .'

She didn't want to hear about his children, about his wife. What did he know about Robbie? What did he care?

She stood up and asked him to go. She was tired. No, she wasn't crying, she had a cold, her nose always ran when she had a cold, and could he please leave now.

She tried not to think of him.

She roasted mutton, potatoes and kumara. She cooked cauliflower in a white sauce instead of the usual boiled cabbage, and made bread and butter pudding studded with currants and sultanas.

It was Robbie's last evening at home. All through dinner Katherine did not know what to say. What do you say when you may never see someone again? What do you say after years of silence?

She held him in the doorway as he said goodbye. He enveloped her, shielded her from the southerly. When had he grown from a boy to a man? She did not want to let him go. She hugged herself as he walked into darkness.

She shut the door, blew her nose and climbed into bed, all about her the emptiness of the house, wind rattling the windows, buffeting the weatherboards.

She did not know whether she wanted Yung to come. Everything ached. Grieved.

She closed her eyes, felt bright flashes of lightning. She fell asleep listening to thunder, rain on the iron roof, a silver dark world etched on the back of her eyelids.

LAST NIGHT

Robbie knew his mother had cooked all his favourites. They ate their last dinner together quietly, interrupted only by her blowing her nose into an embroidered handkerchief. 'This cold's a blimmin' nuisance,' she said.

Sometimes he looked up and saw her dabbing her eyes or, worse, found her staring at him. He quickly looked away. She didn't need to say anything. It was in her silence. In the way she plied him with food.

He had two helpings of everything. And then he didn't know what to do. What to say. He needed to walk it off, to blow away the cloying air of his mother, to have one last look around the city at night.

She fussed. What about the southerly, what about the rain coming in?

He wanted to say, Who's going to worry about rain at the Front? but thought better of it. 'Mum,' he said, 'you know how I like a good southerly.' And he meant it. The wind made him feel alive, the way he had to fight with each muscular step.

He put on the gloves Edie had sent him, dark green wool knitted purl and plain, purl and plain. They fitted exactly, and he marvelled at how she could get them so right and yet get his socks so wrong. They were at least three sizes too big. You have to allow for shrinkage, his mother said, but the ones she had knitted were only one size too big. He could see Edie sitting at the front of her classes with her friend Alice, from Timaru, both of them knitting for the war effort while they waited for lectures to begin; his mother of an evening knitting in front of the fire.

He kissed her on the cheek and let her hold him as long as she wanted, then pulled his hat down, turned up the collar of his greatcoat and stepped out into the wind.

He turned once and waved at the figure silhouetted in the pale yellow glow of the doorway. She seemed smaller than he remembered. Or was it he who had grown taller? He shrugged off a shiver, put his hands in his pockets and walked down Adelaide Road towards the Basin.

The moon hadn't come up yet, just street lamps and rectangles of light falling from still-open shops and dully lit windows. As he passed by he heard a man and woman yelling, saw their shadows behind closed blinds. He shut them from his mind and hummed, walking in and out, then into the light again. Here was the tram rattling and wheeling down the track, the whine of the motor, the hiss of brakes.

He'd gone riding all over the city today, on every route to Miramar, Island Bay and Karori. His mates had tipped their caps and had a yarn between clipping tickets. He'd gone on every tram – the double-decker, the Hong Kong Toast Rack, the Wellington Palace – and no one asked for a fare. Dave had given him his cap, the leather money bag and clippers, and he'd clipped a few tickets for old times' sake.

Before he'd left for camp, all the trammies and Dorothy the office girl and Kevin the manager of the depot had got together and given him a silver cigarette holder. It was in his top pocket along with a photograph: Dot, Kev and some of the others, him smack in the middle, outside the terminus.

He felt his father's watch through the wool of his gloves, the smoothness of the glass, the gold links of the chain, the greenstone amulets hanging off. He could hear his boots ringing on the footpath;

could feel his body, bolt upright, arms swinging, the sound of hundreds, thousands of boots, marching.

He'd dreamed of this when he marched up and down on parade, even as he drilled at cadets. Now the waiting was almost over. By midnight he'd be back at camp. Monday they'd take the train to the city again, then march to the troopships to the sound of the army brass band. Already he could feel the charge in the air, an expectation of rain, of history in the making.

This is how he walked that night, by the tram tracks, past wooden cottages and shops, towards the Basin and the city. Something drew him and he didn't understand why. So absorbed in dreams of battle was he, of heroism in the face of the enemy, of victory over evil, that he didn't know where he was going, didn't realise until he marched right into the light, the long rectangles of light thrown into the street, into his face and eyes. Was it the colours, the shapes, the textures shining out of the bright window? The pineapples like strange unlimbed reptiles; the yellow bundles of bananas suspended like the AVRO 504K he'd made from balsa wood and paper and hung with string from his ceiling; the apples, innocent as Snow White's cheeks. Was it the wind dropping, the silence of his stilled boots?

Sounds, vibrations he would never have noticed during the day echoed in darkness.

He used to lie awake in bed listening, his ears, his body suffering the slightest of sensations – the sound of his mother's steps retreating down the stairs, the click of the back door opening and shutting, the heaviness of his heart beating.

Then his feet cold and bare on the gritty footpath. The click of the gate into the backyard behind the shop – his mother disappearing. And he left behind. Nothing but the mocking display of fruit – apples, oranges, pears – in the darkened window.

ONE FLUID MARK

When the soldier came into the shop that night, Yung was cashing up, rolling bundles of notes and fixing them with rubber bands, counting and stacking sovereigns, half-crowns, florins, right down to pennies, halfpennies and farthings, rolling them in paper, folding over the top and bottom, then writing the amount on the outside.

It was quiet for a Friday night, perhaps because of the weather. Not many came out on a cold winter's night with the expectation of rain. Shun Goh had gone down Haining Street to check his *pakapoo* ticket and play a game of dominoes; Mei-lin had gone upstairs with Wai-wai. And so Yung started cashing up, leaving just enough float to last until closing.

As he counted and folded he thought about Katherine.

When he'd prepared his banquet to celebrate the death of President Yuan, almost everyone he'd invited had come. They drank tea and rice wine, joked and told tales, raised their glasses to the new order. But now the leftovers were eaten, and already China had disintegrated into factions, each area dominated, manipulated by its own warlord and bandits. Depression could settle now, an old cotton quilt that had to be re-spun, a mantle so heavy that he'd wake in the mornings exhausted.

Katherine had not come to the celebrations. She did not know his

214

dashed hopes. She had other things on her mind.

'He's only eighteen,' she'd said. 'Why is he doing this to me?'

Eighteen, Yung thought. He was married then. His wife was expecting twins, though at the time he didn't know it. It seemed so long ago – another lifetime. 'I leave China, eighteen years old,' he said.

'You chose it! Robbie isn't just going off to make money. He's going to war! What if he doesn't come home? What if he comes back with no . . .'

Yung reached out across the table and took her hand.

She pulled away. 'How would you know what it's like anyway?' She was sobbing now.

He thought about Joe Kum-yung, the others who never made it home. He thought about those left behind; felt a sudden, inexplicable loss. He'd never even met his sons.

She told him to go. She was tired. No, she wasn't crying, she had a cold, her nose always ran when she had a cold, and could he please leave now.

Sometimes he challenged her. Provoked her. He knew that. Sometimes she got angry and pushed him away. But there were many ways to see the same circumstance. Even his wife and son, even the chaos back in China.

He would go to her tonight. Take her flowers. She would be upset – her last night with her son. He would say nothing, just listen. Isn't this what women wanted?

He would take her in his arms . . .

It took a moment for Yung to register, to translate the sound of footsteps into his consciousness, aware as he was only of the paper-wrapped coins in his hands, of his penis, the way it throbbed as he thought of her, a rudder for his body. Without looking up, he expected the Marshall boy – he always came in about this time. His father

215

smoked two packs of Capstan Navy Cut cigarettes every day, one of his better customers, and Yung and his brother never sold tobacco after 8 p.m. But already he knew the footsteps were too heavy. This was a man, not a boy.

The soldier stood looking at the stacks of fruit, the collar of his great-coat pulled up against the cold, his lemon-squeezer pulled down over his face.

'Cold enough for you?' Yung asked, smiling. He liked the irony. After Katherine first said it to him he'd practised saying it each night as she came to his door, until at last she'd laughed and pinched his arse hard and told him to shut up. *Shut up.* Part of his new vocabulary, her lips touching, silencing his.

The soldier didn't answer.

All right, Yung thought, so he doesn't have a sense of humour. Or maybe he's not much of a talker. 'Pineapple very good,' he said, watching the soldier examine the fruit. 'Smell it. Nice and ripe. Very sweet.'

The man did not seem to know what he wanted. He picked up an apple. Put it down.

'Apples very good too,' Yung said. 'Crisp and juicy.' He picked up the paring knife from the shelf behind the counter, walked over and selected a red-cheeked Jonathan. As he cut, a little juice splashed on his hand. He gave a slice to the man, cut another and placed it in his own mouth. 'Help yourself,' he said, leaving the apple with its white missing wedge, the knife, on the stack.

He walked back to the till and continued cashing up.

Looked up. The man had not eaten; the apple slice was still in his hand. 'Eat *la*, very good,' he said.

The man lifted his face from the collar of his great-coat, and Yung was struck by the air of something familiar. He pushed back his hat and looked Yung in the eye, and in that moment Yung recognised not the eyes themselves, because they seemed very cold and blue, but something around the eyes, the red hair of his eyebrows, the pale

216

freckled skin, and the lips, those same full, wide lips. This was barely a man and he had the lips of his mother.

Yung could see the angle of his jaw, the hate, or was it anger mixed with fear? And yet all he could see was *her* face. He could not look at him and not see the desperate love of his mother. He saw the mouth open and close and open, the twist of the facial muscles, the gesticulations of the hands and arms, the advance towards him.

'You are too quick,' his brother always said to him. 'You do not think. What is the use of your learning if you do not think?'

Now as Yung watched he did not need to think. He watched this man who was barely a man. How he wanted to be a man. Yung breathed. It was as simple as breathing. The in-breath and the slow out-breath. This was the dream, the first breath and the last.

He is a figure lying in the bottom left corner of a landscape. Mountains rise craggy and bare through mist and water. He is very small, at the edge of the painting. He rests under a twisted pine, surveying the world. A world of air and water. A world of white rice paper in which he is one fluid mark, forgettable under the wash of mountains.

THE SEND-OFF

Katherine spent the weekend in bed, getting up only to go to the lavatory or have a cup of tea. Once she ate a little leftover bread and butter pudding cold from the meat safe. Another time she made a hot drink of lemon and honey. She felt weak, and went back to bed and slept.

Yung did not come. He knew she was sick, that she was grieving for her son. Why didn't he come? The least he could do was climb into bed and hold her. But she felt too sick to care. She slept. And slept.

On the Monday morning she rose and brushed her hair, bathed. Her head had cleared, though her throat still hurt. She felt light-headed, as if her body needed to readjust to being upright, her legs learning to walk again. She drank a hot cup of lemon and honey, ate some porridge with sugar and no milk. Felt better.

She took a tram to the railway station, already more crowded than usual. As it travelled down Adelaide Road, she looked for the shop, tried to catch a glimpse of him through the shop window.

It was shut. Strange, she thought. When did they ever close except Sundays and public holidays? Could it be a feast day? She knew they closed for Chinese New Year. She leaned over to take another look, and stepped on a foot.

'Sorry! Are you all right?'

'Yes,' the woman smiled. 'Are you going to watch the parade too?'

Katherine tried to smile back. 'My son is embarking today,' she said.

'It's so exciting, don't you think? I come and watch every parade. There's nothing like the bands and all the gallant young men. Don't they look fine in uniform?'

Katherine looked at her again and realised she was just a girl, perhaps the same age as Robbie and Edie.

They got off the tram together but quickly lost each other in the crowds. Katherine searched the rows of men in uniform and eventually found Robbie. As he moved off she followed him from Government Buildings along Lambton Quay, down Willis Street, Manners and Cuba, pushing her way through the people lining the street, following the sound of the Trentham bugle band, three brass bands, watching Robbie march, back straight, arms swinging in formation. The girl had been right. All the beautiful boys in their freshly pressed uniforms, their lemon-squeezers set at exactly the same angle, every step in time with every other, the rhythmic sound of hundreds of boots hitting the road, the hush of air in between. If only it was dress-ups and marching to the band, Katherine thought. And yet it was hard not to be caught up in the fervour as the men of the 14th Reinforcements, the engineers, the artillery and infantry, the men of the 4th Maori Reinforcements, all of them big brawny men – and Robbie, how he'd grown – marched past the waving, roaring crowds, down to the wharf, as they boarded, got rid of their kit, then surged over the decks.

The noise from shouting between ships and shore was terrific. All around a sea of handkerchiefs waving like victory flags. Everyone waving except for Katherine. Her handkerchief was too damp, and as she looked about her she realised most of the other handkerchiefs were white, waving madly as if an army of lunatics were declaring a truce but were all too excited to notice.

Katherine looked everywhere for Robbie and then found him standing on deck in the midst of hundreds of other boys – men:

219

hundreds of men with their smiling, unafraid faces. He'd been so impatient to go overseas, to go on his big boys' adventure. Friday night he'd left to return to camp, his face flushed with excitement, to say goodbye to Wellington he'd said, maybe ride a night tram and look over the lights. Yet here he was looking out from the boat deck – and could she see correctly? Was that really him among the waving surge of soldiers, so very still, his expression flat, unsmiling?

She watched as the ships one after another slipped their moorings, as all around her the shouting and cheering intensified, as it throbbed and pulsed like one great heart beating. She waved, but Robbie did not raise his hand. She watched as tugs towed the ships out of the harbour, as the figures on deck got smaller and smaller until all she could see were specks of movement on little toy boats, now under their own steam, pouring forth their plumes of smoke. She watched as the background hum of the crowd dissipated, as snatches of conversation and tobacco smoke were replaced by gulls screeching and soaring and diving, by the smell of salt and fish.

Why didn't he wave?

The sky was fading, an appearance of winter warmth swallowed by late afternoon. She walked through town, avoiding the wet footpath outside fish shops, almost forgetting to listen and watch for trams, carts, motorcars. As she came up Adelaide Road she went into Paterson's. She didn't know what she'd have for dinner but the smell of fresh bread made her hungry.

Mr Paterson smiled at her. 'He'll be all right, love. You just wait, he'll come home wearing a medal, that boy.' He passed her the loaf and gave her change. 'Terrible thing next door, eh. Looks like it was a robbery . . .'

Katherine felt the colour drain from her face. She could see Mr Paterson's mouth moving, the white tips of his teeth as his lips parted, pursed, then closed and opened, the brightness of his eyes. 'Where have you been? Friday night. Left the John for dead, he was. Dead. Used his own knife. The coppers were here but I couldn't really help them. First thing I knew was them knocking on the door . . . Two of them stood guard outside the shop right through to this morning.'

Which one? she wanted to ask. Which one did they leave for dead? But she was too afraid. He hadn't come Friday night . . . Saturday . . . Sunday . . .

Katherine walked out of the bakery and down the alley, her legs weak and wobbly as blancmange in summer. She opened the gate and walked across the yard to the back door, her thoughts flying ahead of her – what if, what if, what if, she's got to wake up now, please, please wake up, wake up! She stood at the door, next to the bags of vegetable trimmings, knocked, heard footsteps coming. She gasped as it opened, just a little.

Mr Wong, the elder, looked out and slowly opened the door, let her in.

Katherine could feel the words trapped in her mouth like small, fat birds. And then they spilled out, disembodied, shrill, flapping their wings in the air.

He shook his head, sat down at the table, face in his hands.

'What happened?' Katherine's voice grew louder, more shrill. 'Tell me for God's sake what happened!' She could feel her hands twisting in the air, her body, her voice out of control.

He didn't look up. 'I come home and she clazy, clying. She hear bang door, call out, velly frighten. Velly quiet. She go downstairs. Yung lie in shop.'

Something crumpled inside her. She put her hand out, steadied herself on the table, sat down on a hard wooden chair. There it was. The loss of hope. No going back.

For a long time she was silent, but then she heard her own still, small voice asking, 'Did anyone see who did it?'

He looked across at her. 'No one see,' he said.

JASMINE

She hunched into her woollen coat, buried her face further into her scarf. She could not sleep and she could not wander at night from room to room. And so she walked.

She followed the routes she once walked with him, feeling his presence in every step. In every shadow. She knew she should find new paths but all she could see was the garden where he stole a rambling rose, or the gutter where she found the heart-shaped stone, the lamp post under which he swept the air on one of those nights of the comet.

Even darkness reminded her. Of his hair, his eyes, his lips on her throat.

The last time she saw him, she sent him away without a kiss or even a squeeze of the hand. No goodbye, no wave of a white handkerchief. She'd turned her back and hadn't seen him leave, just heard the click of the door as it shut.

She wished she could take it back. When he came to her, tried to embrace her, she wouldn't push him away. She'd take him. She'd rip off his shirt and she wouldn't care if a button flew off, if a sleeve tore from his shoulder. She'd fuck him. She'd make him pay. And pay. For dying. For leaving her when she still wanted him.

She'd take him to her bed and lie with him, her face nestled into his chest, her arm wrapped round his smooth body.

If only she could speak to him one more time. Smell him. Touch him.

He'd wanted her to join in celebrations for the Republic. She would have been the only white face, a sea of Chinese faces speaking an indecipherable tongue.

He'd wanted her to come for dinner. 'I am very good cook,' he'd said. 'Cook many dishes.' She'd looked at his earnest face, his slender, slightly trembling hands, and she knew it was true. He would have spent hours in the kitchen, preparing beautiful dishes.

He'd wanted to walk her home in daylight, for her to walk openly to his, to take the cable car together to the Kelburne Kiosk, to take Devonshire teas.

If only she could have changed his skin. But then who would he have been?

If only she could have spoken to him in his own language. If only he could have spoken freely. Fluently. 'Do not let anyone steal from you that which is yours,' he would have said. She could almost see his face, almost hear his voice. 'Never be afraid of language. You are your own master, Katherine. If you master language, you master a world.'

She had been walking for over an hour. Every step reminded her, every road seemed to lead to another and another, and there she was again, fleeing shadows.

And what was that fragrance? As if to torment her. She reached through darkness and touched the foliage as it tumbled over a wooden fence, the clusters of thin buds, the flowers like small stars. Once she would have picked a sprig, or perhaps he would have. She pressed her face into the leaves, the flowers; closed her eyes. So close, so far away – this black-hearted expanse of sky and the stars threading through it.

THE KEEPER

Always, it had been Yung who wrote to their parents, his characters flowing elegantly down the paper in even columns. Like a child learning to write, Shun could see the square each character should occupy on paper, each stroke building into a wall or roof or foundation, each word finished like a well-made house. But no matter how hard he tried, his own words seemed to collapse down the page like a village in an earthquake.

Before Yung came out, a village cousin had written Shun's letters, sometimes, like Yung, adding witticisms or lines of poetry that Shun had never heard of. But he had gone home seventeen years ago.

Today Shun walked Wai-wai to school. Just in case. He had several hours yet before he had to collect him. He left Mei-lin asleep upstairs. He could not leave her for long. Not even in daylight. In the evenings he did not go down Haining Street. He went to bed early. He took Mei-lin in his arms when she woke screaming.

Shun locked the back door, turned the handle and pushed. He looked at the milky sky, shrugged in his woollen coat and walked down the steps into light rain. He examined the yard, looked for any unexplained shadows, then walked through the gate and up the alley. He nodded to Mr Paterson through the window of the bakery. Mr Paterson nodded back. He paused on the street and gazed at the

CLOSED sign hanging on the door, at the unsold fruit sitting in the window. Then, hands in coat pockets, he walked down Adelaide Road, around the Basin Reserve towards the city.

What would he write? He was the oldest. He was his *brother's keeper*. Wasn't that the phrase he had learned? He wiped his face. Even light rain accumulated over time.

A motorcar blew its horn and Shun jumped back into a puddle. He cursed, looked both ways along Tory Street, behind him and up ahead along Buckle. He crossed, breathing in the smoky exhaust, quickening his steps before an approaching tram, weaving behind a horse and cart. He passed Mount Cook Police Station, his feet squelching in his shoes, the bottom of his trousers wet against his ankles.

Yung's son was already on his way. He would not arrive in time. He would not see his father lowered into the grave.

Shun crossed the road and turned into Cuba Street. Fong-man's reputation as a calligrapher was not as great as Yung's, yet he was educated. He and Yung had shared poetry. He was Yung's best friend.

Fong-man was wrapping a cabbage when Shun walked into the shop. He looked up, nodded, handed the parcel to the woman and put her coins in the till. He called his son to come and serve.

Shun followed him out the back. He gazed at the spot on Fong-man's head where the hair had thinned, where the paleness of his scalp showed through.

He did not know what to say.

THE KIOSK

Mr Wong, the elder, visited Katherine on the Thursday afternoon. He stood on the back porch and declined her invitation for tea. The funeral would be at 10.30 the following day, he said. At the Chinese Mission Hall in Frederick Street. Yung would be buried at Karori cemetery.

Katherine thanked him and watched him walk away. She could not see anything of Yung in his brother.

The next morning Katherine splashed cold water over her face. She bathed and put on her finest clothes – a cream dress and hat Mrs Newman had bought as a birthday gift from Kirkcaldie's.

At ten she put on her woollen coat and caught a tram to Lambton Quay. She could feel the damp in the air, the threat of rain, but she still climbed the staircase to the upper deck, gazing at the hills, at the smokestack towering from the cable car powerhouse at Kelburne. She watched the drift of smoke, its direction a weathervane for the city, and remembered Robbie's words before he walked into the night. 'Mother, you know how I like a good southerly.' She wrapped her arms round herself. Shivered.

Light rain fell as she disembarked at Cable Car Lane. She bought a ticket and chose an exposed seat, alone, at the back of the trailer. The trailers were rebuilt Palace trams. This is what Robbie had told her. Why did she remember such meaningless facts? Why did she remember? She wiped the back of her hand across her eye and – through dark tunnels, over viaducts – watched the city fall away before her, the ring of the bell at Clifton, Talavera, Salamanca, past the windmill to the top of the hill, Upland.

Oh, the grandeur of the Kelburne Tea Kiosk: the twin turrets, the orange-tiled roof, the great windows and veranda.

'Madam?' the conductor asked.

She roused herself and climbed down to the path, walked the short distance to the steps, the ornate balustrades, up past the white picket fence. She was relieved it was raining, that it wasn't Sunday. That the Kiosk was almost empty.

She gave up her coat at the desk, took a table by the windows and ordered two Devonshire teas.

The waitress brought a tray with pots of tea and hot water, a jug of milk, bone china tea cups with matching plates and saucers, silver teaspoons and knives, two large scones, and a bowl each of raspberry jam and whipped cream.

'Should I come back?' the waitress asked. 'The gentleman has not arrived?'

Katherine stared at the starched white tablecloth, at the bowl of sugar cubes. She closed her eyes, shook her head. Her lip trembled.

'Are you all right?' the waitress asked.

She burst into tears, covered her face with her hands. She could not stop shaking. 'Please . . .' she said at last, 'just leave . . . the tea . . . here . . .'

She heard footsteps as the waitress retreated. She blew her nose. Looked out the window at the buildings of the city, the tiny wooden houses, the dark, lumpy green of Mount Victoria and the town belt; at the harbour, at Leper and Somes Islands, at the distant hills like layers of torn, grey paper – the darkest layer meeting the water, the palest

228

disappearing into the milky sky. She watched a boat leave the wharf, move across and disappear behind Point Halswell on its way into the Heads.

She lifted her watch. Quarter to twelve. She sighed.

It was the first time she had taken tea at the Kiosk.

She took the teapot and poured. Added water from the other pot. Weak, black, unsweetened for him; white with one sugar for herself. It would be cold, but she didn't care. She cut the scones in half and spread them with jam and cream.

She gazed at the empty chair. At the cup of black tea, the scone with its swirl of cream over an ooze of jam. She lifted her cup to her lips.

Outside the Kiosk she took the bus, sat as it jolted over the rough, wet roads. She barely noticed the scarred landscape, passing trams, only the smell of engine oil, the groan as the bus struggled upwards, the graunch and jerk of the clutch and gears, her fingers gripping the seat as it turned corners, as it ran downhill.

She had come this way only once. A lifetime ago.

She disembarked into a puddle. The bottom of her cream dress now wet, ingrained with mud. She didn't care.

At the sexton's cottage she asked for directions. Did not look into the man's curious eyes.

All around the hills. Above and below the sweeping paths, row after row of gravestones, trees planted in disarray between them. Strangers. Lovers. Lives lived and forgotten.

The crowd was mostly black or grey haired, white garbed. Only a few dressed in black. She stood behind a tree and watched from a distance; could not hear anything but the wind rustling leaves, the soft patter of rain, birdsong. The smell of wet earth.

As they dispersed, his sister-in-law looked up.

Katherine waited until everyone had left. She gazed at the space where they had been. Do people leave something of themselves – more than memories – even when they are gone?

She took the tiny flowers from her coat pocket. They were bruised. They released their sad, creamy, pink-edged fragrance.

She walked towards him.

SHADOWS

Sometimes Mei-lin would see him. Late at night when the shop was shut and everyone else was sleeping. She would wake, or perhaps she had never gone to sleep, watching the slight rise and fall of the bedclothes. She would look across at the father of her son, his face wrinkled yet childlike in sleep. Shadows would move across the pale ceiling. A morepork's call. She would rise and go down the stairs towards the kitchen.

Always something would make her turn and open the door into the shop. A flash of light perhaps, a shadow, a sense of someone moving. The first time she had almost cried out. He had been so full-bodied – as if made of muscle and skin and bone – that for a moment she had mistaken him for an intruder. And then she had recognised him. His long, aquiline nose, the way he moved as if at ease in his body.

She had seen him half a dozen times. Sometimes he was bending, looking at a stack of fruit, reaching out as if to take an apple in his hand. Sometimes he was walking away.

Afterwards she would always wonder why she did not call out to him, but he did not see her and, in the moment, somehow, she could not speak. Light would fall from the street lamp through the shop window, casting pools of brightness across the room, everywhere half-remembered shadows. She would look again and he would be gone.

She did not tell anyone. They had found another shop in Tory Street, a little smaller, but without lives that needed to be forgotten. She wondered what would happen after they left. Would he still reach out as if to take fruit in his hand and find only shoes or bottles of elixir or, perhaps, nothing? Would he know where to find them?

She would look out the window into darkness, into shadowed light, then turn and walk back again, close the door behind her. In the kitchen she would pour half a cup of cool boiled water from the kettle, drink, then slowly walk back up the stairs.

MOON CAKE

Katherine was surprised to see her at the door 'Please,' she said. 'Come in.'

She made tea. Poured it weak and black.

'I'm sorry,' she said, 'I have no cake or biscuits to offer you. The children are gone and I . . .'

Mrs Wong smiled. Her eyes were soft, warm. It did not matter. 'I see you,' she said. 'By tree.'

'Yes,' Katherine said. 'I'm sorry.'

Mrs Wong smiled. 'No sorry,' she said, then after a pause, 'do you know Moon Festival?'

'Yes,' Katherine said. Yung had told her about the fifteenth day of the eighth lunar month, the night each year when the moon is fullest, when Chinese families come together to eat and drink and gaze at the moon. He'd shown her a Chinese calendar – a small, fat block of pages, one for each day, the years, months, days all signified by numbers. How do you live in two different times? she'd thought. In two different worlds.

'I make moon cake,' Mrs Wong said. She took a brown paper bag from her basket, gave it to Katherine. 'No good. No good cooking.'

Katherine saw the flush of pleasure on Mrs Wong's face. She understood that she had made the cakes herself, that this was

233

something she did very well. There were two inside the bag, each of them wrapped in greaseproof.

Katherine brought out plates, a knife, napkins. Yung had given her moon cakes. He'd told her the Chinese gave them to family, to friends. Always an even number.

She cut one in half. They ate quietly.

Katherine did not know what to say and yet she realised she liked this woman.

As she left, Mrs Wong told her they were moving. 'Tory Street,' she said. 'By Stein's pawnshop.'

Katherine watched her open the gate and close it. She had not been back to the shop all these months. She raised a hand in the slightest wave, watched her walk away.

On the night of the full moon, Katherine walked through the city, through the gardens between Cambridge and Kent Terraces. She stopped at the statue of Queen Victoria and placed her cheek on the cold granite pedestal.

'Come,' he'd said, and Katherine turned. She could almost feel the warmth of his hand.

She walked to the harbour and along the parade. What had he said? Why did people die? Not of drinking. Not of driving motorcars . . .

She climbed the steps of the band rotunda and gazed at the moon reflected in black water. At the scattered lights of the city.

People died because they failed to go out on dangerous water. Because they failed to gaze at the earth . . . as it turned overnight to silver . . .

She looked up at the stars in the great expanse of blackness.

Where are you? Where are you now?

She walked back down the steps and around to the water's edge. Dipped her hand in its coolness.

Among the rocks she found a patch of fine stones. She smoothed

234

them with her palm, then wrote with her finger: three small words.

From her coat pocket she withdrew a paper bag. The cake was smooth, glossy, with a Chinese design – perhaps a word – pressed into the satiny pastry. She traced her finger along the grooves of language and wondered how it translated.

Again from her pocket she drew a small bone-handled knife. She sat down and carefully she cut the cake into quarters. Pieces of yellow moon fell from its centre. Salted duck egg, he'd told her. Sweet red bean paste surrounding a boiled, salty yolk. She looked up at the moon. Sometimes she'd seen it when it was yellow, but tonight it was white and very large.

The bean paste looked black, smooth as oily water. She took one quarter and tasted its sweetness, its heaviness on her tongue. The gritty saltiness of the moon. She licked her fingers.

The coolness of the stones seeped through her woollen coat, through her skirt and petticoats. The southerly was picking up, moving through her hair, over her cold face, her damp fingers. She placed the remaining three pieces of cake inside the O of the middle word in the stones, stood up, and put the knife into the paper bag and back in her right pocket. From the left she withdrew a sprig of jasmine. Breathed in the lingering sweetness, placed it on top of her offerings.

Would her words lift and travel over the harbour out to sea? North to Flanders, to the still-warm dead, the freshly shocked and the living? South to the dusty tomes of Dunedin? Out to that other place where he dwelt now, she knew not where?

She looked again at the moon, water, at the earth turned silver. She remembered the flutes he fashioned out of bamboo; the violin he'd played in his room one night (before his brother knocked on the door and yelled at him in Chinese), the small round belly of the instrument, one side covered with snakeskin – the dark patterning of the scales reminiscent of gardens, desire, the plucking of fruit – its belly held between his legs, the way his hand, arm, body moved the bow back and forth between the two strings. She could still hear the tune, *Butterfly Lovers*, he'd said, the way it haunted her dreams. But she could not sing it, hum it. All she could bring forth was something that rose out of her bones, her voice thrown out into the night air – *Should auld acquaintance be forgot and never brought to mind, should auld acquaintance be forgot in the days of auld lang syne . . .*

FIELD OVER HEART

Katherine knew it would happen, and yet as she passed by on Adelaide Road it still shocked her: the empty shop, its dark windows like dead eyes, the FOR LEASE sign fraying about the edges, like the edges of the mind.

To think of, to long for. 'Si,' he'd said, the sound of the word in Chinese. Now she could not remember how it had started, how they'd come to this word. Somehow the reason had been lost – all she had left was the journey.

He'd come to her from behind, so that her back leaned into his body, his arms around her. He took her hand and wrote onto her palm with his finger – the word for *field*, and underneath, *heart* – and she remembered the characters of his name. Was this what the Chinese longed for, she thought, that piece of land called home always falling over the heart? She could feel the quaver in her voice, the smallness of it speaking into the air. 'Do you . . .' she said, but now he was kissing her hair, the back of her neck, moving across to her ear, his tongue gentle, insistent, flicking over the lobe. She was shaking, just a little, a shoot coming up from darkness into a slight breeze. She could feel her body loosening, turning, his lips on her eyelid, her nose, the side of her mouth. And she was kissing him, small star-kisses that opened, unfurled inside her.

On the bed he asked if he was hurting her, the way he tugged her upper lip, tenderly, into the warmth of his mouth. 'No,' she whispered, almost afraid to look into his face. Almost afraid to see the way he looked at her.

She stood outside the shop, staring in at the blank walls, the empty shelves. *There is nothing more empty than that which was full.* For a moment she thought she saw oranges piled high, apples, pears, the intense green of spinach and silver beet, bananas hanging from the window. For a moment she thought she saw movement: his hand cradling an apple, the long fingers that had written on her palm, traced her lips.

She closed her eyes. She'd always had so many thoughts inside her, thoughts that never came out. Always felt so awkward in her pale, freckled skin. But now she understood. He'd given her language: his language, a new opening into her own. And he'd brought her home in her body. He'd brought her home.

PART IV

DUNEDIN & WELLINGTON

1918–1922

A tree shifts in the wind, just a little, the way a southerly presses its shape into the trunk, traces its coolness over branches, messes with the dark and light of leaves. Blood-flowers. Day after day, needles of blood fall, a scattering of red on the earth.

Katherine McKechnie

Black Blancmange

Robbie can still hear the shelling, can still see the flares – crimson, yellow, green – the earth vomiting flame. They're coated with mud; it fills their kit and boots and plasters their clothes to the skin; it stops up their rifles. They're wading through black water up to the waist, the duckboards washed away. With each step, mud sucks them to the knees. A few days ago the man in front, Tracy, fell in a shell hole and disappeared, and they couldn't find him, just two bubbles that broke the black surface. There are arms, legs sticking out of the mud walls, sometimes a black face with its staring white eyes. Rats as big as rabbits slip over the parapets, their fat oily bodies slow from feasting. The putrefaction makes you gag, but you've got to inhale. The smell clings to your skin and you never wash it out.

The rain won't stop falling. With each shell the mud shakes like black blancmange. Robbie can't feel his feet any more, despite the greasing with whale-oil. Jimmy's feet swelled double, and then the screaming started as the toes turned putrid and the flesh fell away.

They're cold. They're hungry and wet and bloody cold. And the lice drive them crazy – they crawl out of the seams, out of every seam, you run your nail over your seams, crack, crack, crack, to break their backs, they crawl over the skin, and if you crack them with your nail blood comes out. Your own blood. One minute Robbie's talking to

Billy, they're talking about getting out of this hell-hole, getting back to Billy's girl, Linda, she's got a dimple just here, you've never met her have you, Rob, you know, he says, you won't believe this but she's got red hair, she looks a bit like your . . . and the next, a flare's gone up lighting the whole goddamned landscape – shell holes, water, barbed wire – everything bathed in silver light. The sound of shells, artillery, dirt flying up. Robbie feels something warm, soft on his cheek. He drops, turns to Billy. He's got a look of surprise on his face, Billy, staring eyes, a mash of brains spilling out.

Robbie. Robbie. It's raining, it's always raining, and the walls keep on shifting and the doors hang loose. A woman is calling, she's calling your name, and you know that voice, you know it, but you can't work out who.

A Loose Collection of Bones

The doctor told Edie it could be on account of the shells. 'A bursting shell creates a vacuum, and when the air rushes back in it disturbs the cerebro-spinal fluid.' He told her this as though he were breaking good news, as though he had just won a large sum of money. He grinned from a mouth jammed too full of teeth.

Edie tried not to stare. His mouth reminded her of an ill-kept graveyard, tombstones untended and falling over. She stared at the top button of his white coat. She still had a year and a half left at Medical School and felt flattered that he spoke as a colleague. After all, how did his enthusiasms differ from her own? Yet Dr Fisher's lack of tact in his diagnosis of her brother seemed almost indecent, or as Mrs Newman would have said, it indicated a certain lack of breeding.

'Geoffrey,' he said, 'call me Geoffrey.' He looked into her eyes, shook her hand again, holding it longer than necessary. 'There are, of course, other possible explanations,' he said as she extricated her fingers. 'French and German neurologists don't believe it's caused by organic trauma any more. They say shell-shock's a *functional nervous disorder arising in a premorbid personality . . .*'

Premorbid personality. Edie had never thought to apply such principles to her family.

'The symptoms,' Dr Fisher continued, 'are actually the same as for traumatic neurasthenia.' He smiled. 'What the common man might call hysteria.

'The latest opinion is that any circumstance, including shells exploding, might bring about onset. But the predisposing cause is fear combined with gradual psychic exhaustion . . . of course, here we are dealing with a neuropathic individual.'

Edie thought about Robbie. *Neuropathic?*

'So what is the course of treatment?' she asked.

'Encouragement, persuasion, fresh air, exercise, nutritious food, work – yes, it's the work that's important, that's what Dr King would say . . .'

Dr Truby King. After Mrs Newman's ravings, it was a disappointment the superintendent was away in England. Edie wanted to see for herself, to compare the myth with the man. Now she would have to wait until their class visit next year. She'd heard Dr King would discuss cases of insanity, even parade his favourite patient – the infamous Lionel Terry. Apparently, Terry would put on quite a show. With guards on either side, he'd give a speech, recite poetry and have students calling for more, wondering what he was in for.

'. . . we'll get Robert out in the garden,' Dr Fisher – Geoffrey – was saying, 'digging round the rhododendrons, tending the beans and lettuces.' He grinned. 'By the time he gets out of here, he'll be a right Chinaman, you'll see. Come, I'll take you to him.'

He was sitting in an armchair, staring out the windows onto the garden. Even with sunlight falling across his face, his thin body, he looked cold. He had a greyish pallor that seemed inconsistent with the brightness of his hair, his freckled skin. And his clothes fell over him as if loosely wrapping a collection of bones.

Edie spoke his name, but he did not turn his head. 'Robbie,' she said, her voice an echo. She pulled up a chair and sat down beside him, searched his face, looked into the opaque blue of his eyes.

Even after Dr Fisher's descriptive lecture, it was a shock. Robbie had always been so annoying, so full of himself. She remembered a game they played after dinner, their father conjuring words like a magician. She should have loved it. After all, she was the one who got up quietly in the night, took the dilapidated dictionary down from the shelf and read it by flickering candlelight. But she could see her father's impatience – letters and words already forming on his tongue, archaic derivations, obscure meanings ready to leap in ambush from behind his waxed moustache – and even as a word and its meanings rose in her throat, she'd swallow them down again, almost crying for the lack of something amusing to say.

It was Robbie who loved the game. Robbie and their father. She would watch the delight in her father's eyes at Robbie's *stupid* responses, the way he praised him, laughed with him, played with him, and she'd hope and pray that her brother would die or be crippled or simply disappear, that her father would forget he ever existed, that now he'd tell *her* his jokes and outrageous tales, make *her* toys from balsa wood and empty cotton reels, take *her* to cricket at the Basin.

Even after their father died, Edie still resented her brother. Their mother fussed over him, worried about him, fought with him. He was the braggart, the larrikin, by his loudness the centre of the known world.

She looked into Robbie's blank eyes. He was like the leather cover she'd wiped dirt from, wrapped in tissue and hidden at the bottom of her drawer – all its words ripped out.

She took Robbie's hand, but he did not respond.

This was what she studied. Life. Medical disorders. Death.

The day before at the anatomy museum she'd studied wax models of the human embryo. One had a round, protruding forehead, wide-set eyes, a squat nose, and an open mouth with tongue poking out. The bulbous face reminded her of something she couldn't quite put her finger on – some mythical beast, something not human . . .

She pressed Robbie's hand. He turned, but there was no flicker of recognition.

She had worked at the hospital and seen horrific injuries and diseases. During the flu epidemic she'd watched patients spit pus and phlegm, greyish-white and bloody; watched them drown in their own secretions. They lost their hair, fingernails, toenails; lapsed into coma or delirium. Great strapping lads and men in their prime, boys like George McAlister, the varsity wrestling champ, the suddenness of it all, his skin translating to deep crimson then, just one look away, and he'd turned, in an instant, jet-black . . .

And yet this was worse. This was her punishment – her prayer had been answered.

She stared at Robbie and did not know what to say. Realised she didn't know what she'd say even if he were well.

She'd stood on the wharf waving goodbye to Dr Bennett, just as she knew her mother must have done to Robbie. What had this war done? Dr Bennett had risked everything serving the wounded in Serbia. Bombs landed beside her, she contracted malaria, her beloved brother died at Passchendaele . . .

Edie held Robbie's hand. She opened her mouth, let words stumble out.

BIRDS

Katherine looked out the window as the train passed through Port Chalmers and left the harbour. Gulls disappeared as they climbed the hills; through the trees glimpses of blue water. Edie sat making notes from some thick medical text. Perhaps it's easier like this, Katherine thought, the rock and jerk of the carriage over rails, drumming in the ears. Easier than fractured conversation.

The carriage filled with smoke in the tunnels and the lighting was too dim for reading. Even without looking, Katherine sensed the stillness of Edie's pencil - as if caught in photographic plates - then pressed to paper again as they were thrown into daylight, as they rattled down along the cliffs above Waitati.

Katherine gazed at the beaches, the seaside cottages. She remembered laughter at Island Bay, Edie collecting shells and stones, molluscs, small marine animals, Robbie kicking a ball over sand. They passed through rolling sheep country, and before she realised it the porter was calling, 'Seacliff! Seacliff!' and the train lurched to a halt.

Edie packed her books into her bag and they disembarked.

We don't know how to be together, Katherine thought. We don't even know how to be silent. She glanced at Edie, bag swinging heavy in her hand; looked at the road ahead of them. Ten minutes, Edie had said. Ten minutes' walk.

'Does he speak?' she asked at last.

'No,' Edie said. Softly. Like a sigh.

The sound of their shoes on gravel.

'Does he know you?'

'Mum, are you sure you . . .'

'Does he recognise you, anyone?'

'I . . . I don't know.'

'What do they say about his . . . prospects?'

'I think it's too early . . .'

Edie kicked stones along the road. Kicked again and again.

Don't. Don't, Katherine wanted to say.

'Why is it so hard?' Edie asked.

What are you asking me? Katherine wondered. *What can I say to make any of this easier?* She gazed at her daughter, all of her life ahead of her. 'There's so much we don't understand,' she said at last.

Sunlight fell warm on their skin. They walked listening to birdsong, everywhere lush green, flowers blooming, the sky too blue. *Why is it so beautiful? Is this supposed to make it bearable?*

'Why didn't you tell me, Mum?'

'What, Edie? What didn't I tell you?'

'About Mr Wong.'

Katherine took a sharp breath. 'What do you mean?'

'Why didn't you tell me about you and Mr Wong?'

She knew. All these years she knew . . .

'I . . . I didn't think you'd understand . . . didn't think you'd approve . . .' She stopped and looked into her daughter's eyes. 'I didn't want to have to choose between you.'

'But wasn't that choosing?' Edie kicked a stone ferociously into the grass. A bird flew up across their path, a flurry of brown wings.

'I'm sorry, Edie . . . I . . .'

Edie stared at the road ahead of them. 'You loved him, didn't you?'

Katherine blinked. They walked in silence.

'We're here,' Edie said at last. They turned through the hospital gates, up the twisting driveway, past the orchards and raspberry beds to the huge greystone building.

Katherine took his hand, squeezed it, and he turned. She took him in her arms and held him, his cool face against her throat. She could feel his bones, the thin strips of his ribs, his shoulder blades like wings. 'Robbie,' she said, a whisper into his hair. 'My son.' She felt the slight weight of him, the subtraction of what she had known. She kissed him lightly, afraid if she pressed too hard he might dissolve.

He leaned into her, held onto her, and she felt him begin to shake, small sobs wracking his thin body.

Afterwards Katherine could not return to her rooms. Edie gave her a hug – how long had it been since Edie embraced her – and then went back to Medical School, leaving her to wander the city. She walked up Lower Stuart Street into the Octagon, stared at the statue of Robbie Burns sitting on his tree stump, quill in hand, scroll at his feet. As she watched, a seagull flew down and settled on his head. It looked so ludicrous, Katherine almost laughed. It could happen to anyone, even the high and mighty. Life could come out of the blue – and crap on your head. She started to shake but it was not laughter that came, that wrenched itself in waves from her body.

She fled, trying to control her weeping, trying to control the shaking. She heard horns, the screech of brakes, almost collided with someone whose face she did not see. She tried to slow down her breathing, tried to slow down.

Wiped her face with a handkerchief. Opened her eyes.

The building represented everything she did not believe in, its spire reaching into the sky as if to strike the fear of God into the city. First Church. The One and Only unyielding God.

She walked through the iron gates, passed the manicured lawn, the quiet trees, up the bluestone steps, let the limestone swallow her.

In the foyer, she walked through the open door, into the belly of God.

The church was empty. Late afternoon sun fell through the rose windows, leaving highlights on the western pews and across the straight-backed seats of the choir. She sat in the last row, looking over lines of wooden pews to the front of the church where pipes like silent cannons reached upwards. Two British flags hung from the wooden archway, one on the east, the other on the west, overhanging the altar. She sat alone, fragments of pink light streaking across the ivory walls.

In the silence words resonated, words like forgiveness. Redemption. But she had no words to speak, no words to share. She looked down. On the back of the pew in front of her someone had scratched in angular letters, GOD IS. What? she wondered. She had heard many words. Righteousness. Justice. A consuming fire. And words like love, which could slip off the tongue too easily. A word spoken with the mouth or eyes, with small acts of sacrifice or large. A word with many facets, capable of great clarity and great misunderstanding.

What would she have done differently if she had known? What would she have chosen?

She buried her face in her hands.

THE WATCH

Robbie was weeding the rose garden when the stranger came upon him.

'It's only fools who believe roses are symbols of love . . .' The voice was strong. Authoritative.

Robbie looked up.

The man was clothed completely in white. He had long, slightly wavy white hair, a long white beard. Like an Old Testament prophet. Like God. He was flanked by attendants wearing Seacliff uniforms. 'What do you say, son?'

Robbie looked down again, concentrated on the rich, brown soil, the feel of it between his fingers, under his nails.

'It's the colour that's of utmost importance,' the man was saying. 'Take white, for instance – white roses symbolise eternal love, but did you know they also indicate secrecy and silence?'

The man laughed. 'People don't usually think of love hiding secrets, do they?

'And black. There's no such thing as a black rose. In truth they're more the colour of dark crimson or red, but such is the power of symbol. Death, my son. Mourning . . . Personally, I don't see any reason for mourning. Death is inevitable. Sometimes it can even be used to prove a point.'

The man bent under a rose bush, in an area Robbie had already weeded, and pulled out a poor straggling stem with fine root hairs, flicked it onto the weed heap. 'You let one small evil take root and within the blink of an eye the land is overrun with unspeakable horror.

'What's your name, young man?'

Robbie didn't know. Nothing seemed to fit. But he kept hearing the same name over and over. Robbie. Robbie. He heard it in his dreams.

'Has the cat got your tongue?'

Robbie's throat felt dry, as if words no longer lived there. He tried to cough. A nomad crossing a desert.

One of the attendants said, 'His name's Robert. His sister calls him Robbie. He doesn't speak. Just spends all his time in the garden.'

'Robbie,' the man said thoughtfully.

Robbie looked up at the man's face, surprised by his silence. Suddenly he remembered his father – it *was* his father – opening the back of his pocket-watch to reveal the cogs with their tiny teeth clicking, clicking in never-ending circles. 'Nothing is still,' his father had said. 'Even if we don't know it, even if we do nothing. The earth turns, and everything in it . . .' His father spoke so quietly that Robbie did not recognise him. He gazed into the middle distance, seemed to forget Robbie's presence. 'Is this all there is? Are we just cogs, our lives running inexorably to their conclusion?'

He turned, looked Robbie in the eyes. Suddenly laughed. 'Don't look so serious, son.' He ruffled Robbie's hair. 'Off to bed with you now. Everything always looks better in the morning.'

But it wasn't, was it? In the morning. That's when they'd pulled him out of the water.

The stranger was talking again, his speech forming a disturbing background hum, but all Robbie could see were greenstone amulets, his father's ink-stained fingers, and water, endless water, closing over . . .

252

THE RETURNING

From the first-floor window in the room he'd inhabited as a child, Robbie looked down on the garden. The rata was still there, the wooden battens he'd nailed to the trunk, the overhanging branch he'd sat on, raining down on his sister small stones, acorns, boiled Brussels sprouts he'd squashed in his pocket from dinner. The grass was very long, full of dandelion and daisy that in summer would bloom again wildly. Once there may have been a vegetable garden, flower gardens, in a time before they moved there, but all his memories were like this: weeds like too many thoughts run rampant.

He had lain in the white softness of his bed for almost a day and night after the long journey by train and boat from Dunedin. He'd drunk his mother's vegetable soup, performed the rites of the invalid. The room was the same as he'd left it, but he did not fit any more – like the clothes his mother had kept hanging in his wardrobe or folded in the oak chest of drawers. He tucked his shirt into his trousers, which hung from his bony hips till he fitted the braces, pulled on a jersey to cover the gaping at his waist. Then he took down his model aeroplanes, trains, the postcards and posters on the wall, shoved them in a heap at the bottom of the wardrobe.

He did not want to remember.

He grimaced as he squeezed his feet into shoes and went down the stairs.

He did not stop to reassure his mother, just walked out the back door, through the grass that tugged and pulled at his ankles with its long wet leaves, and on to the iron shed. Inside, bright motes of dust drifted in the morning light. On every shelf and surface, grey-brown dust settled in a layer of dirty felt. There, between the wooden ribs, he found spade, rake, pruning shears, trowel.

He had never dug in this garden before, having from an early age inherited his mother's disdain for gardening. But his time at Seacliff had left its green-fingered mark, and now he could not look upon a neglected wasteland without envisaging an English garden, a garden *à la* Truby King.

Every morning after breakfast he entered the world of his garden. He slowly walked a full circuit, examining each corner, every aspect, planning his work for the day. Then he extricated the tools he would need, long shafts of wood and metal that came to feel like extensions of his limbs, his own body.

Over the days, weeks, he found in the shed small pleasures: a collection of nails, a hammer and a saw, a stack of wooden boxes. He levered and banged out the nails from the boxes, and then at the back of the garden built one much larger: tall, bottomless, with a sheet of wood that sat on top, and a few holes around the base to let in air. There he layered grass clippings, sweepings from the range and fireplaces, vegetable and fruit scraps from a bucket his mother kept in the kitchen. Earth to earth, dust to dust, the promises of sun and rain.

Pansies, fairy bells, lilies, lavender, roses. Rhubarb, cabbage and parsley. He would build a trellis to hide the outhouse and train climbers over it. Honeysuckle, his mother had said, or maybe clematis. Why not jasmine? he wondered, but he didn't care. He just wanted flowers. The shy awakening of spring bulbs, the drunkenness of summer blooms. He wanted their living, breathing colours, their seductive smells.

254

Winter passed into spring and spring into summer. Light slipped under, around the edges of the blinds, onto sleepy skin. If Robbie were a cat he would have purred. He lay in bed and did not know where dream and its awakening lifted and drifted apart.

He ate porridge with his mother, stirred sugar crystals and milk in a thick whirlpool in his bowl. He drank tea with milk and two sugars.

His mother was running water to wash the dishes – he knew she was about to get the kettle from the range – when he bent down and kissed her lightly on the cheek. He picked up the scrap bucket, opened the door, walked out into the garden. Into the bright morning air.

PINEAPPLE

Katherine had never bought pineapple, never tasted it. The spiky skin seemed too daunting, like a huge fruit half-pretending to be a cactus, but Mrs Newman had offered ten shillings extra a week and Katherine felt like celebrating. She was walking down Tory Street, thinking of buying cakes – Queen cakes or doughnuts or kisses – when she saw the pineapples in the shop window. She stopped and stared, and when she looked in she saw Mrs Wong smiling, motioning for her to come in.

'Pineapple very good,' Mrs Wong said. 'Come, I cut for you.'

Katherine followed her out the back of the shop and into the kitchen. She watched her run the pineapple under the tap, then cut off the top and the bottom. Leaves like aloe, Katherine thought, as she watched them tumble into the sink. Now Mrs Wong was trimming off the skin, turning the fruit little by little, bringing the cleaver down quickly.

Katherine watched pieces of skin fall and be swept into the sink – slices of orange-green reptile. She watched the transformation, the pale yellow flesh still studded with dark verrucas. Mrs Wong turned the pineapple at an angle, slid the knife in, first on one side of the ingrowths, then the other, slicing long Vs down the flesh like trenches.

Katherine marvelled at how quickly she worked, how the fruit turned before her eyes into a soft yellow barrel covered with spiralling trenches. Now Mrs Wong sliced the pineapple into rounds, and the rounds into quarters. She washed her hands, took from the shelf a flat porcelain bowl, and from a cupboard a large glass preserving jar.

'What's that?' Katherine asked, watching her spoon white crystals into the bowl.

'Salt,' Mei-lin said, pouring water from the kettle over the salt and stirring with her fingers. 'Make it sweet.' She dipped a slice of pineapple into the brine and handed it to Katherine.

Katherine had never tasted anything like it. Juice spurted out as she bit into it and she laughed, sweetness coating her chin.

As Mrs Wong packed a preserving jar with pieces of pineapple, Katherine thought of Robbie working in the garden. Since he'd returned, he'd never touched fruit – apples, pears, oranges – but surely pineapple would be different.

Katherine followed Mrs Wong back into the shop. A man stood at the cash register, counting out change to a customer. Katherine felt the colour drain from her face. He looked up, nodded to her, and she saw he was very young. She realised it was not him.

That night, Katherine used a fork to spear pineapple pieces out of the jar and into two blue-flowered bowls. 'Pineapple,' she said to Robbie, savouring the word on her tongue as if it were a piece of magic.

She could barely close her mouth and chew without sticky juice leaking out. She closed her eyes. It was like devouring sunlight made juicy.

'Come on, Robbie. Try it. It's delicious!'

When he still did not touch it, she pierced a piece with her fork, held it up to his mouth. *Take some sweetness, Robbie. Take it into your life.*

Robbie knew that fragrance – the slight, sweet, tropical taste of it in his nostrils. A window of light in winter darkness.

He'd lifted the pineapple to his face. Inhaled.

'Pineapple very good,' the Chinaman had said. 'Very sweet.'

Bastard, he'd thought. *Is that how he sees my mother?* He'd put the pineapple down. Next to the apples.

There were four just the same in the fruit bowl at his mother's. But he refused to eat them. He'd heard stories about how the Chows polished their fruit, rubbing them with spittle to make them shine.

'Apple very good, you want to try?' The Chow was looking at him expectantly. Without thinking, Robbie moved the pads of three fingers over an apple. Even through his gloves he could feel the cool smoothness of its skin; the redness of its cheek; his mother blushing. He wiped his fingers against his coat.

But now the Chinaman was coming towards him with a knife, cutting a slice of the very apple he'd touched, somehow placing it in his hand, walking back.

Robbie's mouth was dry, his throat tight. His lips parted, and he heard footfalls, laughter as a man and a woman passed on the path outside. He closed his eyes, then opened them, dropped the apple slice, spat, and ground it into the linoleum. 'Stay away from her,' he said.

A wave of recognition passed over the Chinaman's face. A cloud.

'You hear what I said? Leave her fuckin' alone!'

The Chinaman looked him directly in the eye, unflinching. People said they were easy targets, Chinks, they never resisted. But this one defied him.

Robbie could hear his voice rising as if from a distance, strangled and separate from his body. He was shaking. He was shouting, but all his words were small and tight.

Afterwards Robbie wondered why the John had given him the knife that night. He'd laid it down in front of him casually. An invitation. A dare.

He could see himself but couldn't feel, every movement detached from his body. The way the knife fell into his hand, the way it plunged into the body, the way it thrust up. He was surprised at its ease: a bayonet slipping into a padded sack. As it went in, Robbie noticed the Chinaman's eyes were suddenly round, which for a split second seemed ridiculous. The mouth opened in surprise, but no sound came out. He fell clutching his stomach, where a small patch of red stained the white apron.

Robbie looked at the knife, the stain of red on its pointed blade, the clean fit of the wooden handle, so that he knew of its presence only from a certain weight on his fingers. He watched a single drop of blood fall, heard the clatter of the knife on the white linoleum.

He could not move. There was a Chinaman lying at his feet, staring up at him wordlessly, the metallic smell of blood in his nostrils. He looked at his gloved hands, at these hands which were not his own. What to do. What to do. He walked to the front door, his legs heavy, every step taking an immeasurably long time, as if they were walking under water. He pulled the door to, but a corner of linoleum caught in the doorway. He wanted to scream, could hear himself screaming, but could not open his mouth. He pulled again, forced it hard, heard the spring lock click. The sound of footsteps upstairs. The woman. God, he didn't want to . . . Robbery, it had to look like a robbery. Everyone knew Chinks had money. He grabbed some sticks of tobacco, stuffed them in his pockets, went to the till.

He stuffed the rolled notes, a couple of cylinders of coins into his pocket. Left the till open and ran. Out through the back of the shop. Out the back door.

Opposite the gate, windows from the bakery threw light across the alley. It was wide, wide enough for a baker's cart, too wide and too bright – and was that Mr Paterson that walked past? The house on the other side was dark. Robbie ran blindly, banged his knee hard into the wooden fence, climbed over, heard coins fall to the stony ground, ran across the neighbour's yard and vomited against the fence line. He ran down into Adelaide Road, walked across the street and headed towards the Basin.

A drunk staggered out of the Tramways Hotel. A couple walked arm in arm, she looking into his eyes, he laughing. In the darkness, no one seemed to notice.

Robbie looked at his hands, at the gloves his sister had knitted. He had to get rid of them. He didn't want to touch them. He had to wash his hands.

Lightning streaked across the sky and lit the street, the Caledonian up on the corner. The sound of thunder and then the deluge. Robbie hunched into his coat and ran, bullets of rain hitting the footpath, flying up at his feet, water pouring over his hat, trickling down his neck. Already the gutters were flooding.

He didn't hear a woman scream.

FROM THE ART OF DYING

There are many ways to kill yourself. Some do it quickly, leaving their bodies as a farewell gift, or perhaps an act of revenge. Others, over a whole lifetime, die quietly.

Katherine did not understand what happened. First she heard his cry – low, deep, like that of an animal – then she felt the silver fork, the piece of pineapple fly from her hand, Robbie running, running from the room, arms flailing.

Afterwards he looked out at her with hollow eyes, arms loose by his side. Everything so loose, barely held together, almost as if his body had forgotten the meaning of muscle, ligament, bone.

She found him in the afternoon. One overhanging branch, the one he'd sat on as a boy. He was wearing his blue and white striped pyjamas – the pyjamas she'd proudly bought him, the very latest in men's nightwear – his bare feet a few inches from the ground.

There was nothing under the tree. Only grass, fallen twigs, dandelions that had yet to grow a heady stalk and burst into bloom. No overtoppled chair or box, nothing he could have stepped off into another world. And Katherine realised he had climbed the trunk, his fingers and toes wrapped over the wooden battens. That he'd sat on the branch as he tied the rope, first one end, then the other. How long had he sat there while she typed letters on monogrammed paper and filed newspaper reports into folders? What had he thought as he overlooked the garden: the honeysuckle he'd started to train up the white trellis, the roses whose young leaves were just beginning to sprout?

She did not want to look at his face, the length of his neck, the way his head hung to one side as if looking away, unable to meet her gaze. He used to poke out his tongue as a boy, when he was thinking deeply, when he was tying his shoelaces or even skimming a stone. She hoped he had flown, the way a cicada flies from its transparent skin, leaving a ghostly memory while its true self sits in summer trees, driving the world crazy with its singing.

He had been good at driving her crazy. Perhaps that was his role, the role of any child. To challenge his mother and father. And find them wanting . . .

Mrs Newman takes off her reading glasses. There is tenderness in her eyes – a soft, clouded sky – that Katherine has never noticed before. Her lip trembles. 'It gets easier,' she says.

She gazes into her lenses, places them carefully back over her eyes, looks down at the newspaper.

Grief comes softly behind her. She does not know whose face he will wear. She might be typing a letter or washing a white bowl or looking out from the top of a double-decker tram. She might be at a show at His Majesty's, surrounded by laughter and gilt-edged conversation. And grief will come and touch her arm with his hand. She will turn and there he will be. He will wrap his arms round her neck. He will ask her to embrace him.

AUTHOR'S NOTE

The major characters in this novel are fictional and their stories are works of the imagination; however, some of the minor characters are true historical figures. The most prominent of these is (Edward) Lionel Terry who murdered Joe Kum-yung in Haining Street, Wellington, on 24 September 1905. His interactions with the McKechnie family are fictional but his views, poetry, publications, trial and subsequent incarceration in mental institutions, as well as his popularity, are factual. During various periods at Seacliff Mental Hospital near Dunedin he enjoyed great personal freedom and during others he was subjected to solitary confinement because of his escapes and poor behaviour. He died still incarcerated at Seacliff on 20 August 1952, aged 80 years. Note: some of the 'facts' about Terry as related in the novel, e.g. his education at Eton and Oxford, are not actually true but are what was believed and reported in newspapers of the time.

Dr Agnes Bennett was raised in Australia and England but first came to prominence in New Zealand where she was a popular and respected pioneer of women in medicine and a staunch supporter of female education and rights. Her life's philosophy was to give rather than receive and to 'choose the leaden casket'. Drs Frederick Truby King and Ferdinand Batchelor were also major medical figures, Dr King being most famous in New Zealand not as lecturer of Mental

Diseases at the Otago Medical School or Medical Superintendent of Seacliff but as founder of the Plunket Society supporting mothers and infants. (Elizabeth) Grace Neill was a leading nurse, public servant and social reformer, and Kate Sheppard and Lily Atkinson were at the forefront campaigning for women's suffrage in New Zealand.

Mary Anne (Annie) Wong came to Wellington from Melbourne to marry the Anglican Chinese Missioner, Daniel Wong. He died within a few years but she remained in Wellington working alongside subsequent Missioners before retiring to Hong Kong in the 1930s.

Yue Jackson (surname Yue), son of a Chinese father and Scottish mother, lived in New Zealand and China. For many years he was the English Secretary at the Chinese Consulate in Wellington. Consul Kwei Chih and the incident recounted in 'If the Time Has Not Come', as well as Kwei Chih's son's reaction, did happen, though all other local names are fictionalised.

All political figures, whether New Zealand or Chinese, are real. The only exception is Alexander Newman, husband of the fictional Margaret Newman.

Sir Robert Stout did preside, as Chief Justice, over Lionel Terry's trial. He was a member of the Anti-Chinese League and was, like many leading figures of the day, anti-Chinese. Interestingly, his wife Anna Paterson Stout, a prominent woman of her day, was sympathetic to the Chinese.

Although Chinese New Zealanders in the late nineteenth and early twentieth centuries did have friends and supporters, the anti-Chinese legislation outlined in this novel is historically accurate, as is the general climate of racism and sometime violence. The shooting in Naseby and the murder of Ham Sing-tong in Tapanui are true examples. My paternal great-grandfather, Wong Wei-jung (Wong Way Ching) was brutally murdered in Wellington in 1914. The case was never solved.

Romanisation of the Chinese in this novel was problematic as, although my characters are Cantonese and only spoke Cantonese, many famous Chinese names, places and terms are only recognised by the general reader in Mandarin, either in the *pinyin* system used in modern China or the older Wade-Giles system. There are many different, often non-standard methods for romanising Cantonese and the common spellings in New Zealand are very different from those used elsewhere.

Because *pinyin* did not exist at the time of the novel, I have generally used the familiar Wade-Giles Mandarin romanisation for famous historical figures and places or whichever form they were most famously known by, but generally used Cantonese for everyone else. Sun Yat-sen was Cantonese and therefore recognised by the Cantonese romanisation of his name, and the province is most readily recognised as Kwangtung.

According to Chinese custom, surnames are listed first, though when Chinese entered western countries like New Zealand, government officials often mistook parts of given names as surnames and what with varied methods of romanisation, many Chinese ended up with erroneously recorded surnames which survive to this day.

I have hyphenated the two given names to make it clearer which are surnames and which are the given names. However, people were often called by one of their given names, eg, Wong Chung-yung was referred to as Yung by his elder brother. As the position in the family is so important, Yung referred to his brother as Shun Goh, Goh being the term for elder brother. Cantonese also often refer to people by Ah plus either their surname or a given name.

I have used the standard spelling used by New Zealand newspapers for Consul Kwei Chih. The Chinese 'violin', *erh-hu*; the Goddess of Mercy, Kuan Yin; and the woman warrior, Mu-lan, are all romanised in Mandarin, but most other Chinese words, including units of measure and money, are romanised in Cantonese. I am indebted to Janet Chan of Picador Asia for her help with Cantonese romanisation.

Most of the early Chinese in New Zealand came from three main counties in Kwangtung (Guangdong) in southern China: 增城Tseng

265

Sing (known as Jungseng in New Zealand, Zengcheng in *pinyin* or Tseng-ch'eng in Wade-Giles); 番禺Pun Yu (Poonyu, Pan Yu or P'an-yü); and 四邑Sei Yap (Seyip, Siyi or Ssu-i).

By the turn of the twentieth century, Wellington had arguably become the major centre for Chinese in New Zealand. Media and popular portrayals of the Chinese at the time generally focussed on Haining Street and were usually sensationalist, negative and highly inaccurate. The Chinese community was centred on Haining Street and neighbouring Taranaki, Tory and Frederick Streets though many Chinese also lived above their businesses scattered throughout the city.

Note: the spelling of the Wellington suburb Kelburne did not change to its present day Kelburn until 1917.

This novel is not my family's story nor that of any particular Chinese New Zealand family, though my family did come from Melon Ridge (瓜嶺Gwa Liang or Gwa Ling, Gualing or Kua-ling) and Tile Kiln (雅瑤Nga Yiel or Nga Yiu, Yayao or Ya-yao) villages in Tseng Sing county, and some of the incidents in the novel were inspired or informed by true experiences. This includes the sizeable amount of money raised by patriotic Chinese New Zealanders to support Sun Yat-sen and the 1911 Revolution, and my maternal great-grandfather's (Wong Kwok-min, Huang Guomin or Hung Kuo-min, also known as Wong Hum) involvement.

Although I have endeavoured to be historically and culturally accurate, there are many different and even conflicting views. There were also instances where I was unable to find out the 'truth'. At the end of the day this is a work of fiction, not of history.

ACKNOWLEDGEMENTS

I am grateful for assistance provided by the Robert Burns Fellowship, the Willi Fels Memorial Trust, a project grant from Creative New Zealand, a Reader's-Digest New Zealand Society of Authors Stout Research Centre Fellowship and a New Zealand Founders Society Annual Research Award.

I am indebted to Jane Parkin for her sensitive and perceptive editing and Judith Ludkin-Amundsen for her invaluable reading; my publishers, Geoff Walker and the team at Penguin New Zealand, and Rod Morrison, Daniel Watts, Janet Chan and the teams at Picador in Australia and Hong Kong; as well as my agent, Toby Eady, and Jamie Coleman of Toby Eady Associates. Thanks to Keely O'Shannessy for her fabulous cover, Mary Egan for beautiful internal design and Alan Knowles for his author photo.

Special thanks to Roger Steele, Christine Roberts and Roger Whelan of Steele Roberts who provided support and encouragement throughout the years.

Fiona Kidman gave excellent structural advice on an early draft, and Toni Atkinson, Gilbert Wong, Eva Wong Ng, and members of the various incarnations of my writing groups – including Caren Wilton, Raewyn Brockway, Lynn Davidson, Johanna Knox, Claire Baylis, Sarah Laing, Kate Camp, Catherine Chidgey, Virginia Fenton, Alex Gillespie,

Jay Linden, Michael Gilchrist, Peter Hall-Jones, Naomi O'Connor and Jan Farr – gave feedback and/or encouragement. Thanks to Kate who found the Chinese proverb which inspired the novel title and chapter, *As the Earth Turns Silver*. I have no idea whether this is a true Chinese proverb.

Dianne and Peter Beatson provided their wonderful Foxton writing retreat where much progress was made and Siggy Woolloff and her staff at Aunt Daisy's Boathouse Café gave coffee, sanity and a writing refuge overlooking the water.

James Brown, Catherine Chidgey, Justin Paton, Chris Price and Lawrence Jones, as editors of *Sport, Landfall* and *Nurse to the Imagination: 50 Years of the Robert Burns Fellowship*, published draft extracts.

Linda Cound gave me her 'little orange book' and Forbes Williams assisted with research and discussions about narrative.

The residents, associates, secretaries and the directors – Allan Thomas, Vincent O'Sullivan and Lydia Wevers – of the Stout Research Centre, the staff of the Chinese section of the Department of Asian Languages at Victoria University of Wellington, and many people associated with the English and History Departments of the University of Otago, made me welcome and helped along the way. Other institutions which helped with research were the library, anatomy museum and medical library at the University of Otago; the New Zealand Dictionary Centre; the Alexander Turnbull Library, Oral History Archive, Manuscripts, Music and Reference at the National Library of New Zealand; Wellington City Archive; Wellington Public Library; Porirua Public Library; Pataka Porirua Museum; Te Papa Museum of New Zealand; Otago Settlers Museum; Porirua Police Museum; Olveston; Larnach Castle; Archives Research Centre of the Presbyterian Church of Aotearoa New Zealand; First Church of Otago; Hocken Library; and Anderson Park in Invercargill, where the Ashford table was found.

Many individuals helped with historical, Chinese, military and other research. In particular, Nigel Murphy, James Ng, Eva Wong Ng, Brian Moloughney, Duncan Campbell, Helen Leach, Graham Stewart, Tom Brooking, Aaron Fox, Pat Fox and Edmon Wong, all went way beyond the call of duty.

Thanks also to Jane Malthus, John Stenhouse, Dorothy Page, Barbara Brookes, Howard Baldwin, Alison Hercus, Lynley Hood, David Hood, Bill Keane, Michael Kelly, Helen McCracken, Jenny Gibson, Chris Cochran, Chris Jones, Trevor Garrett, Sophie Giddens, Sylvia Carlyle, Russell Klein, John Earles, Geoffrey Rice, Anne-Marie Brady, Mervyn Thompson, Liz Bryce, Chris House, Hardwicke Knight, Richard Hill, Bronwyn Dalley, Clarence Aasen, Pauline Keating, John McKinnon, Eirlys Hunter, Alistair McLean, Jean Ellis, Joan Henderson, Harry Ricketts, Selwyn Graves, Kirsten Wong, George Wong, Lynette Shum, Bill Wong, Kai Wong, Dan Chan, Ray Wong Tong, Percy and Alice Chew Lee, Nancy Wong, Ng Li Fe Oui, Anita King, Tsan Yew Wong, Yuk Fung Chong, Maurice and Margaret Meechang, Chan Wai Yung Wong, Margaret Wong, Roy Law, Thomas Keong, Bai Limin, Li Kangying, Jing-Bao Nie, Manying Ip and Timothy Woo.

Diana Davies, Steve Yanko, Jo McMullan, Raewyn Brockway and Dr James Ng helped with medical details, and Dr James Walshe and Dr Charles Moore, specifically, with psychiatric history. Philip Simpson, Phil Garnock-Jones and Bill Sykes provided information about plants in early Wellington and New Zealand. Ngahuia Te Awakotuku, Morrie Love and Maui Solomon gave advice about Maori in the early twentieth century, and Dianne Bardsley provided invaluable guidance on early New Zealand English.

Damien Wilkins, Bill Manhire, Adrienne Jansen and Andrew Johnston encouraged me in the early days of my writing. Even earlier, my high school English teacher Peter Exeter opened my eyes with *Owls Do Cry* and was the first to believe in me and inspire me with literature.

Over the years a number of people helped in many and varied ways: Michael Gilchrist, Pepe Choong, Andrea Hudson, Ruth Pink,

Pam Atkinson, Shanti Setyowati-Anderson, Don Anderson, Caroline McCaw, Martin Keane, Lindsay Forbes and Phil Castelow. I particularly want to thank Linda Tyler, Kevin Yelverton and Toni Atkinson, who were always there for me through hard times.

My family are owed the greatest thanks: my mother and father, Doris and Henry Wong – Dad, you gave me the permission to write this story and this is for you – my brother, Graeme Wong, and sisters, Sharon King and Janice Young, and their families, without whose support this book would never have been written, and especially, the best little guy in my life, my son, Jackson Forbes, whose patience and tolerance made this possible.

This novel was written over many years. To those who declined to be acknowledged and also those whom I have inadvertently neglected to acknowledge, please accept my heartfelt thanks.

Many written sources were consulted in the course of research and writing. What follows is only a partial listing. Newspapers included the *Evening Post, Dominion* and *Truth* and websites included the Dictionary of New Zealand Biography www.dnzb.govt.nz/dnzb/. *The New Zealand Medical Service in the Great War 1914–1918*, Lieut.-Col. A. D. Carbery, Whitcombe & Tombs was particularly useful for its descriptions of shell-shock and *Sojourners: The Epic Story of China's Centuries-old Relationship with Australia*, Eric Rolls, University of Queensland Press for its descriptions of opium smoking. The words of Po Lo in the chapter 'More Than Horses' are based on Arthur Cooper's beautiful translation of Lieh Tzu in *Li Po and Tu Fu*, Penguin Books. Lionel Terry's recital in the chapter 'A Fine Example of a British Gentleman' is quoted from his long poem 'God or Mammon?' which he self-published. Dictionary entries in the chapter 'The Little Orange Book' are quoted from *Glossary of English Phrases with Chinese Translations*, Woo Kwang Kien, Commercial Press.

Other books and theses which I particularly drew on included: *Doctor Agnes Bennett*, Cecil & Celia Manson, Whitcombe & Tombs; *Lionel Terry: The Making of a Madman*, Frank Tod, Otago Heritage

Books; *The Shadow*, Lionel Terry, self-published; *Truby King: The Man*, Mary Truby King, Allen & Unwin; *A Brief History of the Chinese in New Zealand*, Joe Y. Sing, self-published; *Black November: The 1918 Influenza Epidemic in New Zealand*, Geoffrey Rice with the assistance of Linda Bryder, Allen & Unwin: Historical Branch, Department of Internal Affairs'; *Old Wellington Days* and *More Wellington Days*, Pat Lawlor, Whitcombe & Tombs; 'Representing Haining Street: Wellington's Chinatown 1920–1960', Lynette Shum, MA thesis for Victoria University of Wellington; *Zengcheng New Zealanders: A History for the 80th Anniversary of the Tung Jung Association of NZ Inc.*, Henry Chan (ed.), Tung Jung Association of New Zealand Inc.; 'The Poll-tax in New Zealand: A research paper', Nigel Murphy, The New Zealand Chinese Association; *The Kelburn Cable Car: Wellington – New Zealand*; *Always a Tram in Sight: The Electric Trams of New Zealand 1900 to 1964*; *The End of the Penny Section: When Trams Ruled the Street of New Zealand*; and *When Trams Were Trumps in New Zealand: An Illustrated History*, Graham Stewart, Grantham House; *Supreme Court (42 Stout Street, Wellington) Conservation Report for the Ministry of Justice*, Chris Cochran; and *Twentieth Century China*, O. Edmund Clubb, Columbia University Press.

Other useful books included: *Windows on a Chinese Past, vols 1–4*, James Ng, Otago Heritage Books; *The Basin: An Illustrated History of the Basin Reserve*, Don Neely and Joseph Romanos, Canterbury University Press; 'Psychiatry & Seacliff: A Study of Seacliff Mental Hospital and the Psychiatric Milieu in New Zealand 1912–1948', Susan Fennell, BA (hons) essay for University of Otago; *Backblocks Baby-doctor*, Doris Gordon, Faber & Faber; *Lady Doctor: Vintage Model*, Frances I. Preston, A. H. & A. W. Reed; *Stethoscope & Saddlebags: An Autobiography*, Eleanor S. Baker McLaglan, Collins; *Wellington's Old Buildings*, David Kernohan & Tony Kellaway, Victoria University Press; *The Chinese Century*, Jonathan Spence & Annping Chin, Cassell Paperbacks; *Songs of Gold Mountain: Cantonese Rhymes from San Francisco Chinatown*, Marlon K. Hom, University of California Press; *Yuan Shih-k'ai*, Jerome Chen,

Stanford University Press; *Reader's Digest New Zealand Yesterdays*, text: Hamish Keith, picture research: William Main; *Anzac Diary: A Nonentity in Khaki*, N. M. Ingram, Treharne Publishers and Distributers; and *Dear Lizzie: A Kiwi Soldier Writes from the Battlefields of World War One*, Chrissie Ward (ed.), HarperCollins.